P9-BTY-900

Angie Was Yards Past Her Home and the Darkness Crowded In . . .

She could smell the sweet, clean scent of the lake mingling with the heavy green smell of wind-washed conifers.

She felt Tye prod her from behind with the tip of the knife blade and she walked faster, into the wind that swept down the moonlit road.

"You turned me away. You never liked me," Tye said.

This she could not deny. Another prod caused her shoulders to jerk forward in automatic response. Oh God, she thought, why hasn't my father called for me yet? Where *is* he?

Tye came alongside and took her arm, dragged her against her weight into the shelter of the trees. "You are coming with me," he said between gritted teeth. "I will leave no one alive to talk about me after I'm gone. No one . . ."

Books by Billie Sue Mosiman

Deadly Affections
Slice

Published by POCKET BOOKS

Most Pocket Books are available at special quantity discounts for bulk purchases for sales promotions, premiums or fund raising. Special books or book excerpts can also be created to fit specific needs.

For details write the office of the Vice President of Special Markets, Pocket Books, 1230 Avenue of the Americas, New York, New York 10020.

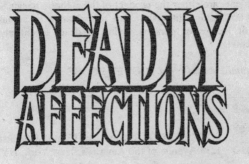

DEADLY AFFECTIONS

BILLIE SUE MOSIMAN

POCKET BOOKS

New York   London   Toronto   Sydney   Tokyo   Singapore

This book is a work of fiction. Names, characters, places and incidents are either the product of the author's imagination or are used fictitiously. Any resemblance to actual events or locales or persons, living or dead, is entirely coincidental.

An *Original* Publication of POCKET BOOKS

POCKET BOOKS, a division of Simon & Schuster Inc.
1230 Avenue of the Americas, New York, NY 10020

Copyright © 1990 by Billie Sue Mosiman

All rights reserved, including the right to reproduce this book or portions thereof in any form whatsoever. For information address Pocket Books, 1230 Avenue of the Americas, New York, NY 10020

ISBN: 0-671-67874-4

First Pocket Books printing August 1990

10 9 8 7 6 5 4 3 2 1

POCKET and colophon are registered trademarks of Simon & Schuster Inc.

Cover illustration by Lisa Falkenstern

Printed in the U.S.A.

For Kathy Williams and Richard Ferguson,
good friends.

Special thanks to Linda Marrow, Michael Carlisle,
and Matthew Bialer.

Author's Note

The places Moon Lake and Clarksdale, Mississippi, are real, but the characters and situations in this book are entirely the product of the author's imagination.

Chapter

1

It could have been one of those cherished, perfect days of youth. Day of rich promise, of sun and water and laughter shared with good friends. Instead it was a day destined to be remembered by Angelina Thornton as the time when childhood ended.

Moon Lake, Mississippi, lay in a cup of fertile bottom Delta land ringed by blue-green conifers. The beauty of the still, cobalt waters was deceptive the way an exquisite woman sometimes harbors a cold, cruel heart. Although Moon Lake seemed to be nothing beyond an idyllic recreational retreat stretching miles across, it was a treacherous pit, site of many drownings, over sixty feet deep once a swimmer waded past the sandbar and dropped into icy depths.

Angie worried about being caught offshore with a crippling attack of abdominal cramps. She hoped the booklet in the Tampax box was right about swimming while on her period. This was one of those times she missed having a mother to advise her.

She shrugged, pulling up the black elastic shoulder straps of her one-piece bathing suit. It was too late now to do anything but take her chances. All the other kids had already changed and were down at the shoreline splashing one another and laughing. Angie had hung behind to protect her privacy. The bathhouse stalls were doorless, affording scant protection, and she had had to insert a tampon before putting on her suit.

"Me and Bobby McGee," a lonely tune by Janis Joplin, screeched from the little portable Zenith radio one of the girls had left playing on the lip of the sink. Angie glanced down at herself, sucking in her slightly protruding tummy. She was going to look worse than the alcoholic, ballooning Joplin if she gained any more water weight.

She bent to gather her clothes into a bundle so as to hide her stained panties. One thing about Tampax. Sometimes they leaked and she was just too fastidious to ever wear a Kotex pad as backup. She hated those thick, scratchy things next to her body, and she didn't know what was worse, the pad itself or the sanitary belt that cut into her skin and always showed through her clothes. She hardly ever had accidents, but of course today of all days it had to happen.

As she pawed through her things she heard a mild cough, a clearing of the throat that was louder than the music from the radio. She froze. Someone was in the bathhouse with her. Someone male.

"Who's there? I'll be out in a minute."

"What's holding you up?"

She recognized the voice as belonging to Tyeson Dompier. Only the cutest boy she had ever seen. Just to look at him made her heartbeat do triple time. Had he come back for her?

"Are you looking for something?" he asked.

2

Angie's heart slowed and the blush that had risen to pink her cheeks faded. She did not like the tone in his voice. It was wheedling. Mischievous. No, not only mischievous, but *mean*.

She glanced at the conglomeration of clothes piled on the cement floor. Shorts, pink and white checked shirt, bra, white sneakers. She had been looking for something, yes. Now she squatted and flung the pieces of clothing apart, her heart again stepping up in rhythm.

"What you're looking for—" His voice neared her cubicle. Then his face peeked around the wall. "—could be in my possession now." His arm snaked around the wall; he held out a closed fist to her upturned face.

Angie heard Joplin wail how feeling good was easy, Lord, when he sang the blues. She could not quite believe Tye had been sneaky enough to steal her panties while her back was turned. But if he had and that was what he now held securely hidden in a clenched fist, then feeling good was an emotion she might never experience again.

She stood slowly and tried to smile, stretching out her right hand until her fingers were centimeters from touching his fist. "Tye, please don't play mean games. Do you have my . . ."

Words lodged in her throat so she could not swallow. He couldn't have taken her underwear. That would make him a monster. And he couldn't be a monster because he was so cute and she liked him so much. If it were a cruel joke how could she live it down, knowing that he knew it was her time of month? Shame was sudden fire consuming everything to dust and she was so young and life, before this terrible moment, so sweet.

She moved closer to him. Her eyes watered. Unbidden tears streaked down her cheeks, infuriating her. She was too old to cry over such a silly trick. He was teasing and she had to learn how to take a joke. Maybe this was how it was with southern boys. She couldn't imagine any of her friends in St. Louis doing this to her.

Joplin ended up her song, the music swelling, the lyrics belted out in a harsh whiskey voice.

Wet strands of black hair clung to Tye's cheeks and forehead. Lake water dripped from his earlobes, sliding down the fault of his neck into the perfect hollows of his collarbones.

"Whatcha gonna do, Angie? Stop me? Go ahead, try to stop me."

Her vision fogged. He weaved before her like a ghost losing substance. She whispered, "Please . . . ," and lunged to grab his hand.

He swung away, laughing. "I think it's funny. Look at you. Poor baby, poor Angie. On her period and bleeding . . ."

"Don't say it!" She clasped both hands tightly over her ears and squeezed her eyes shut.

"A little snob who thinks she's better than everyone else could do with a lesson, Angie." He backed slowly to the door, body tensing for escape. "You come down here to Moon Lake from your fancy St. Louis schools and think you can lord it over the rest of us."

"That isn't . . . that's not . . . Tye, if you're mad because of the date, I couldn't help it, it wasn't my fault. My dad just doesn't think I should go out yet." The thought that he might show the others the panties caused her to tremble. Inside she felt thrown side to side, floundering. "You can't do this, really, don't do it, okay?"

"I *can* too. See?" He opened his fist and let the

4

soiled article dangle from thumb and forefinger. "I can throw it in the air and laugh about it. You'll be a *star,* Angie. Everyone in school will know about you. Wouldn't you like that? To be a star? To make an impression on all these rednecks you're thrown in with?"

"My dad'll get you for this." She wiped her eyes with her knuckles and forced back her shoulders. This was a new, cleaner emotion. Her fists balled. Disgust rode the heels of anger and the tears dried abruptly.

"You tell your father and I'll do something worse."

Such a cold threat! Colder than the threat of humiliation she knew she was about to endure. She believed him. If he was capable of this kind of betrayal, then he might do anything. But why? And how could he want to hurt her just because she wasn't allowed to go out with him? Her dad was just trying to protect her, didn't he understand that? And she liked Mississippi; she was the new girl and it was going to be hard to make friends, but she genuinely liked the other kids, their soft, singsongy accents, their sweet, open, country faces.

Her fingers dropped from tight fists. She flicked them like a runner preparing to sprint. Her throat ached where a spiked ball creaked up and down her esophagus. She had to make a show of bravery. He might respond to spitfire and backbone. Drawing on a buried reservoir of strength she said, "Don't keep threatening me, Tye. I don't find this a bit funny."

He flipped his prize toward her face and back again. She stood perfectly still, slowly breathing in the suntan oil scent of his smooth long arms. Contempt edged aside her fear. She looked him up and down. He wore red bathing trunks, fitting snugly on a lithe frame. He was tall, muscled, sixteen. He had blue eyes that turned the color of the lake during a storm when, like now, he was furious and bent on revenge. For all his beauty he was truly ugly underneath. She grimaced at such hidden ugliness.

He slowly smiled. Angie tried to look away. The smile was a lamplight in the dark of an otherwise forbidding and dangerous face. She couldn't look away and the smile held her. It promised things. It conjured images of sex in night-shrouded parked cars that she had only dreamed about, of illicit fondlings, of kisses long and sensual.

"Don't threaten you?" he asked. "Is that what you said? You got it all wrong. I do what I want and I *want* to do this."

He became a shadow flitting through the bathhouse door, whooping and hollering to get the group's attention from where they cavorted on the far beach and in the chilly lake waters. Angie saw him disappear through trees, her spotted white satin underwear flying aloft like a war banner.

Her stomach rose and then settled. The cramps she had feared earlier returned with a demonic force that doubled her at the waist. She sucked in her breath, hearing raised voices and nervous embarrassed laughter from the beach. Above it all Tye's crazed, excited whoops echoed across the lake.

She had to leave. This was disgrace and it was forever. She would walk the half mile to her house through the woods. She could never ride back with the rest of them in the station wagon. Face them? Not after what they knew, not after she had been made an object of ridicule. They all understood menstruation, sure, of course, it was natural, it was necessary, and the girls, all of them, had periods. But it was not a subject to be bandied about, the mechanics of it made into a tasteless display.

The radio announcer promised "Purple Haze" and a brand-new tune by the Doors, "Hello, I Love You." All over America it was a psychedelic fall, but for Angelina Thornton, a teenager trapped in the rural South, it was merely a time of rioting hormones and innocent fantasy. She and her peers were too far removed from the center of the hippie revolution to be affected by little more than the music of their generation.

The Hendrix guitar strain filled the bathhouse like thick smoke and Angie came to as if slapped. She jerked upright, pressing spread palms across her abdomen, staring hard at the dull gray cement wall opposite. She glanced once at the pile of discarded clothes, bent and snatched them to her chest. In one hand she carried her sneakers. She slipped out the door, leaving the room to Jimi Hendrix, and skirted the squat ugly building. At first she walked rigidly, shoulders stiff, mind purposely blank. She was hidden and they would not see her. Not until—school—on Monday—then they *would* see her and she would have to face it, face *them*. But anything could happen. She might get lucky and die before Monday. Or Tye would die and she'd forgive him.

"I don't care," she mumbled, kicking pine needles and leaves aside. "It's all right because I don't care."

Then she did care and the tears rushed back and she was running, swift and fleet, racing as if it meant her life. Dry, rusty blackberry vines tore at her. Undergrowth snagged at bare feet, limber cedar limbs whipped across her face and exposed chest to raise instant welts.

Of course she cared, she cared so much she could kill him for trying to destroy her dignity with such casual disregard.

7

When she exited the woods onto her father's lakefront property, the sun blazed beyond the rooftop like an Aztec coin. She could smell her sour sweat. There was no purple haze clouding the sun, no mercy in that ball of fire, no mercy in this day. None.

In her bedroom she collapsed on her bed and hid her face in a pillow. Her father would not be home from Clarksdale for another hour. She could hug this pain to her bosom alone and smother it perhaps, squeeze away the bitterness, drain it of sting. Maybe it was not so bad. Maybe the others had censored Tye and made him feel rotten and low-down. Maybe his plan had backfired and he was the one humiliated.

Maybe the world would end and Monday would never come.

She heard a car horn blaring in the distance and sat up on the side of the bed, legs swinging, feet thumping the floor. The sound closed in, intermittent honks going on and on, a madman's Morse code. She raced through the house, throwing open the front screen door just in time to see the familiar green station wagon John had borrowed from his dad for the swimming trip. It rushed past screaming, her friends crowded together and hanging out the lowered tailgate. Angie receded into the shadow of the doorway, but she knew they had seen her. Hoots and derisions floated back on the breeze as the car flew past. An anonymous hand threw something that fluttered to the white gravel lining the paved road.

She closed her eyes tightly, stricken to the bone. Couldn't someone have stopped him? Didn't anyone care?

Angie opened her eyes and pushed ajar the screen door, striding across the small lawn to the gravel. She stooped and retrieved the undergarment, balling it bit by bit into her fist until all that showed were white, quivering knuckles.

She glared after the car until the speck of green vanished down the long vortex of lake road. Standing here, the evening breeze ruffling her hair, her jaws aching from clenching her teeth, Angie discovered a burning seed of hate growing deep down inside where she would not cry, where self-pity and tears were banished. If at that moment she had been empowered to magically wipe the day and the people involved out of existence she would have done it. None of those jerk southern kids would have ever been born.

Especially Tyeson Dompier.

The station wagon swerved back and forth across the center line of the gravel road like a rocket with a malfunctioning booster propelling it. Tye sat in the back cargo area with the other kids, enjoying their vulgar jokes at Angie's expense. He had started something and was able to bask in the fulmination of his efforts. By Monday this group of kids would spread the story of the lake scene through every classroom until Angie would be the pariah he hoped for her to be. Without acceptance and friends at the new school, she would be more vulnerable to his advances. After all, he had manipulated her into the position of being an outcast. But he also could put in a word here and there and lift her from that position. If she played it all his way. *His* way. She must be made to understand he was the one in power and without his guardianship, she was lost.

"Did you see her face when she came out that door?" one boy asked of another, jabbing him in the ribs, laughing. "Looked like she'd been hit with a banana cream pie. Zap!"

The girls were circumspect in making fun of Angie, but they giggled and lowered their eyes. No one was speaking up for the new girl. Tye had not expected they would. The girls knew they could be the next butt of a humiliating joke and did not wish to court that particular fate.

Go against him? None of them would dare go against him.

He smiled and pushed one of the boys over to the side so he could untangle his legs.

"What do you think she'll do, Tye?" John asked from the front seat where he drove. "I hear her ole man's a prof out at the university. What if she tells him?"

Everyone quieted, waiting to hear what Tye might do if called upon by an adult to explain his behavior.

"She won't be telling her daddy," Tye said easily. He prodded the girl nearest him. "Would you go tell your daddy you lost your dirty pants?"

"I don't think so," she said with downcast eyes.

"Of course you wouldn't. You don't tell your ole man you're on your *period*. You might tell your mom what happened, but Angie doesn't have a mom. She won't tell anyone."

The girl shrugged uneasily.

"Aw, c'mon, lighten up." Tye put one hand under the girl's chin and brought it up until he could see her eyes. "Don't go feeling sorry for Angie Thornton. She acts like she owns the world. We have to let her know she doesn't own our little corner of Mississippi."

And she has no right rejecting a date with me, he thought. Who does she think she's dealing with, a redneck?

"You gonna get her to go out with you after pulling a stunt like this?" John asked.

Tye decided John was being just a little bit too outspoken. Questioning the leader wasn't part of the damn rules around here. Where did he get off?

"Well, you don't think for one minute she's going out with you, do you?" Tye challenged.

"I didn't say I wanted her to," John retorted.

"Even if you did, she wouldn't. She's too good for you, John. She *thinks* she's too good for all of us. Today was just an example of how far misguided her thinking is."

Everyone noticed Tye had not answered the question. He saw them looking at him and realized the problem.

"Sure she'll go out with me." He straightened his broad shoulders. "Why wouldn't she go out with me? She just had to be taught a lesson, that's all."

John and the others neglected to argue the point. If Tyeson Dompier said he would have something it had been their experience that he would have it. A car, a girl, being named president of his class—whatever it was, he'd get it. That was simply indisputable fact. Anyone else who had done such a thing would not only *not* get away with it unscathed, they would also *not* have the audacity to think they could turn the girl into a steady.

"Now that she's had her lesson," Tye continued, "she won't be so quick to turn me down next time."

Some of them nodded at the wisdom of this. Then they began to discuss a James Bond movie, forgetting all about the hilarious, if unnerving and unusual, incident down at the lake.

It was just another hot Saturday in September, one day closer to another Monday and the curtailment of freedom. Who could waste it on Tye's convoluted plans concerning the new girl? She was his. What he did with her, whether it was humiliation or protection beneath his wide wing of power, had little to do with them. Besides, while Tye had his attention turned in Angie's direction, they were all spared his somewhat unsettling regard.

Tye wrestled with one of the boys until he had him

flat on the carpeted metal floor of the station wagon and yelling uncle. Throughout the thoughtless shenanigans he participated in on the way to Clarksdale and during a round of root beers at the A&W, he seemed perfectly at ease with himself.

But no one knew that with every minute that passed his mind was obsessed with Angelina Thornton— wondering what she was doing, wondering if she were crying, wondering, when his planned apology came, if she would kiss him with those soft lips and hold him with those lovely dusky arms, letting him have what he wanted . . . anything he wanted. He must possess her as his own, unequivocally, and maybe . . . maybe . . . forever.

Chapter

2

Angie stopped hating John, Helen, Jerry, Marlena, Cory, and Jodie. It was easy. The Monday she went to school following the lake incident all of the kids who had been party to her humiliation at Tye's hands found ways to let her know they were sorry for falling in with him; they were sorry she had been hurt. Yet in the end nothing changed.

The three boys stood together at John's locker that morning before the bell rang and when they saw her coming, they nodded in unison, then dropped their guilty gazes to their shoes and turned, bumping into one another, unable to get away fast enough. That was an apology of sorts and she accepted it with her head held high. Of course she would never speak to them again, it would embarrass everyone concerned, but she held no grudge.

Helen stopped her in the girls' bathroom. "I didn't laugh, Angie. I swear I didn't. I'm really sorry it happened." Helen's voice shook and blotches that marred her otherwise pep-rally-girl prettiness came on her face. Angie told Helen it was all right, she understood, and watched her scuttle out the door, head hanging. There went a girl who might have been her friend. Now this *thing* was between them and Helen would always feel sorry for her. You can't have a friend feeling perpetual sorrow on your behalf. It was too bad. Angie had really wanted Helen for a friend.

Marlena and Jodie chose to sit next to her in the cafeteria at lunch and didn't say a word between them. Once or twice Angie wanted to spill out her fury, scream frustration at how her own sex had betrayed her. Finally she asked in a tightly controlled voice, "Why did you let him do it?"

"Don't knock it, Angie," Jodie said. "You're the one who's getting all the attention."

"What do you mean? You mean none of you care what Tye does as long as he's paying you some attention? Will you people take anything off him? God."

When they would not answer, Angie's indignation grew. Was she that much different from other people? Would they literally take anything from Tye and be happy he even turned his head their way?

When lunch was over and Angie stood with the two girls, emptying their food trays into garbage bins, Tye sauntered past with a gang of boys who kept just a pace or two at his heels. Jodie and Marlena immediately moved away from Angie's side as if she were infected and contagious.

That did it. Now Angie knew the score. Tye controlled a power base at Moon Lake High. He was admired by the boys and lusted after by the girls. Cross him and you were out the door and on the street.

It seemed as if nothing could have been done by the others. Tye was responsible. He didn't have to make her suffer this way. She wouldn't forgive him if she lived to be a hundred and twenty-five.

When she saw him in fourth-period English class, he was already in his desk near the back of the room, lounging in his seat like the lord of Moon Lake High, long legs spread out in the aisle. A crooked smile plastered on his face. *Pretty face.* She couldn't help think it every time she saw him. What a pretty face, prettier than Jim Morrison's. The Doors' lead singer, everyone agreed, with his skintight leather pants and long, curly hair, was sex personified. But Tye's mean smile spoiled it. The smile brought fire to her cheeks and she saw him galloping down to the lake, her panties held high. She so wanted to walk back to him and slap his face. Slap it so hard he'd cry out.

The ember of hate smoldered for him. He had lit it and it was not going to go away. That more than anything was unforgivable.

Before Tye her life had been ordered and ordinary, a mundane kind of existence that she accepted as normal. She was fifteen, a little rawboned and gangly, too tall for her age, but nice looking verging on pretty. She thought one day when she grew into her square, high-cheekboned face, she might even be as pretty as her mother had been. Her father adored her. He might be out of touch with the changing social climate of his world, but stodgy as he was—and all college professors were stodgy by her lights—he did love her and provided for her needs. She was somewhat lonely, but any girl without her mother would be lonely. It didn't help to be from St. Louis where she had been raised in a brownstone and attended urban schools all her life. That life handicapped her for Moon Lake, Mississippi, where cotton grew in long, green fields across from her house and people talked so slow and drawly she could hardly understand them, even the teachers.

Yet notwithstanding her motherless condition, her sense of being uprooted from what had been her home, her height, and her loneliness, she believed everything always worked out for the best. Growing up was one long summer party where at any second she would show up in a princess gown and be crowned the happiest girl alive.

Of course she thought herself different from other girls her age, but all girls thought that. The truth was, however, her instinct was on target. Angie Thornton was more mature and sensitive than most girls of fifteen. She took life more seriously. Already she had definite beliefs and a strong sense of morality. Though it was not altogether clear to her, she also sensed she had become head of the family by default when her mother died. She had stepped into her mother's role, becoming a full partner in the relationship with her father. Without her knowledge, this cut her off from caring about the trivial lives of most teenagers. She was fifteen going on twenty-five.

This serenity of self was shattered when Tye accosted her at the lake. That chilled look from his blue eyes had speared her like a bug to the bathhouse wall. Now chaos had entered her sphere and reality shifted. She had never hated anything or anyone and now she hated Tyeson Dompier. She had never once imagined she would have an enemy—ever meeting one or ever being important enough to lure one. But here he was: lounging in his desk, grinning crookedly, stealing a wink at her when, imagining his eyes on her back, she turned to send a discouraging frown his way. Winked at her! He might just as well have shouted to the world, "I know you. I know all about you. I know the things you don't want anyone to find out."

She sat through English with her hands clenched on the desktop while Miss Burstyn droned about the importance of style in Flannery O'Connor's short stories.

What about the importance of common courtesy? What about the importance of being kind? What kind of place was this, the South, this lush, flat Delta land close to the Mississippi River where boys deliberately hurt you out of spite and then grinned holes in your back?

"Yes, Angie? What is that you said?" Miss Burstyn asked, turning from the blackboard to point her white chalk.

Angie blinked. She knew she hadn't spoken aloud, but she must have grunted or made some kind of sound that brought the teacher's attention. "Uh, nothing, Miss Burstyn. I didn't say anything . . . did I?"

Behind her she heard Tye laugh and once he did everyone joined in and the whole room tittered at her being singled out by the pompous, fat little Miss Burstyn.

"I thought you had made a comment, but obviously not. Tell me, Angie, did they teach you the works of Flannery O'Connor where you came from?"

Angie thought the woman managed to make "where you came from" sound like the other side of the moon. It was a sure bet they weren't going to like her answer either. "No, I've never heard of O'Connor, Miss Burstyn."

Miss Burstyn sucked her bottom teeth, her lip sinking in for long seconds before loosening her stare from Angie and turning again to the blackboard. By her silent reaction she had condemned the whole Midwest. If Angie let herself she knew she could hate that kind of attitude until finally she couldn't help but despise everyone in the South for thinking themselves so separate and informed on all things that mattered. Didn't they know that Mark Twain came from Missouri? What was a Flannery anyway?

When the dismissal bell rang, Angie made a beeline for the nearest exit, glad for the end of a horrible day. She couldn't wait to get home.

The bus stopped, white dust flying, to let Angie off in front of her house. She sighed deeply and did not look back. Inside the cool, shadowed house she dropped her books on the nearest coffee table and flung herself on the sofa. She could hear her father banging things around in the kitchen.

"That you, Angie?"

"It's me, Dad."

"Want some milk and cookies? I got chocolate chip from the bakery in Clarksdale."

His words made Angie smile. He kept treating her like a five-year-old. Sometimes it wasn't so bad. If she could only be five years old again none of this would have happened. "Sure," she called, and stood from the sofa, sloughing off fatigue. He was a good guy, her dad. Dumb as a rock when it came to raising a daughter, but a *good* dumb rock.

She went to kiss his cheek where he stood at the counter, spilling cookies from a white paper bag onto a glass platter her mother had used for roasts.

Beneath her feet she could feel the waves of the lake washing against the pilings. The back of the house jutted out over the water so that when she looked out the window over the sink and the one over the dining table, she felt as if she were on a ship rather than in a house. She was always expecting the roll that accompanied water-going vessels, waiting for the table to lurch sideways and spill the dishes to the blue and yellow tiles of the floor.

"How was school today?"

She stuffed a cookie into her mouth and grunted. He always asked. And him a teacher. He should know better. School was school. Lately, granted, it was a hellhole where no one liked her and people felt sorry for her and Tye made her feel ashamed, but generally what could you say about a school day? It just was. And then it was over and you were glad. Real glad.

"Have you made any friends?" he asked, pouring two glasses of milk.

That was his second boring question. "Too busy learning about Flannery O'Connor." She pulled out a chair and sat at the table. She turned her face to the window and chewed. "She lived in Midgeville, Georgia."

"And she raised peacocks!" He joined her and set the glasses of milk at their places. "A great writer."

"Greater than Mark Twain?"

"You can't exactly compare writers that way, Angie." He kept staring at her. Tye stared at her. The kids stared at her. She was tired of it.

"Well, I like Mark Twain. I don't care what people in Mississippi think."

"Did you have a hard time at school?" His voice had lowered, softened almost to a whisper. He worried all the time, she knew that. Since it was his idea after her mother died that they move back to where he had been born and raised, if she didn't fit in he'd have made a terrible mistake. He'd have been a bad parent. It wasn't his fault.

"It was okay, Dad," she assured him. "I don't think the English teacher likes me, though. She asked if they taught me about Flannery O'Connor where I came from—like St. Louis was some kind of weird, dirty city that didn't teach anything worth teaching. I guess I'm just different, that's all."

"Well, you know you're different!" He reached out and touched her cheek. "You're more beautiful than they are, that's what it is. They can't help but know how different you are."

"Oh, Daddy."

"What about those kids you went swimming with over the weekend? Are they friendly?"

She looked out the window and pretended to be concentrating on a V-shaped formation of ducks flying in low over the horizon. They landed far off in the center of the lake one after the other in a graceful touchdown, wings folded to water. "They're okay."

She heard him sigh and give up. He asked the questions and she answered "it's okay, they're okay, everything's fine" and they both knew she was lying and there wasn't one thing either of them could do about it. She was a misfit. Now more than ever. She was not beautiful as he was fond of telling her. Her mother had been beautiful. Brown hair highlighted with auburn tints, green eyes the color of dragon scales in a children's book Angie kept in her room, lips full and luscious as ripe peaches. A sexy-looking woman. Killed by polio and swept away from them. First her long, beautiful, perfect legs disfigured. Then the fever. And then the slow dying.

Angie remembered whispering into her ear, breathing her hair that smelled like lilac shampoo, "Mother, don't go. I'll miss you. I need you. Dad doesn't know how to get along without you. Please, don't go. You can't leave us alone like this, please . . ."

But she did leave. Quietly, without a fuss, breathing softly against the stark white of the hospital pillowcase one second and not breathing the next. Just gone. And her father weeping in the hallway, weeping in the car driving her home, weeping in his study in the brownstone that Angie's mother had made into a home.

Not more than a month passed before there was a For Sale sign in the yard. A month later the moving van was in the drive and men were packing their things. "Going back South," her Dad said. "I can't live here in this house where Susan lived. Not without her. You'll like Mississippi, Angie. You'll take to it. I've already had a realtor find us a lake house. Moon Lake is supposed to be gorgeous and you love to swim. It'll be perfect. We'll start over again."

Everything so fast. They were hardly unpacked and it was September first, time to go to school. She knew she would have a rough time of it, but she never imagined how rough. She never could have imagined someone like Tye.

"Basketball season starts soon," her father said, handing her another cookie.

She shook her head at the cookie. Too many chocolate chips in it. She liked Oreos better. "I don't know if they have a girls' basketball team."

"Sure they do. I asked people in Clarksdale. They said the girls are active and the team's pretty good."

"I don't know, Dad . . ."

"You're good at it, Angie. It would be a way to get to know people."

"Make them accept me, you mean."

"I don't mean that. How can they not accept you? You're my girl, aren't you? What's not to accept? You should join in the sports program. You take after your ole dad. You can shoot those baskets like nobody's business. Be a shame if the school didn't have you for their advantage."

"I'm not that good. I'm just taller than the other girls."

"That too." He grinned at her, his aging Audie Murphy boylike face lighting up. It made her heart rise. He smiled so seldom these days. He was proud of her, long legs and all, she couldn't deny that. What he didn't see was how her height made her tower over her classmates, except for some of the boys, and how she sometimes caught herself stooping to talk with people so that she thought she'd grow up with a hump on her back. Damn. Basketball was about all she was good for. Long Tall Sally, duck back in an alley. That was her.

"All right," she said. "I'll try out when the season opens."

"Great. That's the spirit. I'll be at every game, sweetie, cheering you on."

Angie looked out the window again and wondered how much that would help. She visualized an auditorium full of spectators and her dad standing up in the front bleacher yelling, "Go get 'em, Angie. Shoot for the basket!" One lone, crazy college professor's voice yelling in the silence so that again everyone would turn his head and look.

Look at her.

The great big misfit girl from Missouri with a father who was trying too hard to be a father and a mother too.

Tye stood behind the lone oak tree across the road from Angie's house. The sun was setting in an orange fireball that tinted all the trees in the distance with rust. He leaned against the trunk and looked out over the empty field. Then he turned and peeked at Angie's front door.

If she came out, he fantasized, he would walk over to her and apologize. Make it brief and sincere, take her hand, explain how upset he'd been when she said she could not date him and how that emotion led him on to goad her at the lake before the others. Just a mistake, he'd tell her. Not one of his better ideas. He was mean sometimes, he'd say, couldn't seem to help it, but he'd change for her; he would never hurt her again if she'd forgive him this once. If she'd let him kiss her, just this once . . .

The shadow of the tree fell across the road and the sunset at his back warmed a spot between his shoulder blades. The door remained closed. She was in there. She belonged to her father. What kind of fair was that, her belonging already to another man, even if he did understand everyone needed a parent.

She should belong to *him*. He could love her and give her so many more experiences than a father. Or any other man for that matter.

She was in there.

Everything blocked his way. The creeping twilight. The closed door. The father. The argument they had. The things he had said to her, done to her.

He was out here.

Alone, getting cold now. Should have worn a jacket. Should walk across the road and knock on the door. Should take her hand and lead her away from the house where he could talk to her, explain.

Explain how much she excited him. How he saw her as so different from any other girl he had known in his life.

But he saw in his head what might happen if he left his post at the tree and knocked on that door.

She would slam it in his face.

She would make him furious.

She would show him how much she detested him.

Then what could he do?

His thoughts slid down a hole, entering a warren of dark twisty turns. Violence bloomed in his mind like a deep purple flower with roots intertwined all around his muddled brain. He saw himself hurting her. He saw himself holding one of her arms behind her back, shoving the wrist up and up while the elbow screamed from the tension and the girl wept. He saw her go to her knees and beg for him to stop.

He reached out with his other hand to her face and crooned, "Baby, baby, it's okay, it's gonna be okay, don't worry. I was only playing. I won't hurt you, I promise not to hurt you anymore. Now come here and let me wipe your eyes. I'll lick your tears and make them mine. Put your cheek on my chest, let me hold you. Everything's fine, it's as it should be, me and you, nothing in all this world but me and you. You know that.''

The fantasy wound down and the dark intruded, causing him to shiver. He looked longingly at the door one last time. It was impossible, so impossible; all thoughts of apology died as quietly as had the sun beyond the trees. He pivoted and ran across the field toward home. Never had he felt so incompetent. For this he held Angie responsible and for fleeting moments as he ran, he despised her.

Chapter

3

The morning of the basketball tryouts for the girls' team Angie could not find her biology textbook, the toast burned, and her father groused about his shirt not being ironed properly by the cleaners. Everything pointed toward a bad-luck day.

As soon as Jason Thornton left for Clarksdale State University in the nearby town, Angie locked the front door and crossed the gravel road to wait for the bus. She was early, but the empty house oppressed her and she felt compelled to flee for the outdoors.

She stood grinding the sole of her right shoe into the side of the road. Mist hung over the lake behind her house like a dirty white miasma creeping onshore. Angie breathed in the dampness and tried to relax. So what if she tried out for the team and failed? So what if her father might face a disappointment? At least she was going to try.

A brisk wind swooped past and set the leaves of the tree at her back to rustling like bony fists knocking together in the dense limbs. Angie turned and for the first time noticed the lone oak supported a rope swing dangling from a thick branch on the opposite side from the road. She walked over to it and smiled to herself. How odd that someone had put up this swing on the side of the road at the edge of a cotton field. Of course by the time they had moved into the lake house, the cotton was gone, hand picked, her father told her, with disapproval in his voice. "Coolie labor, something the South is famous for. Or infamous, from my perspective."

The field stood barren of its crop now, a dark morning October sky crowning it and the wind pushing the lake mist toward its gravel-lined edges. Rows upon rows of brown, straggly stalks dotted the black earth. It was a desolate piece of ground, a boneyard of twisted shapes. It made her want to cry just to look at it.

Setting down the armload of school books, she turned away from the field and sat down on the weathered board seat in the swing. She wrapped her palms around the thick straw-colored hemp and tightened her fingers into fists to feel the rough texture bite into her skin. She looked up at the tree. The leaves were brownish green, curling at the edges, and when the breeze rattled through the limbs, tiny dry missiles dropped at her feet. The tree would soon be skeletal and match the cotton field. She kicked off and began to swing, the damp air pressing against her face like a wrung-out dishcloth.

She dragged her feet along the packed path beneath the swing and holding tight with both hands on the rope, twisted to the left until the twin ropes crossed. She turned and turned, head down to watch the leaves scattering about her. When the rope was so tight her shoulders felt hemmed in, she gave a push in the opposite direction, lifted her feet, and let the swing's momentum take her round and round, faster and faster, until her head spun and the earth whirled rapid as a top.

Just as the swing slowed, the two hanging ropes whipping apart, she heard the growl of the bus coming down the lake road. She halted and stood, but her vision was out of focus and she couldn't manage to see one road and one bus. Everything around her was doubled and moving. She squatted to take up her books and grew instantly faint. The bus ground to a stop, she heard the hydraulic doors hiss open, and she knew the driver and the passengers were waiting, watching her balancing herself in a squat, books in lap, fingertips to each side to steady her body.

The faintness passed, the world slowed, and she took a deep breath. Maybe she should be treated as a child if she still loved swings and the out of control feeling of vertigo produced by turning herself around and around. As she moved toward the bus door she told herself she didn't care if they'd caught her playing in the swing. Doing kid things was all right, now and then. She wasn't an old lady, for goshsakes, she could still swing if she wanted. Besides, something told her that any one of them, including the saggy-faced bus driver, would have done the same if he had been alone this windy, damp morning and he had seen the swing hanging lonesome and unused from the oak tree.

It was amazing to her that her father had chosen to live in such a secluded place after their life on a busy street near downtown St. Louis. It was really the boondocks here. The boys wore uniforms of blue jeans, T-shirts, and dirty sneakers; the girls wore dresses or skirts and blouses she wouldn't be caught dead wearing. There were only two buses which picked up students for Moon Lake High from the lake area. Although Conway Twitty lived in a fancy lake house farther down the road—which didn't impress her in the least; no one liked Conway Twitty when they could listen to the Beatles and the Stones—the lake had not yet been discovered by city dwellers and the population along its rock-strewn edges was sparse. As far as Angie could see in both directions from her own house there were trees and road and fields. The only other habitation in her line of view, if indeed someone actually lived in what looked like a tumble-down shack fit only for barn animals, stood several hundred yards down the road across from them. It might have been a tenant's shack for the cotton pickers who swarmed the fields during season. Except for that one unpainted house, the lake seemed abandoned to the wild.

Tye rode her bus. For three weeks she refused to look at him. He sat toward the front surrounded by a group that made a lot of racket to bring attention to themselves; she sat toward the back in a seat by herself.

Each day when the bus pulled up beside the massive white granite pillars topped with lions' heads that guarded the entrance to where he lived, she cautiously studied his house in the distance. Unlike the other kids picked up along the route who lived in houses similar to her own, Tye's house was an ostentatious display of red brick and mortar. It rose two stories topped by four chimneys jutting from the black roof. It was an antebellum house with a gigantic wraparound veranda. White stone columns braced wide steps leading up to ten-foot double doors.

Angie wondered what it must have been like to have been raised in that house. It was a sedate, stately mansion flanked by two huge cedars at the ends of the veranda. It looked cold to Angie, austere, a Civil War kind of house full of dark rooms and velvet drapes. Since no brother or sister waited for the bus with Tye, Angie assumed he was an only child like herself. But she had shared her childhood with streets full of neighbors and children who poured down the sidewalks in St. Louis like gangs of those small, African deer she had seen on television, hopping as they ran, sniffing the air for adventure. Who had been Tye's playmates? Did he have any? What did he do in the summer for fun besides think up horrible ways to embarrass people?

After weeks of contemplation of both the boy and his home, she concluded he was just one of those spoiled-rotten rich brats who had nothing better to do than to think up hateful surprises. His parents were probably such snobs that even President Johnson wouldn't want to talk to them.

Not that this lessened her animosity toward Tye. In fact these thoughts fueled her dislike. She had never approved of the pretentious rich or for that matter, the pretentious anything. There had been some of them on the faculty of the university where her father once worked. When he brought them home, her mother invariably said, "Jason, if I have to put up with these academic asses past nine o'clock, I'm going to throw the whole bunch out on the street so that I can go to bed. They get on my nerves with their precious theories and their ponderous rumblings."

"Hey, Angie, I hear you're trying out for the team today." Tye's voice broke into her reverie of her mother. She had not heard what he'd said from the front of the bus. He had not spoken to her since the lake incident and she had not expected him to speak to her again, which suited her fine.

She glanced his way, confusion apparent on her face.

"She's deaf, that's what it is," Tye explained to those around him who laughed as if he'd made a funny joke. "I said I heard you're trying out for basketball."

She almost said no, she wasn't, and it was none of his business anyway, but she was not used to lying, at least not without preparation. She nodded and looked out the window at the gray, featureless fields sliding by. Was all of Mississippi flat as a plate and about as interesting? Would Tye . . . would he leave her alone now?

"I play basketball," he said loudly, forcing her to face front again. "We might play some games together, same schools, same nights, you know."

"Great," she said, and clamped shut her mouth. Great. Ride with him every day to school and to games too. Just wonderful.

"I'm glad you think so," he called, and settled again into his seat, back to her. The group turned too and she was looking at a solid mass of backs and shoulders.

I don't think so, she almost yelled. I don't think it will be any fun at all if you want to know the truth.

The bus geared down with a throaty groan to drive into the back parking lot of the old, yellow brick school and Angie tightened her grip on her books. Another day begun.

She wished she were back at the oak tree swinging, twisting around until the world lost pattern and merged into a kaleidoscope of grays, blues, and browns.

Getting picked for the team should have been a cinch. But since when had things happened as they should? Not since Mother died. It was all downhill from there.

Angie was inches taller than anyone in the tryouts except for one skinny black girl who had to top out at six feet. Not only that, but Angie had been center forward on the St. Louis Tigers in her freshman year and had done a whiz-bang job of it, too. Her father had worked with her on the cement drive at their old house, shooting baskets and teaching her to block until the evening turned to darkness the color of India ink.

Dressed out in their green cotton P.E. shorts and shirts, the woman coach lined them up on one side of the court. She couldn't miss Angie's height advantage. But for some unfathomable reason—and Angie thought it was because she was new and an outsider—the coach gave every other girl in the line a chance to show her stuff before she called on "Miss Thornton."

"All right, Miss Thornton, if you and Miss Brite will step out onto center court, I'd like you to take turns being guards and forwards."

"Which one should I be first?" Angie asked, liking the feel of the basketball in her hands, its tight, full heaviness familiar as an old friend.

"Oh, it doesn't matter, now does it?" the woman asked in a surly tone. "Just do it, for goodness sake. It's getting late and our time's almost up."

Angie shrugged at the Brite girl who stood at average height but weighed entirely too much for the quickness of this particular game. Angie figured the girl had thirty pounds on her. "Okay, I'll forward," she said and bounced the ball, maneuvering toward the goal.

Josey Brite went into a crouch, shifting in front of Angie, waving her arms like a windmill gone berserk.

"No, no!" the coach yelled, taking a few steps onto the court. "Don't do your arms like that. Haven't you ever *played* this game, Miss Brite?"

Angie saw the girl wince and lower her arms. The basketball bounced, boom, boom, echoing against the walls, and there was an opening. Angie took it. She came at Josey, faked to her right, and moved quickly again to the left circling her and she was free, the way open. She paused and shot. The ball hit the backboard and slammed into the basket. Perfect!

Angie turned to the coach smiling in triumph as if to say, "See, I'm good, this is my game."

The frustrated look on the coach's face killed her smile. "What do you think you're doing, Miss Thornton?"

"I . . . uh . . . well, I faked her out and took my shot."

"And you didn't give her time to ready for it either, did you?"

"I thought she was ready . . ."

"You thought. You thought. If that's how they play basketball in Missouri, Lord help us. You jump in or break before a whistle and they'll call a foul. Now start again. Do it right." Whispers broke out among the other girls and the coach snapped, "Shut up and sit down."

Angie caught the ball Josey had retrieved and set her mouth in a line to keep from letting the coach see how angry she was. She bounced the ball against the floor. Boom, boom, the sound filling her ears. "You ready?" she asked the crouching, nervous-footed Josey.

"Yeah."

"Great. Here I come. Try to stop me." Coach blew the whistle.

The girl was no match. Angie felt sorry for her, trying so hard, feinting and swinging her jiggling fat arms, but she was not basketball material. She was slow and fearful. When Angie moved, it took Josey seconds to catch up with her. When Angie shot, the girl ducked and cringed as if she were about to be smashed in the mouth.

"Change places!" the coach called after Angie had made four straight baskets despite all that Josey could do to stop her.

Josey took the ball, bounced it, and lost it. The ball bounded away and rolled across the court. While

Angie waited and the coach stewed and rocked back and forth on the balls of her feet, Josey ran duckfoot to pick it up for another try. She never made a basket. Angie took it easy on her, feeling her ineptitude like a wash of cold water coming off her sweating body. She let her get closer to the net than she had to, but even then Josey missed the backboard altogether and hit the wall.

"Halt! That's enough." The coach blew the whistle shrilly.

Angie and Josey walked toward her, toward the girls who had already been separated into team members and losers.

Without looking up from her clipboard the coach said, "Miss Thornton, you're big and way too anxious to prove what a fine player you are, but I guess we'll give you a chance. Go with the other girls and pick up your suit. Practice starts tomorrow."

Angie sighed with relief. She had not thought she'd wanted this so badly, but if she'd been turned down for the team she knew now she would have felt like throwing the biggest, ugliest tantrum anyone had ever witnessed.

"You, Brite . . . I'm sorry, but you need to work on it another year. You don't have any natural talent. This isn't the sport for you."

"Come on, Josey," Angie consoled. "Let's go shower. You wouldn't have liked this anyway."

The girl's lower lip trembled and she was about to cry. Angie took her hand and pulled her off the court to fall in behind the other girls. "Don't cry," she whispered. "Don't let them see you cry. It's not worth it."

"Yeah, to you, maybe." Josey jerked her hand away and ran ahead, laughter breaking out behind her back.

"What's the matter with all of you?" Angie asked

in outrage. "She tried so hard and she wanted to make it. Why do you have to laugh at her?"

Three of the prettier girls, all blondes, all rounded bosoms and perfect snub noses, turned on Angie in the shower room. One of them, the leader of the pack, Angie assumed, since she looked haughty enough to curdle ice water, said, "She's a slut and she's fat. Nobody has to worry about her feelings. What do you care anyway? You got what you wanted."

"And you got what you wanted too—on the team. It would seem you'd have a little feeling for Josey," Angie answered back.

"I notice you didn't have much feeling for anyone since you're the one who made her look bad."

"Oh never mind." Angie tried to walk past them to her locker. She knew girls like this. There was no talking to them, there was no getting through to them. They were dense as a clump of mud.

The girl in the center of the trio grabbed her by the arm and twirled her around.

"Watch yourself in the games, Angie," she purred.

Angie felt blood rush to her face. "What does that mean?"

"Just what I said. Watch yourself. We don't like people who come from up north and try to tell us how to act to our own kind."

"I'm not from 'up north.' I'm from Missouri. Check your map."

"You're a Yankee and Yankees have no place here. And if you ever tell me to look at a map again, you bitch, I'll make you eat one."

"What *you* should eat," Angie whispered slowly, clearly, aware everyone in the locker room was watching now, "is a steady diet of that so-called southern hospitality. It might improve your manners. And your mouth."

The girl hardly waited an instant between Angie's

last words before her hand came up and slapped Angie's face soundly. Angie pushed her back on reflex and the other two girls jumped forward. Suddenly they were all yelling and cursing, pushing and slapping and shoving. Angie was against the lockers, pinned, taking the worst of it. She had shut her eyes and was lashing out as best she could while ducking her head down toward her arms. Jesus God, they wanted to kill her, they wanted to tear her apart!

"Who started this?"

The authoritarian voice of the coach broke through the sounds of girls fighting. Angie found herself alone, bent over her knees, back against the locker. Her face stung and she thought she might be missing a lock of hair from above her right ear. She stood up, feeling around on her scalp for blood, but found none. It still hurt like hell. And she was shaking. Scared. She knew how girls fight. Like panthers. She had never wanted to fight, never. She should have kept her mouth shut and avoided this. But they kept pushing her, always pushing her . . .

"Did you start this?" The coach stood in front of Angie with her clipboard jutted out from her chest, pencil poised as if to take down testimony.

Angie squared her back and held her tongue. So that's the way it was. It didn't matter if she joined the basketball team, the pep club, or the yearbook staff, they'd still blame her for whatever went wrong. They'd hate her. She was in no better position than Josey who had been tagged clumsy and fat. She never should have tried for the team. All it was going to do was bring her more headache.

"It wasn't her fault." Josey spoke up in the silence. "They started the whole thing." She pointed to the three blondes who were busy smoothing their clothes and hair.

"Did not!" one of them yelled back.

The coach chose to ignore Josey. "For the rest of the week I want you to dress out, Miss Thornton, and run around the football field. Twice," she added on second thought. "Two laps a day, the rest of the week."

She turned to the crowded girls. "The rest of you can expect the same punishment if you fight again. Understood?" She tapped the clipboard with the pencil and strode from the locker room.

Angie nodded her thanks to Josey even though the aid had not helped her. She kept her back to everyone while she changed for the next class. Damn them. Damn all of them. For every Josey there were a hundred little hateful pep-rally girls ready to do her in.

Would living on Moon Lake, Mississippi, ever get better? She doubted it sincerely.

But it might get worse. Downhill all the way.

Chapter

4

Angie's favorite possession was her transistor radio. It went everywhere with her. She slept with it playing next to her ear in bed at night. She carried it in her purse. She would have bathed with it had she been able.

It ran on a six-volt battery and lost power within a few hours, but she used the savings from four weeks' allowances to buy a supply she kept in a shoebox in the bottom of her clothes closet. While the Beach Boys were crooning their way into obscurity, Bob Dylan was making a comeback with "Lay Lady Lay."

Afternoons after school and weekends found her patrolling the lake edge, following the shore in each direction from her house, radio in hand, little earphone stuck in her ear sending messages in song from exotic places like Baton Rouge, Louisiana, and Jackson, Mississippi.

The lake was endlessly fascinating. It was deep and wide, changing colors according to the time of day and the weather, lapping languorously against the rocks and the pilings of her house when calm or, during a storm, rearing like a hell-bent stallion to pummel the land with frothing whitecaps. It performed like some misplaced ocean stuck in the middle of the Delta. It was man-made, she discovered, and not that old, possibly ten years, but it had already spawned legends. Her father told of a story he had heard from one of his students in Clarksdale. She thought for a while he might have made it up to frighten her, to prevent her from swimming too far out into the water. But the story had a ring of truth, and besides, her father was not a prevaricator. He taught freshman and sophomore English composition. Every day he dealt with the truth, with history, and had no experience in creating stories himself.

The story went that one summer a wild group of kids took a fast speedboat out onto the lake. One of the girls wanted to water-ski so they put her on the ski rope and hauled her as fast as they could go up and down the lake. She fell. They turned to come back for her and she was missing, her skis left floating where she had fallen in. Some of the boys dove in and looked for her, but the water was too dark and muddy, the bottom growing a virulent thick weed that kept them from searching. Finally help was called in and the lake was dredged. The girl was found, snagged with a gaff hook and brought up from the bottom. The horror of it, worse than any drowning accident Angie could think about, was that the girl was covered with moccasins. Clamped to her. Hanging off her body like strips of brown slime. They believed she had fallen into a snake pit and been bitten to death.

"I doubt that's an entirely true story," her father admitted when he finished repeating the tale. "I've heard of snakes in water, and I guess it's possible there could be a pit of them, but the real reason I'm telling you about it is that the lake *can* be a dangerous place. Even without a population of venomous snakes, it's very deep and I want you to be careful."

Angie shivered at the thought, staring out at the water glittering softly in the last rays of October sun. All the times she had walked the lakeside, she had not come upon one snake. She was afraid if she did, she'd never have the courage to explore it again. But it was *possible,* even probable, that moccasins were afoot, if not beneath the water's surface.

She intended to be careful. She had never intended otherwise.

Tiring of the shoreline and the sound of birds punctuating her lonely thoughts, she moved through the woods circling it. She would come out on the gravel road and follow it home.

Breaking through dead winter undergrowth and carefully pushing aside sticky cedar branches, she stepped into the open. Directly across from her stood the old shack she had seen so often while sitting in the oak tree swing. And on the leaning porch steps of the shack sat an obese black woman wearing a blue and red plaid handkerchief tied about her head.

"Hello, girl," the woman greeted.

"Hi." Angie took the earphone from her ear and turned off the radio to save the battery. "I didn't know anyone lived there."

"I live here. I'm somebody. Not somebody important, though."

Angie was charmed. She had never really held a conversation with a Negro. Blacks and whites shied from one another's company since the civil rights marches in Selma, Alabama, led by the Reverend Martin Luther King.

Angie crossed the dusty road, kicking gravel as she went. She approached the bare yard cautiously, not sure she was actually invited onto the woman's property or not. "I'm Angelina Thornton—Angie, really.

Everyone calls me Angie . . ." She was babbling and now she was nervous. Maybe she should go on home.

"Hello, Angelina. My name's Varna. Jenkins, it is, but that's no matter. I see you moved in with your daddy down in the lake house." She pointed one stubby finger down the road.

"Yeah, my dad and I. My mother died last year . . ." Damn. Why had she said that? She didn't mean to say that.

Varna's eyes, round and bulbous and yellow-tinged all around the brown irises, lowered their lids. She looked sleepy and Angie wondered if indeed she was about to doze off right in the middle of a thought.

Angie stood still, waiting, not daring to move. Finally Varna Jenkins spoke:

> *"And nothing can we call our own but death;*
> *And that small model off the barren earth,*
> *which serves as paste and cover to our bones.*
> *For God's sake, let us sit upon the ground,*
> *And tell sad stories of the death of kings."*

Angie stood aghast. For a Negro sitting on a porch stoop in the middle of a cotton field to spout poetry was about as shocking as to dive through dolphin green water and find a tangled nest of water moccasins snapping their mighty jaws. It was unheard of.

Angie knew she was standing there with her transistor radio in her hands, mouth hanging open. For the life of her, she couldn't get it closed.

"That was Shakespeare," Varna explained. "From *King Richard the Second*, act two. I don't know what line. I can't never remember the lines they come from."

"It was . . . it was beautiful," Angie said.

"Oh yes, oh my, yes. Shakespeare was a beautiful man."

"We haven't studied him much yet in school."

"Varna's studied him long and hard and to good measure," the old woman said, hugging her knees with big hands that looked like purple-black slabs that rightly belonged to a man.

"Well . . ." Angie itched to be off, but she didn't know how to do it politely. She had to think about this. If her father had quoted Shakespeare, she would not have blinked an eyelash. But who read him and cared enough to memorize his words except college professors and such? She'd just have to think about it.

"It's getting on night," Varna said, as if reading her mind. "Best you be on your way home. It was nice to know you, Angelina. You come back, you hear?"

Nice to *know* her? Varna sure talked funny even if you dismissed the poetry.

"Yeah, I guess I should. My dad worries if I'm out at dark."

"Will you come back?"

The question had such a plaintive tone that immediately Angie was nodding, backing away, and saying, "Sure, I'll come back. I'll come back to visit you sometimes." She laughed. "You're my only neighbor for miles, why shouldn't I?"

As she walked toward home she repeated the question to herself. Why shouldn't she? There was no one to talk to. Her father was always grading papers and working in notebooks. And he was sad; maybe he told sad stories of kings to himself; maybe he missed Mother too much. Of course he missed her. Susan Thornton had left a hole in their lives, a vacuum they could not fill. Her father was awfully quiet, that's all Angie knew. Thinking by himself and holding all his hurts close.

Varna was nice. The first nice person she had met

41

in all of Mississippi. And she could tell she was sorry that Angie's mother had died. Most people got nervous about it when she told them or they treated her like a poor lost puppy or something. Varna spoke of having nothing to call your own but death, and that was right. She couldn't even keep her mother from going away.

Tears formed instantly and Angie wiped them away with the back of her hand. In the end it was a big joke. You thought you owned things like your parents and your house and your happiness and you never really owned anything at all. How could you stop them from going?

The deep twilight laid a blanket over the flat land, over the calm lake, and Angie, hurrying toward the lighted windows of her house, glanced back to see the shack smothered in darkness, not a light shining anywhere in sight. She had a feeling Varna sat on the steps even now, watching her until she was safe.

That night after dinner Angie said to her father, "I met the woman who lives down the road in that old house."

Jason sat at the table, student papers spread out beneath his hands. "That's nice."

"She talks strange. She quotes poetry."

"Uh-huh."

"She has two heads and was eating snakes."

"Good. Good, Angie."

At that point Angie decided she would have more luck doing the dishes and attacking her homework than talking to her father. Huh. More luck talking to the wall, to the lake sitting silent and bottomless outside the windows.

One thing for certain, she was going down to see Varna tomorrow afternoon. She wanted to ask her about the cotton and what it looked like when it was planted and coming up in the spring. She wanted to ask her if the story of the girl bitten by snakes in the lake was true. If they became better friends, she might even ask her what women do with men who do not hear them when they talk, men who, for all intents and purposes, have gone as far away as someone who has died.

Tye lay on his bed thinking about Angie. He had followed her along the lake's edge in early afternoon. She had bebopped along the shore with whatever music she was getting from the radio she carried around and plugged into her ear. It was cute, kind of, seeing her that way, completely unaware of his presence, bopping on down the lakefront like a little kid or something. He wondered if she listened to the same songs he liked. He wondered what she must be thinking as she stopped now and then to stare strangely out at the flat blue-gray water.

When she broke through the undergrowth and crossed the road to old Varna Jenkins' house, he had hidden behind the trees and listened to them. That crazy old nigger mama. Talking her Shakespeare and making her riddles. Most everyone thought her nutty as a fruitcake. It surprised him to notice Varna and Angie seemed to hit it off together. What could they have in common? No self-respecting white person along Moon Lake Road went around making friends with the tenant shack niggers. In the first place it just couldn't be done. The cotton pickers and cotton gin workers didn't want to mess with white people. Why should they? And for another thing, didn't Angie know the worst thing she could do to her reputation was to be known as a nigger-lover? This was not Missouri, he'd have to tell her. This was not the damn frozen great white north. People knew their places here even if they did have to share bus seats and water fountains now. No one who knew anything thought that had really changed the rules. You still didn't associate with coloreds and you sure as God didn't go visiting them at their stupid shacks.

Angie was strange. Once she was his he had to reeducate her completely. Show her how things got done and what things one did not do.

He would have to keep a closer eye on her. If she was bent on making Varna her friend—and he'd heard her say she'd come back to visit, hadn't he?—then he would have to watch her carefully. Black people had peculiar notions and Varna had a goodly portion of those plus some odd ones of her own to add. That was not good for Angie. All that down-home, earthy philosophy. All that homespun silly shit. And who better to know than he, the boy Varna helped tend while he was growing up?

He shifted uneasily in the bed. Varna knew all kinds of things she might start saying to the girl. Now that wouldn't be nice of her, but he wouldn't put it past the old cow. She had lectured *him* enough times, he should know how her crazed old mind worked.

Yes, he would have to keep an eye on this development. Angie was turning into a full-time project. Not that it mattered. He knew she was worth it. Nothing in his entire life had ever been as worthy of his time and best efforts.

Chapter

5

Angie's misgivings about joining the basketball team gave way over a period of weeks during practice to a sense of accomplishment, if not acceptance, on the court. She played center on the first string and she played the position better than anyone who had come along in a decade. The other team members begrudgingly acknowledged her agility and skill, but once off the court the silent treatment continued. Angie realized in a final way that she was an outcast and nothing she did during the rest of her life in high school could bring her into the camp.

The second time Tyeson Dompier approached her after the debacle at the lake happened on an adrenaline-filled night when both the boys' and girls' teams played games against Clarksdale High.

Angie played brilliantly, but the Clarksdale team was leading in number one place while Moon Lake held a shaky fourth place. Still, Angie's team took possession of the court and out of sheer gut-busting energy and excitement, began to give Clarksdale a run for their money. In fact, they had a chance to beat the biggest, meanest, toughest girls' team in the county if their grit held and the southern God that watched over their piece of Mississippi happened to be on duty for the night.

It surprised Angie when the first temper flared. A guard deliberately knocked her backwards causing her to drop the ball, and the crowd, Angie's father screaming the loudest, yelled "Foul!" The referee did not agree. He had been looking elsewhere and had not seen the illegal move.

Violence escalated. Girls knocked into girls, jump shots were blocked without respect to the opponent's anatomy, and name-calling turned into an incessant, ugly cacophony. Angie felt drops of sweat pop out on her brow. She tried to play out the game without further incident. Violence scared her, made her edgy and unsure of herself. Taking jabs in the ribs and rude, bone-cracking falls on the polished blond floor weren't her favorite ways to wind up a good game of basketball.

Moon Lake's only black team member, Tolly Gaynor, happened to make a lucky last shot from center court and won the game by a mere two points in the last five seconds before the end bell. The crowd and team screamed themselves into near hysteria. A roar filled the auditorium and the Clarksdale girls crouched together in public defeat, mouths downturned and fists clenched.

It was unfortunate that the opposing girls' teams had to share one locker room for changing. Some of the Clarksdale girls could be heard griping about the close win and how it was all a cheat any-damn-way, everyone knew Moon Lake couldn't whip a wet bitch dog.

"Well, this was one dog that whipped *your* little mangy asses," someone yelled out.

"Two points!" came a reply. "And you had to let the nigger girl do it for you, you bunch of lazy white trash. If you think two points is whipping ass, have we got a lesson for you!"

The fight erupted. It had been building to eruption since the two teams first walked out onto the court and bowed to the audience. Girls pulled hair, tore bra straps, ripped blouses to shreds, cussing like sailors set to sea for a year.

Angie had her shorts off and was in the process of pulling the sweaty red and white Moon Lake jersey over her head. She heard shouts and an unknown assailant pushed her hard against the rough cement block wall. She cried out in surprise and jerked the jersey over her head. She stood in her underwear watching the melee escalate. Girls surged to the middle of the long narrow room and locker doors banged and rattled like mortar fire. The scents of burning anger and sour sweat suffused the place. Reason was lost to the winds. Before Angie could decide what she was supposed to do Coach Lanahan slammed open the locker room door and rushed in to separate the girls nearest her.

"Stop it! Stop it this minute! This is a vulgar display and you'll all get expelled."

Clarksdale's principal and several teachers struggled in to help break up the fight. They grabbed arms and jerseys and forcibly hauled girls off one another.

Angie watched with fascination until it dawned on her that she was unclothed and there were grown men in the room. She grabbed her jeans and began struggling into them, color rising in her cheeks.

It was over as quickly as it had begun. The two teams parted, jeers and curses still swapped in whispers, and for twenty long sticky hot minutes they all had to listen to Lanahan's stern lecture. The air grew dense with resentment. If looks had been knives every girl in the room would have been fatally impaled.

Angie was relieved to reach the cool dark of the bus. She found a seat in the back to be away from the other girls who would want to gossip over the recent excitement. Angie didn't want to discuss it. Violence and anarchy were alien to her nature. Though only fifteen she had formed deep-seated convictions about certain aspects of the world and found she had a thorough dislike for physical confrontation. When her father, who was generally a refined man, became a fan of boxing, Angie would leave the house to him and the blaring television, unable to stand the sight of dedicated savagery. She could not endure the sight of pain inflicted or endured. It reduced her to tears to see dogs or cats lying mutilated on the highway. She grew ill in biology class when they had to dissect small reptiles. The locker room fight had left her weak-kneed and queasy, the flight mechanism still urging her to retreat, to hide and to wait for calm.

"Your pacifism is too highly developed for you to get along in this world, Angie," her father had told her once he noticed she escaped the room on Saturday nights when he switched on the fights. "If you don't develop some toughness about it, I'm afraid you're letting yourself in for a lot of unnecessary pain. Boxing, for instance. It's a beautifully choreographed sport."

"It's blood sport," she said. "It's vicious."

"No, no, it's not. These men are some of our best athletes. They train for this. Their hands are padded with the gloves, there's a civilized time limit, referees, and doctors on hand."

"That's so when one of them passes out with brain damage or dies, they have someone who can write out the death certificate."

"Angie . . ."

"I'm sorry, Dad. I just don't see the point. It's ridiculous to stand in a ring and beat up people. It isn't at all civilized to me. We aren't cavemen, you know. We aren't Romans who need to see the Christians devoured by the lions."

Angie mulled over that conversation as the bus lumbered its way across the twenty-five miles back to Moon Lake. Maybe she had been wrong. Perhaps men were still Romans and had handed in togas for three-piece suits. Was something important missing from her personality that caused her to turn away from girls fighting? Had she been the only one to step gingerly away into a corner of the dressing stall, hoping not to be noticed, praying for intervention before someone was really hurt?

Tye stood at the front of the bus facing to the back. The bus driver asked him to sit down; *asked* because Tye was not a student one could command with any authority.

All eyes followed Tye's progress to the back, some of the jittery laughter dying down into softly voiced bets on how he would make out. It was common knowledge the new girl was a challenge, one Tye had not yet conquered. She was quiet, she had not been out on a date, and she seemed to care little for Tye's smart aleck advances in the school hallways and lunch line.

Angie looked up at his approach and groaned inwardly. It was not the night to have to deal with him. She was tired and confused over the fight. She only wanted to be left alone, to rest, to get home and to her bed. She glanced out the window to the ghostly flat fields rolling past in the night under a waning Halloween moon. She would rather be walking alone along the deserted, moonlit road than be here. Rather be anywhere but here.

Tye sat down heavily next to her. He carried his basketball jacket in his left hand and it lodged between them like a fish caught between rocks.

"You played a good game tonight. I watched you. You're a natural," he said.

If he had not reached out and patted her on the leg in a familiar way and if she had not been nervous, she might have reacted differently.

She gazed at his hand which did not leave her leg, but which lay possessively on her thigh. Slowly she picked it up as if it were a dead mackerel and put it in his lap. She hunched her shoulders to make herself as small as possible against the cold metal ribs of the bus beneath the window.

Tye, undaunted by her casual rejection, pulled the jacket from between them and dropped it to the floor. He moved closer until their shoulders and legs pressed together. He put an arm around her and pulled her away from the window.

"What do you think you're doing?" She searched for his eyes in the darkness, uncomfortably aware the others watched them from in front.

"Getting to know you better. Can't you be friendly?"

"I don't think so." She removed his arm by bending forward and unwrapping it over her head. Again she dropped his hand into his lap. Her heart fluttered like a wild thing. He looked so good. Why did he have to look so damn good anyway? But she would never forgive him for what he had done to her and she could never trust him not to do something horrible again. She mustered whatever ragtag courage she possessed and turned away.

"Were you in the locker room fight?" He seemed nonplussed by the way she kept brushing him off.

"No. I don't like fighting." She bit gently into her lower lip. He would think she was a child.

They'd all hear whatever she said. She must not speak to him.

"Is that right? I guess people in St. Louis don't go in for self-defense, huh?"

She refused to be baited. She could feel him breathing close to her ear and knew he had shifted perceptibly toward her again. She experienced a tiny tremble that started somewhere in the center of her body and radiated outward to her fingertips. An unnamed stirring accompanied the trembling. It was like the feeling she had had in the flickering light of a shadowed downtown theater when a boy first kissed her, but this was a stronger anticipation, more intoxicating. It shook her that she would think of Tye in that way after the humiliation he had heaped upon her head. It was like asking a motionless Doberman if it were ready to turn you into lunch meat.

Without looking in his direction she could feel his intense gaze on her. An impulse seized her imagination. She wanted to turn to him and trail her fingers over his cheeks and onto his lips. She wanted his arm around her shoulder again. She wanted . . . but no, she didn't, of course she didn't want anything to do with him, he was a monster, a spoiled, rich, mean boy . . .

"I like the way you wear your hair long like that." He delicately brushed aside a still damp lock to nibble her earlobe.

A delicious thrill shimmered down the length of her body and she tightened her legs. His lips now moved steadily, inexorably down into the hollow of her throat. She arched her neck and felt her breasts thrust forward as if awaiting capture. She wanted this, wanted him to continue, to follow the line of her pulsating throat to the gently heaving tops of her breasts. But at the same time she feared he might try that very maneuver. It was all too confusing. It was too hot in the bus and she detected the mingled, giddying scent of male flesh and musky cologne. She felt at war within, the city towers falling over with thundering crashes, the streets of her mind crumbling into scattered bricks and fluttering ashes. How could she yearn for him so strongly and yet distrust and even dislike him?

A muffled cough brought her head up. She leaned away from Tye and nearer the window. She tried to glance surreptitiously through the darkened bus. Were they all watching? Had they seen her moment of fire and longing? Why was every event connected with Tye incumbent with rushing shame and guilt?

She pressed an open palm against his hair just as Tye leaned over and planted his lips lightly against her left breast through the material of her blouse. She drew in a deep breath and said, "Don't do that." She felt his soft breath leave the material ringed with warmth as he withdrew. She turned to look at him, shocked at how brave, how manipulative he could be. It was a tactical mistake. As soon as she faced him his hands came from the darkness and held her head in a vise. His half-closed eyes loomed out of the inky black and his lips closed on hers.

Taken totally by surprise, her eyes wide open, Angie shuddered uncontrollably. She tried to pry loose, hands pushing his chest from her. His teeth strained against her lips and his tongue darted out to force open her mouth. Breathing heavily, blood racing, being drawn closer and closer until she was pressed against him, Angie panicked and heaved him away with all her might. She sucked in breath with a gasp. His mouth had tasted of rainwater, slightly metallic, yet cool and fresh. She had no idea kissing could be so lovely. And so dangerous. Her heart beat as if it would break out of her chest and fly down the aisle of the bus like a red bird racing for freedom.

A catcall sounded from the front and a dozen people began to chortle, whistle, and yell.

Tye sat back in triumph, his eyes shining like polished black stones, his forehead slick with fragrant sweat.

That stupid, glorious face. So arrogant it should be chiseled and set aside in some big city museum where people spoke in whispers. Angie felt embarrassment sweep over her in a cold shiver. He had set the whole thing up. Maybe it was a dare. He had told them all to watch how easily he could control Angie Thornton. Just watch how simple it is to divert her attention and to make a fool of her in front of the whole school.

"You liked that, don't tell me," he said, keeping his voice low so that only she could hear. "I liked it too. You're different, Angie. We belong together. Stick around and I'll teach you a few other things besides kissing."

She said nothing. Had he really liked it or was he confessing this was simply one more of his sneaky tricks and since he was master of the game, he knew all the rules?

Suddenly he had her hand, in the dark, guiding it to his lap. She drew in air, eyes facing forward unseeing, mind falling completely out of sync. It was several mindless seconds before she had the strength and courage to take her hand from him.

What had he done? Jesus, who did he think he was? Though her hand was once again in her own lap she still felt the shape of him imprinted on her skin and more so in her mind. Another new sensation, one more alien to her than the kiss. A fearful thing, an erection. Large and hard and unrelenting in its strange existence. She had never even imagined what it would feel like and could never have predicted her first experience would be when Tye forced her to clamp her hand around the evidence of his excitement.

The very thought of having touched him turned her cheeks to flame. She needed water, needed air, needed space and time and to be away from this boy who had the audacity to make her fondle him in the dark surrounded by dozens of people.

Teach her things, he had promised. No. He would not. She would not permit herself to ever be alone with Tye. Ever. His threats seemed to be ever growing, flooding her with new, coppery fear that coated her mouth and shut off her breath.

Chapter
6

Next time it would be for real, he thought with satisfaction. None of this kiddy stuff for the clowns up front who wanted a show. No more playing around, a little French kissing, a little feelie in the dark to prove to her he was ready when she was ready. No, next time would be the real thing whether she wanted it or not. But she would want it, he could tell from the way she kissed him. They all wanted it. Three girls this year had already come up to him in the hall and offered themselves like the little whores they were. Nothing subtle about what they meant, either. They simply sidled up when he was alone and asked if he wanted to go out for a drive soon, have a good time, drink a little booze, and see how it all came out.

He could stand to wait for Angie. She would never offer herself like the other girls. But he could not wait for long and not forever. He wouldn't want her to forget how much she wanted him. He knew Angie had never been made love to. Hell, that was apparent to any bystander. She was as prissy and stiff as if she had the Hope diamond hidden beneath her skirts. What she had she would lose. To him. Only to him because they were both special people.

Why did she have to keep being such a hard case? He had done all the proper things. It had all started out prim and proper as you please. Smile at her. Ask her for a date . . . then . . . got shot down like some goofball. That had really steamed him good. He could almost hate her for that. Couldn't tell him her ole man wouldn't let her date yet. God, she was fifteen years old, what kind of father did she have, a throwback, some Missouri kind of prehistoric dodo bird who thought his little daughter too precious to go out like other girls? Most of the girls around Moon Lake had been going out since they were twelve, thirteen. Man. How was he supposed to believe her when she gave him that excuse? He never would have embarrassed her at the lake if she'd just played along. But she got mad, always had to get mad, and look at him as if he were some kind of crippled frog or a slug or something. He lost it then and he was out the door acting awful when in truth he hadn't meant to, really wouldn't have done it had she given him the slightest hint that she liked him.

Well, he'd have to teach her not to lie to him. That's all there was to it. Teach her to behave when he wanted something.

Like next time. Next time he'd show her how it was done. How to bare her breasts and sit on top of him and rear back like an angel in ecstasy, that's what he would teach her. And after the first time she would love him for it.

But why did she have to be such a hard case? She was no better than any girl he had known. Well, that wasn't true. She was special, he accepted that. She was a fine looker. Brown shiny hair the color of deep loam shot through with mica glinting in the sun, dark eyes that showed every emotion, every thought, and her long, lanky woman-girl body with the new full breasts, little rounded bottom, legs like a racehorse. She looked *good*. Fresh and wholesome. Untouched.

He was certain of that. Untouched. Until now. She was his now. Branded. His girl. No matter what she was thinking in her pretty empty little head. It didn't matter whether she could go out on dates or not. What a Dompier wanted a Dompier got. That's how things worked on Moon Lake. Since Angie didn't know that, it was one more rule he would have to teach her.

He patted her leg once more, leaned over and retrieved his jacket from the floor. The bus turned into the high school lot where car and truck lights crisscrossed the night, engines running at idle, mothers and fathers waiting to pick up their charges.

His brother Brody waited for him in his stupid yellow Cadillac. He'd want to tell Tye all about his day's surgery schedule at Clarksdale Memorial, want to brag how he cut out some guy's gallstones or hernia, or some old lady's yellow tumor that was always, according to Brody, big and tough-skinned as a watermelon, but not so tasty. Jesus. Why couldn't he have had a sister instead of a brother? Some soft touch who would do anything for him instead of a nutty brother who got off on blood and trailing intestines? Not that it bothered him any, really. How could it bother him since he had watched Brody operate on his taxidermy animals since he had been old enough to walk? He'd seen him eviscerate everything from a bull mastiff to a snow leopard and lay them out clean as wax paper so that he could fill them with sawdust and stitch them elegantly shut with the finest, thinnest catgut. Hell. No big deal, dead things. Nothing to it.

"Bye, Angie. See you around the lake," he said,

hopping from the seat and slinging the jacket over his right shoulder.

He pushed toward the rear exit and jumped to the ground, the night air slapping him in the face with a hint of coming winter. He spied the big babyshit-yellow Caddy and waved his arm.

Brody chewed on his ever-present unlit cigar and tapped his fingers on the wheel.

"We won," Tye announced, sliding into the buttery comfort of the leather seat. "And I copped a feel off Angie. Now tell me about surgery today."

Brody Dompier slipped the transmission lever into drive and pulled smoothly from the lot. "Well, Tye, let me tell you," he began, shifting the cigar around his mouth as he talked. "I copped me a feel today, too."

"That right?" Tye turned to his brother, amused. Brody was thirty-one years old and lived at home, a confirmed bachelor. He was balding, paunchy, and he always smelled like the inside of a bottle of rubbing alcohol mixed with stale tobacco. Tye could not think of him on top of a woman. A bear maybe. But not a woman.

"Was this woman, see," Brody said, mangling the cigar. "Had her scheduled for a mastectomy . . ."

"What the hell is that?"

"Take her tit off. Had cancer."

"Oh."

"So's when the operating crew's got its back turned doing their shit, I cop me a feel too. I thought, Hell, it's a shame this tit's got to come off, but before it's gone and while it's still warm, I'm gonna get me some of it. Couldn't do that proper when she came to me with the lump that was hurting her. Can't do that, you know, when the nurse is there in the way."

"Guess not." Though Tye knew instinctively he

should feel some revulsion for what his brother had done to a woman drugged out on a hospital gurney, he was surprised to find he was secretly excited by the idea. What was the harm? Like Brody said, she was about to lose it anyway. People were all wrapped up in their dumb moralities, that's what Brody said. They expected doctors to be goddamned saints, not men who saw what they saw and wanted what they wanted like any other man.

"Wasn't much fun anyway," Brody continued. "Thing was misshapen by the cancer. Had a knot on top of it like a rock."

"But you did it, huh? Felt of it?" Now it was disgusting. Rocky boobs could not be beautiful to behold, Tye figured. He could see wanting to touch a gorgeous, perfectly formed breast, but something knotted up and weird? Uh-uh. That was all Brody's territory. But what could you expect from a guy who collected some of the ugliest animals in the history of the world and spent hours lovingly restoring them to stuffed statuary?

"You betcha. Nice nipple. Shame she lost it. I could tell her husband isn't gonna much like her when she gets out of the hospital, flat on one side, poking out on the other. Can't hardly blame the son of a bitch. The scar's gonna look like holy hell. Nothing I can do about that."

On the way home Tye thought about what was beneath a woman's breast. He figured there were ribs there, like on his own chest. And if the breast were scraped off, it would look like three miles of bad roadwork, for sure. Not a pretty sight, he guessed.

He wondered idly if the knot his brother spoke of was really hard as a rock, hard as his own hard-on he had made Angie touch tonight. Then he naturally thought about losing his penis and the thought scared him so much he scooted nervously in the car seat.

Damn, he hoped he never got cancer and if he ever did he'd just take a shotgun and blow his fucking head off before he'd let Brody get near him with a surgeon's knife. Damn right. Brody was the best this side of the Mississippi River when it came to cutting, but there was one thing Tye knew that Brody's patients didn't know.

He liked it too much. Brody was a man who joyed in his work. It was downright unappealing when taken in the light of day and if you had to go under his knife. Too awful to even think about seriously.

Tye thanked God his dick was safe and his brother was his brother and not his doctor. There were a lot of things in this life he could be grateful about.

"So your team won?" Brody asked, sensing Tye's lack of interest in mastectomies.

"Yeah. And our girls' team won too. By two points."

"Who scored the basket, your new love, this Angie girl?"

"No, that Gaynor girl, the nigger they got on the team. She did it."

"Hmmmm. The Gaynors. From across the lake. Whole passel of them over there. Don't know how they ever got land this close around. I told Daddy we should have bought up all the lake property. You mark my words, in another ten years this is going to be the biggest resort area in the state. Lookit, already we got Conway Twitty living here, him and his mama. Other big stars are going to find it soon enough. If we owned it, we'd have been set for life."

"I think the Gaynor girl's parents were sharecroppers and ole man Conroy gave them the house they're in. They still pick for him when cotton is high," Tye said.

"Every jig in Mississippi is a cotton picker. Always

have been. Now they're sending their young 'uns off to white folks' schools just like they think they're going to get 'em some doctors and lawyers in the family. And she dunked that ball, did she? Won the game for Moon Lake? I'll be damned.''

"Lofted it right from center court."

Brody chewed his dead cigar and tried to picture it. He turned into the Dompier driveway and pointed a thin, beautifully tapered surgeon's finger ahead. "Looks like Mama and Daddy are still up."

Tye looked at the lights glowing golden and serene from the front windows. He was tired and would have to hit the sack. He wished he did not have to say good night to his parents first. Wished it every night of his life. But it was protocol; it was the way the Dompiers judged it should be and therefore he could not shuffle off to the far west wing that housed his room until he did it.

When Brody parked the car and turned off the ignition, Tye set his teeth and advanced on the front steps leading to the veranda. He could hear the music from inside, wafting loud and unruly as a pack of howling dogs to his ears. He hated Bach and Beethoven and all those longhairs his mother played on the stereo. He hated them since the time of remembering. He especially hated the screech of violins in an orchestra. It set off a nervous tic at the side of his mouth and made his jaws ache.

He opened the door and turned to his left. He stood at the edge of the Persian carpet and waited their attention. Finally his mother noticed him standing there and waggled her fingers at him.

"Good night, Mama. Good night, Daddy," Tye dutifully stated.

Neither of them responded other than a nod of the head and he was released for the night. The sound of a sonata followed him down the hallway, a great stone at his back urging him to walk faster until he reached his door. Once inside his room, there was safety and the music was but faint smoke infiltrating his consciousness. He could handle it. He could sleep. And if he were lucky he would dream again of Angelina and his plans for having her as his own.

He finally dozed while thinking about Angie and how fluid, how graceful she had looked jumping into the air, the basketball poised against her palms, wrists cocked just as she was about to shoot a basket. He could love her. If she ever gave him half a chance, he could honestly love her.

Chapter
7

"They're bad people, Angelina, bad to the bone. Bred in them and passed down like blue eyes or black hair. And the worst of the lot is Tyeson. It's likely he got stuck with a truckload of bad. Leastwhile, that's how Varna sees it. And I don't talk against folks as a habit, don't mistake me."

Angie had come to visit after school. Varna took her inside the sagging, rusted screen door into her home. Home consisted of four rooms. In the bedroom to the right of the front door stood a double bed with a flaking white-painted metal bedstead. A worn, creamy chenille bedspread covered what looked to be three or four mattresses piled one atop the other. In the bed's center against the plumped pillows lay a black fringed throw pillow imprinted with a colorful sequin-and-glitter map of Hawaii. Across the top it said: I LOVE YOU, MOTHER.

The living room was the most crowded living space Angie had ever seen. There were little dark wood tables sitting everywhere—one by an easy chair, two flanking an ugly fifties-style deep gray and silver-threaded sofa, one next to the wood-burning heat stove, one by the door holding a Mason fruit jar full of fragrant cedar limbs. Another shorter maple coffee table stood in front of the sofa and on it rested a plastic and cardboard chess set. It looked as if a game was in play—pieces had been moved from each side.

Against the far wall from the door stood a small, rickety wooden bookcase full of books peeling and shucking off their old, dry, cornhusk covers. A huge handmade rag rug covered most of a wood floor scrubbed down to a gray patina sheen.

The room behind the living room was a walk-through kitchen holding a bare wood table, two ladder-back chairs, an old white gas stove, and a short, ancient, rust-pocked refrigerator.

To Angie's right as she entered the house was another room, obviously a second bedroom. It must have been used to house Varna's children for it held three beds, one double and two twins on either side of it. They were made up neatly and coated with quilts. A chest of drawers, a chiffonier, and a slatwood humpbacked seaman's chest filled the remaining space.

Angie saw no bathroom and knew if she stepped out the back door she would see a weathered outhouse. Everyone today had indoor plumbing. How could Varna live this way?

Neither the chess set, the books, nor the tidiness of the house especially surprised Angie. But what did surprise and shock her sense of justice were the walls. They were covered from baseboard to open rafter ceiling with newspapers glued to the one layer of bare, rough-milled wood. Some of the paper had deteriorated over time to yellow confetti and cracks let in the waning evening sunlight. Angie knew this house in winter must be like living in a tea sieve. There was nothing to keep out the shrieking wind or the damp cold that would soon gather over the lake and drift through the house as if it were no more than a stand of trees.

Varna placed Angie in the one faded flower–upholstered easy chair with the crocheted doilies on arms and headrest. She brought her a glass of iced tea and a plate of fried apple tarts that tasted as heavenly as they smelled.

Angie began to talk to the old woman about her move from Missouri, her father's work at the state university in Clarksdale, her boredom at school with the courses because she was far ahead of the other students, and finally, she spoke of Tyeson Dompier. Not of the things he had done to her, but of how she was inexplicably involved with him without knowing how it had happened and without knowing how to diminish his interest in tormenting her.

"Bad people," Varna mumbled, sitting on the sofa and playing the chess game with herself. She moved a black rook up the board and took a pawn. She stood, circled the little table and, holding her chin in her hand, contemplated the move she had just made from the point of view of the white contender.

Varna seemed to have forgotten Angie was there. She blocked Angie's view so that she could see nothing but the navy blue and white print dress hanging from the immense plateaus of her flat, wide hips.

"What do they do that is so bad?" Angie asked her hostess' stolid behind.

"If Varna told all she knew, there'd be no end to the trouble that'd get stirred up. I know enough so's the whole lot of them Dompiers would be put under the jailhouse if I had a mind to tell."

"Why don't you tell then?"

"No one would listen to me and if I told, they'd all call me a liar—besides some other names I have no hankering to hear—that's why. If anyone ever learns the truth about them, Varna'll be right there with the law to confirm what she knows."

"How did you overhear these 'bad' things?"

"I used to be the cook at that house. I was there, on and off, ever since little Tye was a baby. Now they don't call me in to work much no more. They hired them a little deaf gal from Clarksdale to do the cooking and cleaning. Can't hear word one. They write out her jobs for her on a sheet of paper and leave it in the kitchen on the counter. And she's outta there by five o'clock every day. The Dompiers don't like no witnesses hanging 'round."

Varna moved a white chess piece and again circled the table. She sat down heavily on the sofa to study the black side's next move. Her eyes and concentration never left the chessboard, but Angie knew she heard perfectly every question raised.

"Witnesses to what?"

Varna picked up the black knight, shook it in the air in thought, replaced it where it had been, then went back to considering the next move. "Not proper for me to carry tales. Nothing of interest in it for a nice girl like you, nohow. They just bad, that's all. You need to stay away from Tyeson. He got all the girlfriends he wants. Always was a pretty boy." She took the black knight again from the board. "This here piece is the one that's Tyeson." She glanced at Angie to be sure the girl was listening. "He's the black knight. He rides in on his black horse and black clouds trail him. Everywhere he goes there's some darkness creeping over things. I look at this chess piece and I think, 'He's never gonna be good. He don't know how.' "

"I don't like him," Angie confessed.

"Nobody likes a Dompier, honey. Put up with them, but not like 'em. Mr. Dompier, he's a lawyer man, best one in the county. If I got law trouble I'd call him in a minute. He's smart, cagey as a gopher in a garden full of ripe roots. Knows what he's about and all the little holes for crawling through. My line for him is: 'The most patient man in loss, the most coldest that ever turned up an ace.' That's *Antony and Cleopatra*, act five.

"Brody, now, he's Tye's brother, he went off to some fancy college up north and become a surgeon, world class. Man can cut open a body and sew it back up like lightning zipping open a pine tree trunk. They made him hospital administrator, too. He only cuts on people he feels like cutting on now."

"What about Mrs. Dompier?"

Varna scooted her black queen across the board and took a white bishop. "Ah ha!" she said. "Didn't see that one coming, did you?"

Angie thought it very odd Varna addressed herself as another person entirely when she played chess with herself. She had never seen anyone do that before. But it was harmless, she supposed. It passed the time when there were no cooking jobs or cotton to pick. She was about to repeat her question when Varna stood, circled the table, stood with her big cliff hips blocking the way and said, " 'The setting sun, and music at the close, As the last taste of sweets, is sweetest last.' "

"What?" Angie asked, confused by the Shakespeare.

"Setting sun, girl. Music at the close. That's the nail and hammer of Mrs. Dompier. She don't do nothing but sit on committees that plant roses down the middle of Clarksdale streets and throw coming-out dances for debutantes and raise money for local charities. But that's not what she *does*. What she does best is dance, I guess you'd say. What she does best is listen to music and then dance it. If you can rightly call it dance."

"At parties and stuff? That doesn't sound like anything."

"It's all that one's good for. She sure didn't make a go at being a mama. Weren't fit, by my book. Head in the clouds. Thunderclouds at that. Shot full of sound and blue streaks of electric."

"How many children did you have, Varna?" Angie asked, tired of the Dompiers and Varna's cryptic innuendos.

"Eight."

"Eight?!"

"First three died childbirthing. All stillborn. I worked the fields too hard and too long, I think, couldn't help that. But they're my children all the same and they all got names—Marjorie, Joby Lorraine, and Paulie Lancaster—and I remember their birthdays like I do the other five. Went on to have three boys and two girls what lived. Grown now. Gone. Left Mississippi."

"Where's your husband, Varna?"

"Buried—'longside the three children."

"Oh, I'm sorry. I shouldn't have asked."

"Okay to ask. I'll be going to be with them one of these days. They ain't gone nowhere too far off where I can't find 'em."

Angie thought about her mother and swallowed against a constriction that ringed her throat. How far off was her mother? Was she in the St. Louis cemetery where they had left her or was she here, having followed them south? Did the dead stay nearby, hovering like good angels and waiting for you to join them?

Varna must have moved a white piece. She circled the table and sat down, knees spread wide, leaning over the chess game. Her brow furrowed and looked like freshly dug rows in black earth. It was easy to imagine green shoots struggling to poke through that forehead.

"You like playing by yourself?" Angie asked.

"I wouldn't have a game if I didn't play alone."

"And you like games, huh?" Angie smiled.

"Just chess. It takes mind. I didn't learn to read and write until I was forty-six years old. I had no time for school books. Was married to Mr. Jenkins when I was thirteen. But when I got forty-six and my kids got grown up, I went down to the library and I ast that woman behind the counter how I could learn to read and write. She took me to a table and went and got a little book about Dick and Jane and Spot. We started that very day.

"Once I could read I read the whole Bible through and through. Then I read Shakespeare the same way. Then I read other books I picked up cheap at some auction sales. But I liked Shakespeare best and went back to him. The Old Testament prophets wrote beautiful work when they put down God's word, but Mr. Shakespeare knew how to make words sing and clap hands and turn somersaults.

"One day at one of those auctions the box I bought had this chess game in it too. I liked how all the pieces are shaped. I went back to the library and Miss Quani set me at the table again and taught me how to play. It's the only game I know how to do. Miss Quani said it would improve my mind because it took lots of thinking out, thinking ahead, lots of figuring and seeing into the future. She was right. She's a great woman, Miss Quani. I'll always thank God she was there when I was ready. God provides . . ."

The days were shorter and while Angie was engrossed with getting to know Varna Jenkins, the sun slid toward the horizon in a blaze of rust streaked through with purple. The shack darkened in imperceptible increments until Varna was nearly nose to nose with the chess pieces and Angie sat forward in the easy chair, straining to see.

Suddenly Varna sank back against the silver-threaded sofa that glinted like fireflies around her massive shoulders and closed her eyes, her hands out at her side, light palms turned upward. "Dark's come," she said simply. "Twilight's done."

Angie jumped, noticing the starry sky beyond the window at Varna's back. "I have to hurry," she said, rising, taking the empty tea glass and tart saucer to the kitchen table.

Even when Angie said good-bye at the screen door and thanked Varna for the after-school snack, the black woman did not speak, but sat quietly, eyes closed as if in sleep.

A perplexed Angie rushed down the gravel road barely able to see where she was going. She did not know yet that Varna was not ignoring her out of impoliteness. Varna had just moved the black queen into position and checkmated the white king. She had won her game and when she won, she always sat back, eyes closed, to rest.

Winning meant that her offensive plays on the other side of the board had produced a loser. It was a lesson she thought she should think about each time it occurred. Had she won or had she lost? She had won *and* lost; she must experience both triumph and loss each game, dual emotions, opposite sides of the coin.

This contradiction in experience teased her into applying the concept to larger issues. As a person she was both winner and loser in life. It was all a matter of balance. She'd won when she took Hollyoak Jenkins to be her husband. She had lost when her first three children were born dead, never to suckle her breasts, never to breathe a sigh against her cheek. She'd won in having an optimistic disposition. She'd lost in allowing that disposition to expect things she could never have.

And so on. And so forth. Until she understood. Until she accepted the give and the take of existence.

At the end of each chess game, this was her meditation. Loss and gain, up and down, joy and sorrow, black and white.

Chess and Shakespeare and the Bible and the great biographies she studied, they all were her instruments to salvation. Understanding was salvation. And until she understood and until she accepted losing as easily as winning, there was to be no salvation for Varna Jenkins. This was her gospel and her quest.

She wished fervently she had seen things in this light before her children were grown so that she might have taught it to them. They were too old now. Oh, Lord, yes. They would never listen to their old mama now. But God had sent another child, pale and innocent as a shorn lamb, motherless and lonesome as an abandoned lamb left out of the flock, into her safekeeping. She might be taught. Gently and slowly and lovingly. Given time and world enough, Varna might yet pass on to her Maker having imparted one small pearl of wisdom. If ever she could pry that nugget from the shell of obscurity for herself, that is.

I liked the winning, she thought. *I played the black and won and liked it. Did I mind the losing when I was white? I minded it, yes, I did. I didn't want to lose my white king. And when I did I yelled inside from being mad.*

I can't do that forever. One day I'll lose and I won't mind. I'll win and it won't matter either.

I get that far and I'll have something to teach Angelina. Something mighty fine and good. I know it. Wisdom and the power to use it. I just know it.

Chapter

8

Angie saw the blond boy from her English class coming her way across the cafeteria. He looked intently in her direction, tray in hand, not watching where he was going. The split second before Tyeson barreled at him down the crowded aisle between long tables, Angie saw the collision coming and raised her right hand into the air as if in this way she would stop a catastrophe.

Tye's tray went under and up, lifting the other boy's tray high into the air and dumping the contents over his head and shoulders. Balancing his own food tray precariously, Tye backed off in pretend horror and guilt. "Oh, gosh, what a shame, Dana! I didn't see you there, man. I must have been daydreaming or something." He glanced over at Angie when he said this and then turned back to grin at the mashed-potato-and-green-pea-covered Dana Percy.

The tagalong gang who always seemed to surround Tye laughed uproariously, slapping one another on the shoulder, bending over, holding themselves in gleeful mirth.

Dana moved dumbly to the nearest table and took the proffered paper napkins a girl held out to him. He ignored Tye while wiping gook off his button-down pale yellow shirt. He looked up once to see Angie staring at him and smiled the shy smile of a dupe, but not a conquered, shivering dupe. Pride held his shoulders straight and his head high despite the gravies and sauces dribbling down from his plastered hair to his shirt collar.

"Oh, God, you look just awful," Tye said, taking napkins and rubbing Dana down the shirtfront, scrubbing the stains into the material. "You might have to go home and change clothes."

"Right, Dompier. The minute after I speak to Angie, that's what I'm going to do, too." He put a hand to Tye's chest and pushed him gently aside and walked over to Angie's table where she ate alone. "I'm in no shape to ask you out, which is what I was gonna do before Tye dumped on me, but I did want to say hi. I saw you in the Roverton game and you were great."

Angie's heart went out to him, this brave boy who stood up against her enemy. She hated to have to tell him her father's rigid dating policy. He would think it had something to do with the dollop of potatoes on his collar and that wasn't fair. "I can't date," she blurted. "I mean, my dad, he won't let me yet. I guess he's just old-fashioned. I've been trying to change his mind, talk to him . . ."

Dana shrugged and a green pea rolled down his long-sleeved shirt. He laughed as it dropped to his feet. "Aww, that's all right. My dad hardly lets me drive the car unless he's along and I already have my driver's license. He's an old Elmer Fudd, too. Maybe I can just come by your house sometimes and we'll talk. I don't live that far from you on the lake road."

"That would be nice, Dana. I'd like that."

"Terrific. This Friday night? Would that be all right, do you think?"

"Sure. Friday night."

Dana grinned, turned and gave Tye a high sign sure to infuriate him, and left for the bathroom.

Tye joined Angie immediately. "What'd he want?"

Angie refused to answer. She kept eating, her eyes on her tray. It felt exhilarating to have someone interested in her besides Tyeson. Dana was her secret weapon now. What a fine thing, secret weapons.

"You'll go out with him and you won't go out with me, is that it?"

"I'm not dating, Tye. I told you that." Why was he so dense, anyway?

"Then what did he say? I saw you smiling at him."

"It's really none of your business, is it? What I do doesn't concern you."

"You're acting the royal bitch, Angie. I don't like that. I told you you were my girl."

Though surprised and angered he thought of her as his possession, like Dana before her she shrugged and kept eating as if the mush they served them at this school was a gourmet delicacy of the highest order.

"Angie, I . . ."

Hearing him pause uncharacteristically, at a loss for what to say, she turned to see his face. She had never seen him anything but cocksure of himself. "What?"

"I thought you were different. I thought we would . . ."

"I *am* different, Tye. You made sure of that. You made sure everyone in this whole lousy school knew it, too. You told people about the lake, I know you did. The way people look at me, I can tell what they're thinking. I don't have one friend in this place. Not one. I went out for basketball because I thought I could make a friend there, but that backfired, too. The girls are all jealous or hateful and they know you aren't going to leave me alone and that makes them worse. Because of you I eat alone." She stabbed the plastic maroon tray with her fork. "I go to class alone, I ride the bus alone. I'm this freak from Missouri and it wouldn't have happened without your help." She was breathless, livid, her fork gripped like a dagger in her fist. "So yeah, I'm different. Thanks a lot. You did a great job making sure of it."

"But I . . ."

"Shut up," Angie raged, her cheeks flushed. "Just shut up and don't talk to me. And the next time you go around dumping food on Dana, I'm going to dump food on you. How would you like that?"

She stood with the tray, hesitated a second as if debating upturning the remains onto his head, and then walking stiffly, left him at the table staring after her.

She thought she heard him call her bitch again, but it didn't matter. She had not felt so good since the first day of school. But she expected to feel even better Friday night. She might even show Dana the swing in the cotton field. She had an inkling he was the kind of person who would appreciate it.

"Come in before it gets too late," Jason Thornton called to his daughter as she and Dana Percy walked across the gravel roadway to the lone oak tree.

"I wish he'd let up," Angie groaned. "He wouldn't be this way if my mother were alive. She wouldn't let him treat me like a baby."

"How did she die?" Dana found the swing right away and stood behind it, holding it still for her to sit down.

"Polio."

"Oh geez. That's terrible. I thought polio was

wiped out or something. Hardly no one gets it anymore.''

''Yeah . . . well . . .''

''I'm sorry, Angie. I shouldn't talk about it, I guess.''

''I miss her something awful.'' Angie hung her head and let Dana push her in the swing. Her below-shoulder-length hair flew behind her and the wind whistled past her ears. Miss her, miss her, she heard in the wind. Misssss her. Misssss her.

''Tye's told everyone you're his property,'' Dana remarked.

''Not likely.''

''I've never seen Tye not get what he wants.''

''You see it now. He's cruel and mean and . . .''

''He's just had it all. It's not good to have it all so soon, maybe.''

Angie thought about that, but she couldn't decide if she agreed or not. She had never ''had it all,'' so how could she know?

''I've seen his house. It looks like one of those old Civil War plantations,'' she said.

''That's what it is. Behind it in a grove of pecan trees there's slave quarters. Old Jeremiah Dompier used to work slaves back then. The family has been around Moon Lake for ages.''

''They should have torn down the slave quarters.'' Angie thought of Varna Jenkins working in a house where outside the back windows she could see mute testament to her ancestors' slavery.

''They don't tear down anything. They buy up land and try to sell it to tourists. They think Moon Lake's going to be worth tons of money one day.''

''Maybe it will.'' The wind rushed past her face, bathing it in lake-damp night air. She swung up to the stars and back to earth, Dana's voice carrying to her on the upswing like the breath of reason whispering into her ear.

"Maybe," he said, though from his tone of voice she could tell he was not convinced the lake might ever be a playground for the rich. "I don't think I'd like to see it full of tourists and A-frame cottages and hotdog stands. It's too pretty for all that."

Angie dragged her feet and slowed her swing. "Here," she said, standing. "Let me push you. Watch the sky. It looks like it comes right down into your face."

Dana bashfully sat and kicked off. "You don't have to," he said when she pushed him.

"Let me," she insisted. "I want to."

"Okay."

She watched him turn his face to the star-studded heavens and drink in the night. For a while they didn't talk. The darkness enfolded them in the swish of air and sail of swing, Angie pushing, coming off the ground with each great lunge, and Dana swinging, legs straight out before him pointing to the sky.

When he left at eleven o'clock, he leaned toward her face and she let him kiss her. It was sweet, his lips warm, friendly. Not at all like Tye's insistent, hot frenzy that scared her. Not at all like the stolen matinee kiss when neither she nor her partner really knew what a kiss was about. Dana kissed her in a way that communicated thoughts without words: I like you, he said wordlessly. You're pretty, he said. We're friends, he said, bound to be good friends, dear Angelina.

When her father asked about Dana on Saturday morning over hotcakes and link sausage, Angie said he was her only friend. And why couldn't she date him? Why couldn't she go out with boys? She was old enough. Did he want her to grow up incapable of having a conversation with the opposite sex?

"Your mother and I talked about this," Jason said. "She thought fifteen was old enough to begin dating. I told her I didn't agree . . ."

"So Mother said that I could?" The idea they had planned out her life while her mother lay dying weighed her down with sadness. Poor Mother, deciding the coming years of her daughter's life while her own life waned. It was almost too melancholy a thought to keep in her head without letting it crush her into silence.

"Well, we talked about it, Angie."

"And you both decided I had to be sixteen to date? When was this—when I was thirteen, fourteen? And did you decide what college I should attend and what my major should be and how many children I should have? And did you tell her you were moving back to Mississippi and leaving her there in St. Louis just as soon as you could manage it?"

Jason did not speak for several moments. And he did not look at her. "Angie, I think that was an ugly thing to say to me. I want you to apologize. I also want you to know that I made this move for you. I think you know that, too. I couldn't stand living where I'd shared a life with your mother, but there was more to it than that. I thought if I took you away and opened up a new life for you . . ."

Angie was instantly contrite.

"I'm sorry, Dad. I shouldn't have said it. I know why we left. I know you missed Mother too much to stay there. This place makes me say terrible things. I'm so . . . lonesome here. I miss her, too, you know. I'm alone, too."

Jason stood and came to where she sat. He went to his knees and put his arm around her shoulder, his cheek against hers. "Yes, we're alone now. She's gone and we're all alone in this. If you think I'm wrong in the dating thing, I'll change it. You can date if you want. Your mother knew best about these things. I don't think I'm very good at it, Angie. You'll have to help me as we go along."

"All right, Dad. I'll tell you when you're wrong."
Her lips stretched into a grin. He turned her face to
his.

"You can go to public dances, to the movies, to
skating or swimming with this young man of yours.
As long as there are adult chaperones there, it's all
right with me. Does he drive? Does he have a license
and a car? He doesn't drink, does he?"

"I don't think he drinks, Dad. He's not wild like
that. He has a license, but his dad is like you—old
fuddy dud. He rides with him a lot. He's a nice boy,"
she added. "I like him and I can talk to him."

"Good. Your mother and I could always talk. It
makes a big difference, Angie, if you can talk."

Yes, Angie thought, that's the truth, Dad. Then
why is it we hardly ever do any of it? Why is it you're
reading the Saturday Clarksdale newspaper now the
minute after you almost began to really talk to me?
I have to make you angry before you listen to me.

Waves slapped against the pilings beneath the kitchen
floor, messages in code from the heart of nature,
and sun glinted brilliantly from the slate blue lake.

"Dana thinks people should get married at sixteen," she said, testing her father's attention.

"Um-hmmm," he said from behind the paper.

"When he asks me to run away to California so we
can hang out in Haight-Ashbury and take LSD, I
might do it."

"That's good. Um-hmmm."

Was that really such a farfetched idea? she wondered. Thousands of kids were running away from
home and heading for San Francisco. Tuning in, turning on, dropping out. Kids older than her, mostly, but
some of them were even younger. One of her friends
in St. Louis had dropped out. She had told everyone
where she was going and no one took her seriously
until one day she just vanished. Rumor was her par-

ents went west to look for her and never found a trace.

If Angie ever disappeared that way her father would die. Nothing could make her leave him. If they were alone now at least they were alone together; there was mutual support at a workable level, if not a close one.

No, she would not run away from this despicable cotton field, man-made lake, Delta world that wished to spit her out like a watermelon seed. She would sink into its black, fertile ground and grow roots and send out tendrils and hug the South to her until it accepted her on equal terms. She would defeat it and make it her own. She would not run from it.

She had not been exactly truthful with her father. Dana was not her only friend. She had two now, Dana and Varna. Two more than she had had days ago. Things were looking up. Moon Lake might be livable one day after all.

"I'm going swimming." She left her father with his nose in the paper and went to the bedroom for her bathing suit. Outside the windows a warm fall sun heated the water and the land. It might be a little bracing for a swim, but she could stand it. After a swim she would go to see Varna, maybe beg another fried apple tart from her and ask what she knew about the Percy family. Consulting Varna was like doing research in the library on Mississippi Delta history. If a family lived on the lake, Varna knew them—background, childrens' names, occupations.

Her father called good-bye as she went out the front door, a towel over her arm, transistor radio in hand. She stopped on the lawn and looked up at the clear azure sky. Not a cloud in sight. In St. Louis this time of year she would be wearing her coat and muffler, gloves and galoshes. It was strange to suit up for a swim two weeks before Halloween.

Halloween, one of her favorite holidays. She had heard that in downtown Clarksdale the kids from all over the county got together on the street and linked hands to perform the Snake. As far as she could tell from overheard conversations this performance consisted of hundreds of kids arm in arm running and screaming through town, twisting and turning and snapping like a long human snake. If you were unlucky enough to be late and wind up on the tail end of this chain, you could get lifted right off your feet and slammed into store windows from the force of the snap. It sounded like good excitement unless she had to join onto the snake end. Given that choice, she would not get involved. What she did not hunger for was a broken arm or leg or her face cut into unrecognizable ribbons.

Boy, these people sure knew how to think up odd little entertainments, she had to hand it to them. If a bunch of people made a human snake on the streets of St. Louis the cops would come in battalions to break it up and throw the rabble-rousers into jail.

Her thongs made loud flapping sounds as she went down the embankment and through the trees to the lakefront. The transistor radio earphone was plugged into her ear. Bobby Vinton's mellifluous voice filled her head with "Blue Velvet." Angie thought it was a sappy song and usually changed the station when it came on, but she was too busy maneuvering along the rock-strewn shoreline to bother.

She followed the shore until she came to a natural clearing a few yards up from the lake edge. She threw her beach towel onto the cushiony browning grass. On top of it she placed the radio. She took off her shirt and shorts, kicked off the thongs. Back at the water's edge she tested the water temperature with one foot. She let out a slight gasp and stood thinking it over. It was pretty cold, all right. Was she a chicken liver? Nah. Would she rather go back home and watch the boxing matches with her father? Nah. The water wasn't *that* cold; she could take it; she was a big girl. It would be fun, a test of her courage to fling herself into that icy October water and swim out to the middle of the lake, float back to shore. The sun would warm her once she came out. She could do it. Sure she could.

Something rustled in the underbrush behind her. She whirled to see what it was. "Someone there?" she called, her voice shaky. The hateful image of Tye sneaking through her things in the clearing came to her instantaneously. The bushes were still and quiet. She dismissed the thought as paranoid fantasy.

She was just trying to find ways to keep from diving in, that's all. Chicken liver. Big slimy black chicken liver if she didn't do it right now. Right . . . NOW!

The shock of the cold water set off detonations in every pore of her body. She came up through the dark water breaking surface like a porpoise blowing air, letting out a high-pitched yell, flapping her arms on top the water in awkward arcs. "Oh Jesus, oh God, oh *damn* it's colllddd."

Her teeth chattered as she swam out through the big flat glassy of the lake. From water level the trees on the far side towered like ten-story buildings. The sky was a distant universe. She clamped shut her teeth and breathed through them as she turned and swam back to shore. A dead tree lay out across the water from the bank, its bark stripped, limbs bare and scratching at the sky.

"Chicken liver, hell," she mumbled, swimming faster, kicking furiously until water furled behind her and made a small wake that spread to each side of her passage. "Idiot. Dumb idiot."

She scrambled ashore and ran through the thicket to

the clearing and the towel. She stood stamping her feet on the grass, beating it down flat while rubbing her arms and chest and face and legs with the towel to get the circulation going again. Her fingers were *blue*. She had learned a valuable lesson. Just because the sun shone gently down in a Mississippi late October, it was deceiving to believe swimming might be a good idea. It was a very bad, an incredibly stupid idea. A Missourian "Show Me" attitude certainly was not the best mode of operation on Moon Lake.

That damn lake was downright frosty.

She shivered and hugged the towel around her shoulders. She buried her face into her two towel-covered fists and tried to think about warm things: hot yeast rolls, hot water bottles on the feet, wool coats, knitted afghans . . .

A rustle interrupted her reverie and she ceased all movement. Held her breath. Someone was here. Her gaze darted around the perimeter of the clearing, searching each tree trunk, each clump of bushes, every wall of thickets. Was it an animal? Or was it a person? She felt uncomfortable enough for it to be a person. Who . . . who was watching her?

And why . . . Oh God, why?

Chapter
9

He appeared from between two large pines. Smiling.
Hands in jean pockets. A lock of raven hair fell in a
wave over one eye.

Angie's heart came up and lodged in her mouth like
a lump of sodden bread. She could not swallow or
speak. Had she been a mustang, an independent,
wild, free beast, she could have run from him. If she
had not been a young girl on the brink of maturity,
she might have suavely outmaneuvered him. Her first
instinct urged that she run. She unconsciously slid
her feet across the grass one at a time toward the
treeline, but his hypnotic eyes held her from breaking
into a sprint. Whatever evil dance he planned was
about to begin, preordained and inescapable. This
was not something articulated in her conscious mind,
but something she knew instinctively. She had no
way to avoid this moment in her life.

"It's too cold for swimming," he said, moving into
the clearing as she slid away foot by foot. "Do you

remember what I told you the night of the basketball game?"

She shook her head idiotically. She remembered, but she did not want him to speak of it.

"I said I'd teach you things, Angie. You're not a little girl anymore." His voice was liquid, confidential, but menace lurked there, hidden like snakes beneath water. "You may think you're not grown up, but you don't play dolls and you like what I can do to you. You like the feeling I can give you." He licked his lips and a nervous chill caused her hands and arms to tremble. "Would you like to find out what it's about, Angie? I want to teach you. I want to be the first one. There's no one else who can take care of you the way I will."

"I don't know what you're talking about."

"I'm talking about making love, doing it, having some fun. You know what I'm talking about." He stepped forward. "Come here."

His presence was as commanding as the heady sway of a cobra. He seldom blinked; his stare never left her. She felt her knees weaken at the images his words conjured. She did not want to stay and listen to him obscenely tease her this way, but she was too off-balance and frightened to make a break from the clearing. She had the fleeting thought she must have used all her courage on the dive into the lake and had none left with which to save herself.

She backed against a tree, the bark a rough scabrous layer scrubbing her back. Her hands went behind her to hold to the trunk for solace. The towel fell open across her bosom. She glanced down and his gaze followed.

Tye reached her and lifted hands to her wet hair. He felt around the back of her head, wrapping his hands tightly in the heavy, ropy tresses. He stood looking down into her eyes, taking pleasure in her vulnerability. She wanted to hate him, but she feared him more. There was no room inside the fear for another emotion.

"It's easy," he said. "So easy. I'll show you how. I won't let it hurt. You're someone I really want, Angie. We're meant for each other. You're different from the other girls around here. You're *mine*."

Her breath came in uneven ragged gulps that scorched her throat. Her thoughts eddied into dark nooks and crannies where images floated from movies and books about couples engaging in the sexual act. What was he going to do? He would not possibly do what he promised. He was out of his mind if he thought she wanted to have sex with him.

He stepped in closer, his firm, youthful body flush against her. He brought her face to him by exerting pressure on the hair caught in the webs of his hands. She felt her scalp tingle, her body warm to his flesh. His breath flowed satiny against her lips. When he was this close he blotted out the world. "No," she protested, pushing him away, wishing desperately for the world to rush back in.

"Don't fight me. You'll only ruin it for yourself."

"Tye, you've got everything all messed up. I don't like you. You've never let me like you. I'm going to get my things and I'm going home now." She said this as forthrightly and earnestly as possible, though her voice betrayed her by riding into the high registers.

She tried to disentangle his hands from her hair and he caught the fingers of her right hand, holding her arm above her head in an awkward and painful position. Her breasts thrust out against him, taut against the black bathing suit. She had never been more conscious of her physical body, its proportions, its hills and valleys. Her body belonged to her. He had no right to do anything to it without her permission.

"Let me go," she insisted.

"Don't, Angie. Don't fight me. Didn't I say I wanted you?"

"You're crazy. Let me go before I start screaming."

"So scream. Who's going to hear you?" He laughed. It was an ugly sound, confident and mocking. His head was back, and she brought her free hand under his chin, pressed his head farther back yet until his laughter died and his body followed the pressure. His hands came from her hair. "Damn! You're choking me!"

She ran to where her radio and clothes lay in the center of the clearing. She had waited too long, she knew that now when it was too late. Waited in her fear and let him gain advantage. It was a replay of the last time she had been alone with him only this time he was threatening more than humiliation in front of friends.

Before she could straighten and turn, she was pushed roughly from behind and fell to her hands and knees with a yell. She dropped her radio. "Stop it!"

He pressed her down onto the dry grass, grabbed her wrist and flipped her onto her back. She dropped the clothes from her fingers where he had both wrists crushed to the ground. She stared up into his eyes, furious that he would manhandle her. "Stop it. My father will kill you for this."

Tye shook his head. "No. It's time, Angie. It's our time. Come on, you know you want it. You know you're crazy for it."

He lay on her, releasing one of her hands. She felt him as he unzipped his jeans.

"You're completely nuts," she shrieked. "You're not going to . . ." Tears sprang to her eyes. Self-pity welled and pooled in her heart. Oh God, why was the world so unfair? Why did nothing save her ever?

Before she could finish her protest he swiftly reached for the straps of her black bathing suit and slipped each one in turn off her quivering shoulders. He paused, smiling at her. Then he ripped the top down in one quick savage motion. Angie gasped, startled that he had bared her breasts. She pitched her head from side to side. She struck at his hands and tried to roll onto her side so that she might find leverage and get to her knees. He wasn't going to see her this way. He had no right. This was not a game any longer. He was serious and dangerous.

And now she did hate him again as she had before.

Tye held her down with the palm of one hand to her shoulder while with the other he pried the wet, clinging suit inch by inch down her torso. He straddled her legs to keep her flat while he stared at her breasts.

Angie saw naked lust standing sentinel in his face. She had never seen lust in the eyes before and it shocked her, causing her to feel more than naked. She felt stripped to the bone. Down to the soul. She thought it the ugliest expression she would ever want to see. Her own face reddened in shame. Not one person in her life except her mother had ever seen her unclothed. He had no right whatsoever to treat her this way. No right. He could not do this.

Before he had the suit freed of her hips he bent over suddenly and took one nipple into his mouth.

Angie screamed in sudden terror. She beat against his shirt with her fists. "Leave me alone, leave me alone . . ."

He tongued her nipple and then with abrupt fierceness he reached beneath her, grabbing the bunched bathing suit material. He gave a great heave that brought it down past her thighs. He rolled off her momentarily, sitting at her feet. Before she could draw up her legs, he ripped the suit off and flung it into the trees.

Ashamed and overcome with a fear like none she

had ever known, Angie scrambled away from him, the grass scraping and cutting her knees as he caught her ankles and dragged her back to him. Her buttocks were exposed and the helplessness of the situation, the embarrassment of his seeing her made her want to die.

His hands walked up her legs, gripping her by the waist and turning her onto her back once more. He straddled her before she could raise her knees and, using one leg, he opened her as easily as opening a soft, thin-skinned tangerine. He ducked his head from her ineffectual blows and dropped heavily into position. He tried to hold her hands off while he worked his jeans and shorts down far enough to release his erection. Angie was babbling and could not stop. "Oh God . . . oh, don't do this . . . I want . . . I can't . . . you have to stop . . ."

"Shut up," Tye growled, using his hand to guide himself, finding her center and then removing his hand.

Angie bucked up and away, sideways. Tears squeezed from her lids. He held one of her arms solidly to the ground. She hit him in the face and head with the other until the bones of her hand throbbed as if she had been hammering steel with it. She pleaded and begged for him not to do it. Cried and threatened impossible reprisals. All the words rained down on deaf ears.

"Now," he repeated, ready to penetrate her. "NOW."

She felt a ripping and rending of her flesh, heat spreading into her thighs and lower belly, her whole being reduced to one bright shattering burst of pain. She screamed until his hand came over her mouth. Her eyes ricocheted open but the sky, the treetops, the world, dimmed and was lost. The scream ended on an outrush of air. The merciless pounding of an alien force began and Angie, in defense, retreated to a tiny, lightless closet in her mind where she could live out the horror of her defloration without losing hold of sanity.

When he finished and lay sweating atop her, Angie pushed again and Tye rolled off to the side. The slimy trail of his penis brought her the gag reflex and sick sounds issued from her throat. He breathed heavily, eyes closed. She tried to move, to sit, but the pain returned to stab through her. She cried without restraint, her face awash in tears as bitter as green almonds on the tongue. Not fair, she thought repeatedly, her mind stuck on the words like a child who has been unduly punished when innocent. Not fair, not fair . . .

If she could not sit, she would roll and push herself up. She had to . . . had to leave here. She had to . . . had to get away. Though nothing worse could happen now. Nothing in the world could matter now that he had forcibly taken her.

Rape. Not fair. Not fair.

Her hand touched the little plastic radio, her fingers wrapped around its solid rectangle. She brought it into the air and then, sobbing uncontrollably, lunged for him, bringing the radio down and down again on his face, his forehead, his hair until he struck her arm and knocked it from her grip, broken now into bits and pieces, wires and battery hanging loose.

"You nutty damn bitch, what do you think you're doing?" he screamed in outrage. "Shut up that crying! Jesus, you'd think I'd tried to kill you!"

A drop of blood snaked a trail down his forehead and hung like a ruby from his eyebrow. Through her tears Angie saw it as through a prism. Red glints shot into the sunlight. She hugged herself and clenched her eyes tight. She smelled the thick scent of his sweat and held her breath. She heard him cursing while he dressed, stomping around her like a furiously angered man who has been wronged.

Make him go away, God, she thought. Make him go away, disappear, make him *die,* God. Make him die. Strike him dead, turn him to ashes, kill him with a bolt from heaven and let it be done. Make him die hard, with a lot of pain. Hurt him like he hurt me—do it now—let me watch—let me see him die, God, please do it—kill him—I ask You for this—this one favor . . .

The vehemence of her revengeful thoughts brought staggering guilt and she hung her head and cried for herself. Violence scared her. Now that violence had been done to her, she knew beyond doubt that it was evil and uncompromising. How could she know how wrong it was, how against nature, and still wish violence to bear down on Tyeson Dompier's head? But she did wish it, had prayed for it, and could not find it in her heart to take back the prayers of vengeance.

The clearing was silent though it took a while for her to notice. All the noise and fury of the world was locked in her head and screaming for release. Her dreadful prayer for his death whirled her into inner conflict. Her remorse over lost innocence drowned her in deep gray sadness.

Finally she ceased wailing inside and quaking outside. Prints of her hands reddened her arms where she had held herself from falling apart. She opened her eyes and raised her head, looking around. Her clothes lay scattered. Her bathing suit hung from a branch. Her radio was squashed and broken beyond recognition.

She stood with pain. Then she dressed slowly, methodically. If she could only stop crying she thought she might be all right.

The discovery of blood on her legs nearly set her

off into another hysterical screaming spell. She walked like a cripple to the lake and washed herself, wetting the cuffs of her shorts in the process. She went onto her knees and thrust her face under the water. With her face dripping lake water she shook her head until long strands of hair whipped her cheeks pink.

At home she sneaked in the side door and went to the bathroom. Her father found her there late in the afternoon when he began calling her name.

"I'm in here, Dad," she said.

"Taking a bath?"

"Yes," she answered after a long time.

"All right. I just wondered where you'd gotten off to. I'm going to start dinner. How's linguine with clam sauce sound to you?"

Although he received no answer, Jason Thornton wandered to the kitchen and began preparations for a perfect meal taken from *Betty Crocker's Cookbook*. Angie refused to eat when he called for her to join him at the table.

In her bedroom door Jason stood worriedly shaking the change in his trouser pocket. "What's wrong, Angie? Are you sick?"

"Yes. I mean, no. Yes, I'm sick, Dad. I don't want anything to eat, I'm sorry." She turned her back to him and drew the covers over her shoulder.

He crossed the room and felt of her forehead. "You don't seem to have a fever. What's the matter, baby?"

"I think . . . I have a stomachache."

Jason paced the floor beside her bed. "Your stomach hurts and you aren't hungry. What could be causing that?"

Angie heard the worry prevalent in his voice. Since her mother died she could not run the slightest fever without her father falling to pieces. He thought every sign of illness signaled terminal disease.

"I'll be okay. I just don't want any dinner."

"But it's not normal not to eat your dinner. I can get the Pepto-Bismol. I can call the doctor . . ."

"No!" She turned onto her back to look at him. "No, Dad, please don't call the doctor. I'm all right. I might be able to eat a little."

Her words instantly cheered him.

"Oh that would be wonderful. That would make me feel a lot better about you. I'll make a tray and bring it in. You stay right there under the covers and let me get it."

She knew she would not be able to get down a mouthful of food. She could always open the window near her bed and drop the food into the lake that washed beneath her bedroom against the pilings. He would never know and it was a small deceit.

She wanted to tell him, "Dad, I was raped today. He found me alone in the woods along the lakeshore and he forced . . . he tore off my swimsuit and he forced me . . ."

One tear gathered and was squeezed from the corner of her shut eyelid. Tell him? How could she tell her father the truth? Better to let him think she was coming down with polio than to tell the truth. He could handle neither situation; she knew that now. He would crumple before her eyes, shrink and diminish until he was nothing but a blob of unknowing protoplasm and bone. Until this moment she had not realized how fragile her father really was. He had not yet recovered from losing his wife. If he learned she had been brutally raped and emotionally scarred for the rest of her life, he might never come back from the silent places where he now so often retreated. She would be more alone than ever.

When he returned, Angie looked at the fragility that marked his once strong, virile face. In the brown eyes she had inherited, eyes that could not look at her straight on, eyes that avoided contact, a tablet of pain was written down for anyone to read. His fine, sensitive lips twisted unconsciously when he was lost in deep thought. An unhealthy pallor camped on his olive-toned skin and made him appear to be the one ill, fever-ridden. He did not favor the baby-faced Audie Murphy today.

She could not confide in him. She would never be able to share her own pains and betrayals no more than she had been able to open her heart to him about feeling an outsider since her mother's death. He was locked in his prison, she in hers.

"I've brought you a glass of milk, but if you don't want it you don't have to drink it." He fussed over placing the wicker tray across her legs. "They say milk is difficult to digest so it might irritate your stomach. In fact, why don't I take it away and get you a glass of 7-Up instead? Do you want bread? I have some rolls from the bakery . . ."

She let him mother her, let him fret over the milk or 7-Up, wheat toast or roll. Let him plump her pillow behind her head and tuck in her blanket against the still outline of her legs. And when he was gone from her room she opened the window, carefully removing the screen and dumping the pale linguine, the emerald green broccoli, half a glass of warm 7-Up, and a brown roll over the sill for the fish to feed upon during the night.

On Sunday morning after a sleepless night, Angie felt her mind weakening and falling into a worn groove where the word "rape" singsonged like a perpetual incantation. When her father checked on her she tried to get out of bed but her legs felt paralyzed. What was wrong with her legs? Rage didn't paralyze, did it? Maybe it was polio and she could die and go to her mother. These morbid thoughts dominated her mind until she stopped trying to get up. She remained beneath the covers and let him bring a breakfast tray.

By Sunday afternoon, he was frantic, his hair standing out over his ears where he had ruffled it with his hands in worry, the age lines in his forehead deepened into dark creases that looked drawn by a grease marker on his skin.

"I'm going to call a doctor." He wrung his hands and paced. He paused periodically to touch her mounded shape beneath the covers.

"No, Dad. I feel better, really."

"You don't either. You haven't been out of bed today at all. I don't know why you aren't running a fever. Stomach viruses usually have accompanying fevers."

"It's just a cold or something. I don't want a doctor."

"Angie, we can't let this go on. You won't be able to go to school tomorrow if you don't get any better."

The thought of school, of facing Tye, threw her into instant panic. It must have shown on her face.

"What is it? Did you just get a pain in your stomach?" He hung over her, his hand on her upraised knee.

She willfully cleared her mind. She searched for good, positive thoughts—picnics with both her parents alive and at her side, the day in first grade when she ran all the way home and burst into the house with a handful of crayon drawings to show her mother, birthday parties, Christmas mornings . . .

"I hardly ever miss school, Dad," she managed to say. "It won't hurt to miss a couple of days with a stomach virus. You wouldn't want me to go and spread it to other kids, would you?"

"Won't you let me take you into Clarksdale to the doctor? With some antibiotics, a shot of penicillin, we might get it cleared up faster."

She hated to hear him pleading with her when she had to refuse him. "If I'm not better by Tuesday, I'll see a doctor then, okay? I just need to sleep." Her eyes closed and she sighed. It was simply too much trouble arguing about it. Soon she would not be able to talk to him.

He sat on her bedside and took her hand into his. "Are you sure, Angie? You're going to be all right?"

Without opening her eyes to see his expression she could hear the fear running rampant in his questions. She squeezed his hand and nodded her head. "I'll take a little nap," she said. "Sleepy."

He kissed her brow, his lips cool, and left the room. It was another day before she could climb from bed and dress herself. She sat outside by the lake to watch the minute waves lap against the black-tar-covered stilts which supported the back of the house.

She missed her radio terribly. It was as if a part of her had been amputated. As indeed a part of her had—her virginity. She could hear phantom singers and musicians playing into her ear. Perhaps she would buy another portable radio. A larger one. Louder. One that could drown out the whispering despair and make her believe, for short periods of time, that she was as innocent and young and pure of heart as she had been before Tye walked into the clearing in the woods.

Chapter

10

Angie had never wished to appear shorter or smaller. Though racked with insecurity about her height, she had always overcome this with enough self-confidence to hold her head high, shoulders back, eyes straight ahead. Her mother had explained how girls' hormones flooding their systems sometimes caused them to grow more quickly than boys. How one day she would not be taller than the males in her classes, but could look up to them.

When Angie returned to school on the following Tuesday this attitude failed to carry her through. She slumped. She shuffled. She kept her eyes downcast for fear of raising them to find Tye in her face. When she sidled into English class at day's end, the class where Tye sat behind her in the back row staring at the nape of her neck, she slid down in her seat, knees pressed rigidly against the desktop. She could not see past the girl who sat in front. She studied the sallow skin beneath the girl's ponytail and mentally traced a sprinkling of freckles, connecting them dot-to-dot to keep her mind off Tye staring at her in the same way.

The hardest thing in the world, she decided, was to walk through life without notice. She wished desperately to be able to disappear. It was impossible to make herself inconspicuous, and vanishing simply could not be done.

Not once during the day did she make eye contact with another person, student or teacher. Once at her locker she saw Dana coming down the hall her way and hurried off. Thankfully Tye did not approach her or speak to her on the bus or in class. Had he come to her and said a word, she feared she would not be responsible for her actions. She felt like a sullied Raggedy Ann doll with the stuffing pulled out. Nothing cheered her. Nothing amused her. Nothing would ever be the same in her world.

After school she walked down to Varna's house. She needed to speak to someone. Holding the secret within was like sitting on top a land mine. If she moved an inch out of position, she would be blown into unrecognizable bits and scattered to the wind. *Speak it,* she admonished herself, *before you explode.* She must explain how he had knocked her to her knees and stripped off her bathing suit, how he had pushed her legs apart and . . . and . . . hell . . .

At the screen door the first thing Varna asked was, "Where's your little radio, girl?"

Angie worked her mouth to let the truth spill out, but nothing came.

"Well, Varna didn't mean to strike you speechless. Come inside and sit a spell. Sit on your fist and lean back on your thumb." She laughed. Angie didn't. "You look peaked as a peeled turnip, Angelina."

Angie sank into the easy chair and stared at the chess set. It looked as if the white side was soon to be victorious. The black queen had been captured and the king maneuvered into a vulnerable position.

Varna offered tea and molasses cookies which Angie declined. The old woman kept her peace until she took up her place on the sofa and clasped huge, manly hands together in her lap. "Tell Varna what the trouble might be. 'Let me have no lying; it becomes none but the tradesmen.' *Winter's Tale*, act three."

"Varna, what does the cotton look like when it comes up in the spring?" She could not spit out the words about Tye yet. It was not lies which threatened to come from her mouth. It was truth that might poison everything around her if she were to speak it.

"It's acres of green so bright it hurts the eyes. They're short plants that hug the earth until they get full growth, then they come up past the knee. When the cotton bolls come on they're covered with green shells kind of like a pecan. The shell browns and opens and the prettiest, silkiest white cotton boll in all the land fluffs out. It's a pretty sight if you haven't seen it, but if like me, you've worked in those fields most of your life and the sun's burnt down on you throughout the years and the dry bolls pricked your hands bloody, and the long croaker sacks weighed you down and made your muscles cry like babies with mean colic, then you'd near 'bout lose the idea there was any kind of beauty out in the cotton field. Seeing it growing then stops being pretty and starts the ache down in the bones 'cause you know come harvest time, the work is going to be hard and long.

"Not that I'm complaining, mind you. Cotton filled my children's bellies and kept them in clothes. But the cotton crop is a merciless whoremaster. It don't abide no lazy, daydreaming niggers. It takes a mighty lot of cotton picking to fill a tow sack and a heap of tow sacks to make any money for the day's labor. I 'member picking when all we got was this house to live in and some supplies from the company store. Then they went to paying us, but it weren't much—twenty-five cents a sack.''

Angie tried to see the fields full of Negroes, backs bent, long sacks dragging behind them down the rows. The heat in St. Louis during summer was insufferable. Surely it was worse in Mississippi. She could not imagine a life whittled out of backbreaking field labor. She felt ashamed for being white and educated. It was not fair that she live a life of relative ease, her stomach full, her house climate-controlled, her clothes of the best quality, when just down a gravel road an old woman lived with newsprint on the wall, her youth spent picking cotton until her hands were bloodied in order to feed her children. Not fair. Nothing in life ever seemed to be fair. Mothers died. Boys raped. Negroes picked the cotton.

Some of her thoughts must have shown on her face for Varna said, "That's right. You white folks don't know what it's like for people like me out in the fields year after year, but you're not to blame for how Varna made her living, child. It's not your burden to bear. The guilt ain't yours to shoulder. You didn't make the rules no more than I did. Things are gonna change, don't you be fretting about what's done and gone. They'll change one of these days—already changing!—and what I suffered will be no more. They already got machines that pick faster and cleaner than a field crowded with fleet-footed niggers. And my girls and boys ain't picking no cotton out there in sunny California. They're working inside where they's gots refrigerated air.''

"Do you still pick?"

"Me?" Laughter exploded from her. "Nah, I don't do it no more. Varna's done got too old to be worth a poot in the wind. My children begged me to leave this old house, come live with them, but I wouldn't be happy in the City of Angels in some little bitty apartment. I like to see the fields come green and the cotton bolls crack open. This is my home and I don't hate it like they think I ought to. I tell them home is here and I don't wanna go making home somewhere else, old as I am."

"How old are you, Varna?"

Another belly laugh filled the room. "It ain't polite asking a lady her age, Angelina. But if you haves to know, I'll be eighty-one come December tenth. I plan to make it to ninety, Lord willing, but you can't predict them things. The Lord's got his schedule and it's best we don't know it."

Angie sat quietly for a time, her stare unfocused on the worn smooth wood of the floor. Eighty-one. Very old. Terribly old. Her mother had not reached thirty-nine. How did people live to be eighty-one when life was so barren and mean?

"What's bothering you, girl?" Varna leaned forward, arms resting on knees.

"I . . . it's . . ."

"You can tell me anything, it's okay. I'm not proclaiming I know a lot of things, but I *seen* a lot and there ain't nothing you can say what's gonna undo me."

Angie pulled her head up into the air, stretching her neck, trying to loosen the knot there that made her want to cry. If she could only speak, get the pain out into the open, she imagined the relief would be tantamount to rolling a boulder off a mountaintop to save a man pinned beneath.

"It's too hard to even bring up, is it?" Varna asked, her voice softening. "Just take your time then, don't push it. Varna's got plenty of time and knows how to wait."

Again Angie tried to verbalize, but her lips trembled and she swallowed the confession. She lowered her head, tears forming in her eyes. She couldn't do this. She couldn't tell anyone, not anyone. It was too shameful and too ugly. The boulder would kill her if she tried to pry it loose.

"It's nothing. It's really . . . nothing."

Varna sighed and sank back on the sofa. The evening darkened and a chill settled into the room. Angie could smell the lingering scent of fried foods wafting from the kitchen table, and it made her feel queasy. She would have to make herself move. That was the important thing. Move and keep moving, don't think, don't ask for sympathy or help. Why should she? There was nothing to do about it, about the fact, about how dirty she felt and how lonely. Her father or Varna or the angels in heaven couldn't change what had happened to her. What did she want anyway? For Varna to come to her and wrap those soft, wattley arms around her? To hear an adult rise up in fury and seek revenge on her behalf? Of course that's what she wanted. To be babied and petted and cared for so it could never happen again. But it would change nothing, except perhaps the loneliness, and she was almost used to that. Events had conspired to make sure she knew loneliness as well as she knew herself.

"I have to go," she said, standing, going on the move.

"That's fine," Varna said. "And you come back if you want to talk, you hear?"

Surprising her, Varna moved to the door and reached out in the shadows to encircle her shoulders and give her a hug. It was the first time they had touched, the first time a woman besides her mother had hugged her, and Angie suddenly, without thought, turned into the old woman's arms and hugged her back, smelling lavender bath powder and the aging cloth of Varna's housedress. Abruptly she pulled away and was down the porch steps and running along the gravel road, kicking dust in her wake.

I won't cry, she thought. It's stupid to cry. I won't ever cry again.

It was eleven o'clock at night when Angie, sitting dry-eyed and unblinking on her bed, discovered what it was she would do. No more weeping or self-pity. No more longing for a mother to love and protect her, a father who could be happy. No. The plan was not totally formulated yet, but the pieces would fall into place, she was certain.

She asked herself who was her enemy. *Tye*. What did she wish to do to him? *Hurt him*. How could she accomplish this? *By finding out all she could about him*. And how could she discover intimate secrets she might expose or use in some demeaning way? *Watch him. The way he watched her in the bathhouse and the lake clearing*. When would she start her own little sneaky campaign? *Now. Immediately. Keep on the move, that was the important thing.*

Chapter

11

Angie looked at her deceptive handiwork and judged it would pass muster. She had taken a thick blanket from her closet and arranged it folded lengthwise beneath the bed covers. She used a throw pillow at the top to resemble a head on a body. If her father came to see about her in the night, something he had not done in years anyway, he would think her turned away from him and sleeping.

Earlier she had asked her father, "How would you go about finding things out about someone?"

Her father never seemed to care what questions she asked, what knowledge she sought, as long as she *was* asking questions. He was one of those educators who believed all inquisitiveness a rare attitude to be cultivated.

"Well, I'd go to the courthouse, the vehicle registration bureau, and uh . . . the newspaper files. You can find out about anybody with those sources."

She thought about it, but those avenues did not appeal to her. She wasn't going to write a report on the Dompiers, after all. She needed intimate knowledge, not statistics and deed papers and articles about the heading of committees to beautify Clarksdale.

She changed into slacks and shirt, pulled on tennis shoes without socks. She put away her pajamas in the top drawer of the chest. Tiptoeing, she found the flashlight in the kitchen drawer. Quietly letting herself out of the dark house, she headed down the gravel road toward Tyeson's house. He lived approximately a quarter mile away and it was a balmy night for a walk. In St. Louis at this time of year she would have to wear a coat during the night. She followed the cone of flashlight swinging ahead of her steps and listened to the wind in the trees, the lap of the lake waters on shore. No car passed her by and for this she was grateful.

To her right spread the moonlit graveyard of cotton fields. Stubbles stuck up from the earth like leaning and broken headstones dotting the sleeping land. To her left a battery of trees lined the road, effectively blocking the view of Moon Lake shifting and gleaming in the light of the moon. She knew it was there from the sound of little, soothing waves licking the pebbled shore.

At the entrance into the Dompier land, Angie paused and shut off the flashlight. It was obvious to her she should not walk right up to the porch via the winding driveway. There was nothing along the way to shield her approach from view. Lights blazed forth from tall leaded glass windows in the front of the house and from one wing. The Dompiers kept late hours and that surprised her, but was gratifying nonetheless. Had she arrived to find the house dark, the inhabitants asleep, what could she have done but return home, the mission fruitless.

Making a decision, she moved past the stone, lion-topped entry columns and angled out into the field right of the house. She would come at the place obliquely so that if a Dompier happened to walk onto the front veranda or peer from a front window, she would not be detected.

The earth in the field was dry and hard, stone tablets of cracked ground. Clods rolled beneath her shoes and set her off balance so that she walked like a drunken sailor. The unplowed cotton stalks presented the worse problem. They were like iron spikes she must avoid to keep one from penetrating the thin rubber soles of her shoes and leaving her maimed.

After the cautious trek, she reached the side of the house and, with her hands against the bricks, felt her way around front again. Climbing onto the porch without benefit of stairs wasn't as difficult as staying upright and unharmed in the cotton field, but the porch edge was a lip of planks that came chest high on her. She pulled herself up and swung one leg onto the porch to gain purchase. It was then that she noticed the music, loud music, issuing from the front of the house and inundating the yard with waves of orchestral fury. Why did they play it so loudly? It sounded like Bach or Beethoven, something classical and magisterial with heavy cymbals clashing, thundering piano chords and rolling drums.

Coming onto her feet, Angie moved through shadow to the nearest window. She stood catching her breath, back to the wall. Slowly bringing her breathing under control, she turned and peeked through the glass. Heavy draperies blocked her vision. She edged out farther and looked through a sheer beige lace curtain. What she saw stunned her so thoroughly she stood riveted with nose to window, eyes wide and staring incredulously. Had she been seen at that point she could not have fled.

Inside where the music pounded, inside on a beautiful Persian carpet of an intricate red and ivory pattern, inside against the backdrop of cream walls that soared twelve feet and were capped with carved molding, danced a woman.

Danced a naked woman.

Legs and arms moved the nude body ballet-like across the luxurious carpet, toes pointing, hands poised in midair like delicate, pale butterflies lingering in space.

Angie stared, awestruck, saliva collecting in the cup of her open mouth. What was this? What was this naked woman doing and why was she doing it?

Tearing her gaze from the floating figure, she looked around for clues to the mystery. Further incongruities assaulted her youthful sense of what was right and what was wrong, what was shared with the family and what was private. Sitting at a rolltop desk placed away from the walls and windows sat a man, presumably the dancing woman's husband. He was conservatively clothed in a dark blue suit, white shirt, and tie. He sat huddled over photograph albums, piles of papers, and opened stacked books. He seemed to have no thought whatever for the nude activity of the woman.

Doesn't he notice what she's doing? Angie wondered. What's wrong with this picture? she asked herself. It was like trying to find the mistakes in those cartoon drawings they put in the Sunday paper. What is wrong in this picture? Oh, there's just this crazy naked person pirouetting to Bach, that's all. And then there's this man, immune to it all, see, who is paying absolutely no attention to her. And . . .

Oh God. She must be hallucinating. There was Tye and another man coming into the room! They glanced at the woman without the slightest hint of surprise showing on their faces. They took side-by-side positions on a red Victorian sofa. Tye leaned back with his arms languidly at his sides. The other man, older and very fat, but resembling Tye in some ways—his brother?—crossed his legs and swung a loafered foot in the air. He shouted at the woman, "Turn it down, Mama! Jesus, I can't hear myself think!"

Angie watched while the woman, a petulant look on her face, waltzed to the stereo and twisted a dial.

"Thank you kindly, Mama. You do tend to get carried away, don't you?" He said this while shaking his head the way a father might reprimand a naughty child.

Angie almost laughed out loud. Carried away wasn't even close to the truth. The woman had to be stark raving mad. She *was* already stark raving naked. In front of her sons! Had she no pride, no dignity, no sense of motherhood? What kind of family was this?

Mama danced lightly into the center of the room and gave a mock gracious bow to her eldest son. "Life is all about being carried away, Brody. Don't you know that yet?" She did a quick three-turn pirouette, her alabaster skin sparkling in the overhead chandelier light like a polished vase, the muscles of her thighs and slim legs tight and elegant, her small breasts lifting in flight and swinging with the turning motion of her body like small silken white purses. She then hopped into the air like a dancer performing a leap in *Swan Lake*.

"I like the photographs of the Dachau victims better than the Auschwitz victims," the man hunched over the desk said to no one in particular, his voice carrying with it a peeved note. "They're of better quality."

"Daddy, you have been saying that for twenty years. By now we know which you prefer." Brody swung his foot as he spoke, the tassel on his loafer flipping hypnotically. He smiled genially in his father's direction although the older man did not bother to respond or look at him.

"I should play Mozart more often," Mrs. Dompier said, also talking to thin air rather than addressing anyone present. "Mozart was a moody genius. I think he was a child. Wasn't he an alcoholic? But his music was a man's music. A real *man's* music."

"I'm sending for a new book of photographs," Mr. Dompier said, again to himself. "An outfit in Denmark's publishing it."

Brody yawned, the back of one hand at his sensuous full lips. "Another damn book to take up space in your overcrowded library."

Angie watched Tye. He sat quietly watching his mother twirl about the room lost in her own dream of musical genius. Unable to take the sight of senselessness another moment, Angie slipped back from the window and leaned her head against the wall. She closed her eyes and breathed through her mouth. A jumble of impressions collided in her thoughts and warred for dominance. What did this domestic scene mean? What could it possibly *mean?* Was there any meaning in it? It seemed no one connected. It was a play with four characters who were acting out four different scripts. And yet none of them seemed to be bothered by the fact they were not speaking to anyone or being heard by anyone. A kind of insanity was going on in this house.

The music came like a thunderbolt and shook Angie's eyes open. She moved again to the window to see and discovered the room again occupied solely by the mother and father. Brody and Tye had left their parents to their unlikely diversions.

Angie ran across the porch and leaped to the ground. She took the cotton field unmindful of the sharp spiky stalks. She felt full of marvel and question. How could Tye's mother parade around in the nude that way and no one care? How could Tye's father not protest, but ignore the scene in favor of concentration camp photographs? How could the sons of these people sit idly by and say nothing about their parents' grotesque activities? Had it always been this way, even when the boys were small? Had to be or else now as old as they were they would say something about it.

Could this strange family have produced a beautiful, dangerous boy like Tye? Had her rape something to do with the naked woman? Had normal restraints about sex in the Dompier house been dispensed with years ago? Maybe to them what they did in the privacy of their home had nothing to do with the outside world. And maybe it had everything to do with it, although Angie felt ill-equipped to analyze it.

Slowing down when she reached the gravel road, her brow puckered in deep thought. She had heard about nudist camps. No one thought those people maladjusted, did they? Well, not too much anyway. But if the Dompiers were all nudists, then why didn't the father and the sons walk naked through the house, too?

Oh, it was terrifying to uncover such a mysterious secret. First of all she must find out what it meant. There must be much more to know about the Dompiers. Varna had said they were "bad to the bone." Was this what she had meant? Varna might have seen the mistress of the house waltz around naked that way. A cook might have happened on the scene accidentally. Angie remembered now that Varna had also said something about Mrs. Dompier being a "dancer." This had to be what she was referring to. What else did Varna know about the Dompiers that she had not told?

Angie let herself into the house and locked the door

behind her. Now she felt safe and secure, locked away from whatever maniacal stage play was going on just down the road. She was secure against people who lived beyond society's standards, who lived and behaved in ways undreamed of.

Donning her pajamas, she removed the quilt and throw pillow from her bed and climbed into the depression they had left behind. She lay staring into the darkness, listening to the waves wash beneath the house until early morning light lit the windows of her room with palest gray.

Chapter
12

"Tye, do you like Mozart?"

That had been the question. It grew into a nerve-racking litany in his mind. Angie had come up to him during lunch break and said to him out of the blue, "Tye, do you like Mozart?"

He could not fathom why she had asked him that. After asking, she had turned on her heel and left the cafeteria. He had expected anything but that question in retaliation. She might have slapped him in full view of the other students. She might have broken down with a crying jag. She might have spit on him. He had already given up the notion that she could ever care for him. After she beat him in the head with that stupid radio of hers, and after she wouldn't speak to him as if he had hurt that stupid precious body of hers—which he hadn't, of course—he accepted the fact she'd never be his girl, his real girl. Shit. He didn't want any girl for his own. They were all a bunch of stupid dumb shits, he should have known that. Brody knew it. His dad even knew it. Come

down to it, all men knew it. Women, you could take
'em, but you better leave 'em later because . . .

Why did she want to know if he liked Mozart? He
hated Mozart. He hated all those classical hounds,
the pretentious assholes. And what did Mozart have
to do with him and Angie and what they'd done
together? Mozart and sex? Mozart and making love,
what kind of deal was that?

All through the rest of the school day the puzzle
plagued him. It was like a minor rash that spread into
a raging skin condition. What was Angie up to? It
smelled like a plan to him, but she had not given him
enough to go on. Other girls he had relieved of their
virginity didn't act like this. Nothing at all like this.
No one gave him the silent treatment. And then an
idiot question out of left field. The other girls, they
just wanted to do it again. Slavering over him like he
was their stud horse and they were in heat, he had to
service them. Bitches, dogs, they were dogs. Trivial
animals with no brains.

Angie had brains. She wasn't anything like the others. Smart stuck out all over her. Not smart enough
to stay out of his way, but then she couldn't have
known he wanted her the way he did. He smiled
on remembering the day he followed her to the lake
and watched her take the swim. She made him think
of a goddess then, a sea goddess with long wet hair,
the water streaming down over her breasts where he
wanted to put his hands, and take the nipples into his
mouth, make sweet love to her . . .

Mozart. What had she meant? What was she up to?
He'd ask Brody; maybe Brody would know. His
brother was not only smart, but intelligent too and
educated. He had read more books than Daddy ever
even thought about reading. Yeah, Brody might have
a clue to what was going on inside a girl's head.

Once at home Tye made a bologna sandwich and

poured a glass of milk to take with him to Brody's wing of the house. He would wait for him to get home from the hospital.

The rooms were like tombs, dark and quiet, musty with the scent of heavy draperies needing a dry cleaning and carpets his parents had bought overseas before he was born. No one home yet, but him and his mother. He knew where she was. In her bedroom, napping. She slept more than any woman had any right to. Half the day was gone before she woke up and then afternoons she sipped brandy and napped until the Dompier men came home. Daddy often found her snoring in the sheets when he walked through the door. Not that Tye really cared what his mother did. He appreciated the quiet. It was welcome relief after a day spent surrounded by the mechanical droning teacher voices and the adolescent squeal of the other kids.

Munching on the sandwich, he walked around Brody's workroom touching some of the finished projects his brother had done over the years. Beautiful work, but not to Tye's taste. He couldn't get hot over dead things, no matter how beautiful and lifelike they appeared. He touched feathers, fur, underbelly, scale, beak. Checked his fingers. Not a speck of dust. Brody was extra special careful about cleanliness. "Workmanship," he'd once said, "is nothing without the will to preserve the results. You have to care enough to dust and clean and keep out the sunlight, Tye. Or what's the point?"

The only other place Tye had seen such a plethora of taxidermy specimens was in an old museum in Helena, Arkansas, where he once visited his mother's sister. It had been a frightening place dense with shadows and mannequins wearing aged Confederate uniforms caked with many years' accumulation of dust and neglect. The animals there hung from wires attached to the ceiling so that looking up as a child he had experienced the fantastic sensation of being lost in an H. G. Wells prehistoric world of silent death. He had run from the building wiping his hands on his trousers, tears of fear in his eyes, a mad urge in his heart to run away as fast as he could before the shriveled, stuffed monsters came to wrestle his life from its small, inconsequential body.

He finished the sandwich and drained the glass of milk. He opened the right-hand drawer of his brother's desk and withdrew an imported brown-papered cigarette from an antique iron metal box Brody kept there. He lifted a gold lighter from the desk and flicked it into flame. He drew on the cigarette with great deliberation and pleasure. Moving across the room he sat on a leather sofa the color of old wine to smoke and to wait.

He must have dozed in the dim, hushed room for he woke with a start when the door opened and footsteps brushed across the carpet behind him. "I was wondering where you were," Brody said, going to his desk and taking the comfortable chair waiting for him there. "What is it?"

Tye rubbed his eyes to help clear the veil of slumber that had overtaken him. "What do you think it is?" he asked.

Brody drew a wooden tray from the desk's edge into working range. He picked up a quail he had nearly finished and examined the minute stitches hidden beneath the feathers. "I imagine it's girls. It's always girls with you." He smiled ruefully at his brother before returning his attention to the project at hand.

"Not *girls*. Just one girl."

"Oh, that one. What did she do now?"

"First I have to tell you what happened between us at the lake last week."

Brody again glanced up to scrutinize his younger brother's face. He clucked his tongue. "If this is another story of sexual conquest, I don't want to hear it, Tye. It's getting quite boring." He looked up at the ceiling, musing to himself. "In fact, sex is a repetitive endeavor that can't help but become boring. It's the nature of the beast. Take my word." He grinned broadly. "That's why this year I've decided on celibacy. Less hassle."

"Be serious, Brody. I need help."

Brody picked up a pair of tweezers and his attention again on the quail, he waved for his brother to continue.

"At the lake," Tye began, "I caught her swimming. And I . . . I made love to her."

"You had intercourse," Brody said, emphasizing the last word in correction.

"No, Brody. It was different. I wanted her, you know that. I told you that. I liked her. I wanted her to be different."

Again the tweezers waved at the air in front of Brody's face. "All right, have it your way. Go on. What's the problem?"

"She didn't want to make love."

Brody laughed, but he did not look at his brother. "Where have we heard this little tale before, young hot-blooded brother?"

"Will you quit being a shit and let me tell you?"

"Go on, I said." He had hold of a tiny brown and white flecked feather with the tweezers. He worked to make it lie down along the bird's stiffened wing.

"She didn't want to, but I thought it was a show just like it is with all of 'em. But afterward she tried to bash my head in with a transistor radio lying on the ground."

"Music of the spheres," Brody commented.

"Will you shut up?"

A wave of the tweezers. "Go on."

"She didn't come to school for a couple of days. Then today she came up to me and asked me a really dumb question."

Brody glanced up. "What question?"

"She wanted to know if I liked Mozart."

Brody put down the tweezers, sighed, leaned back in the chair. He locked his fat hands together over his midsection and stared at the ceiling. "Mozart."

"Yeah."

"What'd she ask you that for, do you suppose?"

"That's what I'm asking you. It doesn't make any sense to me. Not one damn lick of sense."

"You've never discussed music with her?"

"No, never."

"You've never discussed Mother's penchant for classical works?"

"No."

"Games," Brody pronounced.

"Games?"

"She's up to something. Some kind of revenge game. Maybe you shouldn't have messed with this girl."

"I wanted her."

"You want. You want." Brody pressed forward to his desk, rested the slabs of his arms on top it. "You're always wanting girls, passels of them. It's like you enjoy hunting down trouble. It's like your dick runs you crazy, boy. There should be a new operation invented—temporary castration. Once the adolescent hormones have run their course, get the dick swinging again."

"That's sick," Tye said. "You have a sick mind, Brody." Tye looked away into the shadows where a gray fox stood on its wooden base, caught forever in a snarling pose. "Don't go lecturing me and making up stupid operations. Help me figure this out."

"Mozart."

"Yeah. What's she mean? What does she want?"

"Beats hell outta me. I'll have to have more to go on."

"She didn't say anything else."

Brody picked up the tweezers. "Then wait until she does."

"That's all the help you can give me, tell me to wait?"

"I'm no mind reader, Tye. I have to have a pattern. *Everything* has a pattern if you're patient and observant. Note the pattern of color in these feathers, for instance . . . ."

Tye tuned him out. He stood, put the ashtray on his brother's desk, retrieved the milk glass from the top of a glass case of mice specimens poised on mounds of royal blue velvet. "I don't like it," he said, going for the door.

"I don't either," Brody whispered to the quail as his brother strode into the darkened hallway.

Chapter

13

The second night of Angie's reconnaissance proved as arresting as the first. This time she had brought along a camera, her father's 35-mm that already had some film in it for taking pictures under low light level conditions. The thrill of anticipation was matched by the encounter she witnessed by the light of the harvest moon.

Again the woman danced nude, the stereo blasting. Again the man sat hunched over black and white drifts of photographs, piles of books, stacks of personal memorabilia albums. But not again did the Brothers Grim sit side by side on the sofa. They were nowhere to be seen.

Before going in search of where the brothers might be, Angie positioned herself at the corner of a window and, her breath rattling with excitement, looked into the viewfinder of the camera. She took several photographs of the woman dancing, the man in the foreground huddled over the desk. With each click of the camera, her breath came quicker. There! Mrs.

Dompier's foot raised in the air, arms outspread. There! Her back turned in a pirouette, her lovely body exposed to the lens, her shapely hips, tiny waist. There! Her breasts pointing toward the carpet as she bent with one leg parallel with her body, her chin lifted, a beatific smile on her face. Even if the photos did not come out beautifully, they were at least focused and should reveal plainly who the woman and man were in the shots. It was evident the woman danced and the man ignored. That was all Angie needed; it was enough to destroy this family if she ever felt the impulse.

Sure she had taken at least six good pictures, Angie crept down the long veranda to the next set of lighted windows in search of them. She spied a dining room, elegant and spare with polished cherry wood table and high-backed, delicately carved chairs. Along one wall stood a matching buffet set with silver serving tray and tea set. Next to it sat a potted philodendron grown to a monstrous height all mottled green with irregular pale silver splotches.

Angie moved on, her breath catching at each squeak of wooden plank beneath her tennis shoes. Excitement rode her bared flesh with chariots of goose bumps. She rubbed down her arms from elbows to wrists as if to smooth away the exquisite pain of mounting euphoria. What further mysteries might she unveil? What further extraordinary behavior would she unearth? It felt like Christmas morning and her birthday all rolled into one.

The porch ended as did the lighted windows in the front of the house. She hopped to the ground, bending her knees on impact to lessen the noise. She stole around the side of the house watching for rectangles of light filtering out into the dark night.

Nothing.

A sudden uneasiness gripped her and she halted.

What was she doing? Alone at night. In the dark. Creeping like a thief from window to window.

She looked up at the starry sky. Dippers, small and large, moon a sickle of canary yellow like the scrawny arched back of a tabby cat. And a girl dressed in dark clothes, hair tucked beneath a blue winter cap, sweater pushed up to the elbows, legs trembling, mind falling into chaotic splendor of questioning the real motives for being here carrying out such a strange mission.

But then the troubled spell passed. Self-righteous anger replaced it. Her thighs ached. Her pelvic bones felt rigid, encased in cement. Violation! Tyeson Dompier deserved just punishment for his sin. She could not murder him. She could not imprison him. But she could extract something as precious as he had from her if only she found the treasure worth all her risk. If only she could *know* his most intimate secrets. It would not hurt to have evidence in the form of the exposed photos of his mother dancing nude. Would anyone believe the outrageousness of it if she simply told them? Her, a newcomer to town, an outsider, and the Dompiers so prominent? No, she had to have the proof on hand just in case she wanted to use it.

Controlling her every step, she moved forward into the hedged shadows, feeling before her with outthrust hands. She made the turn at the corner and was greeted by light spilling patches onto the back lawn.

No porch here; the windows too high to peek into. Scouting around the edge of the yard, Angie found a soda pop crate and took it to the brick wall beneath the window. She leaned the crate against the house, planted the toe of one shoe on top, and leaped upward, grasping the window ledge with both hands. There she hung, balanced on her toes, torso pressed against damp, cold brick.

She blinked until her vision adjusted to the lighted

interior. What she saw confused her momentarily. It looked like a warehouse of animals, a veritable Noah's Ark of earth's multivaried species. Paneled walls boasted shelves from floor to ceiling all around the great room. On the shelves birds were poised in flight—owls, bluejays, robins, hawks, falcons, even rainbowed parrots and the humble, gray sparrow!

There were furred creatures, huge and tiny. A black bear reared majestically from one corner, arms outstretched, claws extended, lips pulled back in a mad grimace. Fox, beaver, muskrat, squirrel, rabbit, mountain lion, leopard, cheetah. There were fish—marlin, shark, bass. There were reptiles—snakes, turtles, frogs. And in the center of this motley collection without purpose or reason, sat Tye's brother at a marble-topped desk. He sat with a jeweler's monocle to one eye, the other squinted shut. He held a bobwhite in his hands. A dead bird.

Angie held on fiercely to the ledge, pushing her face against the cold windowpane in order to see more clearly what he was doing. It came as a sweeping, shuddering shock to see that he was positioning one amber eye into a small black socket. It could not be a real eye, she knew that. Taxidermists used fake eyes, plastic maybe or glass, but it *looked* real enough, so authentic in fact that it brought a hint of bile up her throat. She swallowed, clutching harder at the sill, holding her breath to keep it from fogging the glass.

Varna had told her Tye's brother was a surgeon and a hospital administrator in Clarksdale. Well, it seemed he brought his work home with him. He cut and sewed people during the day. He duplicated that work on the animal kingdom at night.

What could I have expected? she wondered. The whole damn family is loony tunes. Out of their trees. One brick shy of a load. She almost giggled at what a cliché the Dompier family was despite their craziness.

Her hold slipped and she hung on tighter. A movement at the far end of the room snagged her attention and sobered her immediately. A door opened. In stepped Tyeson. He wore nothing but his jockey shorts. The sight of his naked limbs made her stomach knot and twist. He had used those strong arms and legs against her. That chest had crushed her flat to the ground.

He padded across the carpet barefoot, then stood jiggling one leg, fingertips leaning down upon the opposite side of the work desk from his brother.

"What is it?" Brody asked without raising his face from the tedious work of placing the quail's eye perfectly into the slot. "You're always bothering me when I'm busy."

"When are you not busy?" Their voices carried clearly to the window. Angie saw Brody's massive shoulders rise as in an exhausted sigh.

"I was wondering . . ." Tye began.

"Spit it out, Tye. Hurry up. I'm trying to make this son of a bitch fit here and you've got my hand shaking."

"Do you think she'll tell anyone?"

"Who?"

"I don't know who. Anyone."

"Who tell what, Tye? Speak English." He sighed loudly again.

"Angie. Think she'll tell what I did?"

"Be a fool to go tell. Ruin her own reputation, have to file criminal charges, go to court." He guffawed. "She'd have Daddy to contend with if she did that."

Tye smiled. "I never thought of it that way."

"Well, think of it. Rest your mind. Now go away and let me finish."

Tye turned and left the room, shutting the door behind him. Angie released the sill and dropped silently to the ground. She covered her face with her hands and ground the palms into her eyes until she saw shooting sparks of white. They had been talking about her. Tye had told his brother about the rape. They had discussed it, the bastards.

The humiliation was such that she sat down on the soggy dewed grass and began to rock, arms around her upper body. She ground her teeth together to keep from wailing like an abandoned child and drawing them to the window to see what was the matter.

Talking about me. Knowing I won't tell. Knowing I have no one to help me. Knowing it doesn't matter what I've suffered. I'm a dog, a slave, damaged goods. I've been used and Tye's brother, a doctor, knows about it and he doesn't even care. No one cares!

On hands and knees, vision blurred by tears of self-pity, she crept to the crate and hauled it behind her across the grass to where she had found it in a clump of high dry weeds. She sat some time until the damp spread from the ground into her jeans, her skin, her bones, and then she stood shakily and circled the house to the cotton field flanking it.

Once home and in bed she slept as if dead, arms corkscrewed tight to her body, fists balled and tight beneath her chin. She dreamed of animals and birds and reptiles filling her room, the entire menagerie crawling toward her as if through mud, sawdust trails leaking behind.

The next day at school she had her question ready. She went to Tye in the cafeteria line.

"Do you like bears, Tye?" she asked. She was rewarded with a puzzled frown and a yawning mouth.

She would get to him yet. And if she could not, she would soon have the photographs and they always said a picture was worth a thousand words, didn't they?

Chapter

14

October thirty-first, Halloween Night. Earlier in the day Angie had helped her basketball team win against their old nemesis, Clarksdale High. It was a slaughter, 86 to 54. For Moon Lake, a small, rural, underfunded school, to beat out the richer, better equipped Clarksdale called for a celebration. The snake dance was to be their big event and they would dominate it. It was going to be more than showing off. It was Moon Lake's way of outright rubbing their faces in it. Angie would not have missed it for anything.

Her father thought her costume excessive. He was cranky as a prudish old woman forced to watch a Las Vegas revue. "I was proud of you at the game, Angie, but don't you think this kind of thing is going too far?"

What he referred to was the mock Clarksdale girls' basketball uniform she and the other girls had thought up to wear. They had dyed shirts and shorts to match Clarksdale's colors, put gobs of hairspray on their hair so that it would stick up crazily from their heads, and for a topper, dripped red tempera paint on their faces, arms, and legs to make it look as if the Clarksdale team they pretended to be had been in a violent car wreck or maybe an industrial machine accident. She looked a fright. Wasn't that what Halloween was all about? She could not understand her father's remonstrations.

"It's just a joke, Dad."

"It's in poor taste, Angie."

She shrugged and left the house early. Dana promised to pick her up in an hour. She wanted Varna to see the costume first.

Varna saw her coming. She sat outside on the steps of her sagging porch wrapped in a baggy plaid sweater that she used to cover her knees. "Lawdy!"

Angie laughed and turned around to show the rips in the uniform, the red smeared down the backs of her bare legs. She expected she would freeze out on the streets tonight in the skimpy outfit, but it was going to be worth every cold minute of it.

"What you supposed to be, girl? Some kinda walking hospital case?" A smile began on Varna's wide lips and spread.

"I'm one of the Clarksdale girls' basketball team! I got myself beat to smut today by the Moon Lake Tigers!"

"I'd say you did, that's the truth."

"You like it? Dad thinks it's an example of bad sportsmanship."

"Oh shoot, honey, it's the best doggone Halloween treat I expect to see tonight. Never did like them nasty little Clarksdale snob girls. Think they're better than country folk alla time—especially *lake* country folk."

"Well, tonight they'll just have to whistle Dixie and cry in their Cokes."

126

"You going downtown to the annual snake dance I take it."

Angie nodded and curtsied, holding out a pretend skirt. "Dana's coming for me."

"Dana?"

"Oh, he's a boy I met. He's nice."

It was Varna's turn to nod. "Here, I got something for you afore you go dancing and tricking around."

Angie waited impatiently at the steps while Varna went in the house. She watched down the road for car lights coming toward her house. She mustn't be late.

Varna returned with the pockets of her big sweater bulging. She dipped in one hand and withdrew a batch of flat rounds of creamy tan candy wrapped in wax paper.

"What is it?" Angie asked, holding a piece up to her face, sniffing experimentally.

"Pecan pralines. I made 'em. Best thing you'll eat tonight, I venture. Picked them pecans myself down offen old man Marlowe's land. Fattest, sweetest pecans in the county."

"Thanks, Varna!" Angie rushed up the two steps and quickly hugged the older woman before skittering down the road toward home. Before she made it a car turned into her driveway and parked. She was out of breath, but she reached Dana before he could go to the door to knock. She grabbed him by the shoulder and, catching a full frontal view of his Dracula costume, said, "You vant to bite my neck?"

"Be careful," her father said softly from the open doorway. "I want you both to be careful tonight, Angie."

"Yes, sir," the couple said in unison, laughing together.

Jason Thornton stood watching as Dana backed his father's Buick from the driveway onto the gravel road. It's just a costume, he told himself. The premonitions

I feel are nothing but my unwarranted worry of teen-agers getting out of control. They'll be all right. They'll have a good time.

Won't they?

He looked at the clear October sky and thought of his dead wife. It's the first time Angie has seemed herself since we moved here. Won't they have a good time? he asked.

The town was alive in the dark. Dana drew Angie by the hand into the forming human snake. Hands latched and the dance began, feet moving to internal rhythms. Whooping and bellowing rang off the emptied black street and the darkened buildings. Angie felt her blood coursing wildly. Though she was not accepted at Moon Lake High no matter how she tried to fit in, it seemed that tonight no one bothered to single her out for exclusion. The snake was formed with alternating boys and girls, the boys in Halloween masks and painted faces, the girls in their basketball team regalia.

The snake grew longer, couples linking up until the chain ran one block, two, three. It began to whip and take on a life of its own independent of the individual members which made it up. Angie and Dana had arrived in time to be situated near the snake's center. Had they come late and attached themselves to the tail, they would have been whipped mercilessly back and forth with such force as to fling them loose, stumbling and falling to the pavement. Laughter filled the city canyon they undulated down. The snake broke up ahead of Dana and he had to pull his half of the human line faster in order to catch up and reattach them all. Angie felt her breath coming quickly, spas-modically, so that she could hardly laugh now through the exertion to keep up. She thought she might never have had as much fun.

To the right and left of them on the sidewalks stood ghosts and vampires and werewolves, princesses and clowns and pirates. But they were not happy Halloweeners. Upon second brief glance, Angie saw how still they stood, how unnaturally stick-like they appeared, as if rooted to the cement walk. They must be Clarksdale High students, the townies, the rivals. And they were not amused at the joke being played on them.

A ripple of apprehension overtook Angie. She almost lost her grip on Dana's hand. Almost stumbled in the ever increasing pace of the flagellating dance.

Surely, she thought, they would not take this ribbing too seriously. Surely they would not get so angry they'd want to fight about it.

The human snake took a turn at a corner and the kids on the tail were whipped out into the intersection amid screams. Angie looked back in time to see half a dozen Halloween monsters flung to the ground, up against curbs, wrapped around parking meters. She let out a little startled laugh though in some way it was beginning to be an unfunny dance. No one was supposed to get hurt, she thought. It was a game; it was supposed to be good, exciting fun. Yet there were casualties already and some adults were rushing to the intersection to be of help to those downed.

Now her and Dana's center position had fallen back to create the new tail of the human line. There were no more than four or five people holding on for dear life behind her. And the street watchers, the still apparitions made up of Clarksdale students, had begun to move, walking in time to the dancers, keeping astride with them along the streetlight-pooled sidewalks.

Angie jerked on Dana's hand, trying for his attention. He must have thought the jerk came from behind them in the line. His face was pointed ahead, unheedful of the urgency in his partner's hand grasp.

"Dana!" she yelled.

His name was drowned in the shouts and cheers and laughter coming like thunder rising from the dancers.

It was all getting out of hand. The ominous watchers who paced the Moon Lakers down the street. The tail end whipping and snapping ever more like a bullwhip licking the street from side to side.

Suddenly all Angie wanted was to be free, to be away from this outlandish scene of revelry gone amok. It was not fun. It was an aberration on the theme of fun. Within mere minutes it had grown into something she did not understand, but nevertheless feared.

She tried to tear her hand from Dana's hand. She shook the hand behind her to free herself. They would not let her go!

"Dana! Stop!"

She saw him glance over his shoulder at her and she saw his mouth open in laughter. He had not heard her plea. He thought she was adding her voice to the general melee.

Out of breath, eyes darting to see how the twin sidewalk crowd glared at them with lowered heads and hunched shoulders, hand working, Angie sagged backwards with all her weight and broke the link between her and Dana. The abrupt break caused her to fall to the street, landing squarely, painfully on her rump. The connection with the boy behind her broke. He fell too. And those behind him swung weirdly toward a streetlight. The sidewalk people moved back, let them crash against the brushed metal pole with clangs and cries. Up ahead she saw Dana being dragged around another corner, his legs flailing the air to keep him going and upright as he was whipped from her line of sight.

Angie tried to stand. It felt as if the bones had been crushed, but she knew she was only badly shaken, bruised. She came onto her hands and knees, stood up to massage her backside. When she glanced up again the sidewalks were emptying, the population spilling into the street, leaving the safe territory like a human deluge rolling onto shadowed pavement.

Panic seized her. "Hey," she said, "listen, it's just a . . ."

She was unable to finish her protest. A gargoyle dressed in rags, face dripping like melting clay, converged on her, hands out to poke at her shaking shoulders. "Smart ass," the face said, spittle flying from the reddened lips. "Dressing up like our girls, you white trash lake bitch! Who do you think you are?"

She was pushed from behind, stumbled toward her tormentor who poked stiff fingers at her shoulder blades again, sending her backward. "Wait a minute," she said, breathless. "You don't have to get mad. It's just . . ."

"Don't tell me it's a joke. I don't want to hear it. You don't come down from Moon Lake and treat us this way!"

"But . . ."

"Shut up!" the gargoyle screamed into her shocked face. "You shut up before I smash your face in!"

Angie broke from between the two people jostling her and ran down the wide street for the corner where the snake had disappeared. She heard footsteps slapping behind her, the air whistling in and out of her lungs. She heard voices raised on the street she had just fled—Clarksdale's angry teenage mob descending on the four or five others she had caused to fall from the dance.

My fault, she thought. I did it. All my fault! Daddy was right; this was excessive, this was dangerous, we're all in trouble. They want to hurt us.

She ran for her life, the October night air buffeting

her in the face, raising the flesh on her naked legs and arms.

Ahead the snake twisted alive and loud, but the sound dwindled on the wind as the noise carried back to her. She would never catch them now, never. She needed help, protection, but more joined the chase from the sidewalks and the street filled with cries of "Get her! Get that lake trash!"

An alleyway stretched to her right. If she took it she might come out on the next street, head off the snake before it was gone, lead the rabble into the jaws of Moon Lake dancers. She veered across the sidewalk, knocking apart two girls trying to block her escape from those in pursuit behind.

The names they called her were lost in the echoing alley. Each time her feet hit the pavement the bruised bones screamed a pain up her spine. She could hardly breathe now, the air a ragged intake of harsh cold.

"Wait for me," she whispered as she ran, clearing the tunnel of the alleyway, emerging onto a side street. A side street of darker shadows, fewer streetlamps, and no one to help her, no one there, not even a trick-or-treating child with his bag bulging with goodies.

The snake must have continued on down the other street. They had not turned again. She'd missed them. She was on her own.

Turning her head side to side, trying to decide where to hide, she spied a garbage dumpster pressed up against the wall of a store building. She ran across the street, paused at the dumpster to look behind her, saw she might have but seconds in which to hide herself. She ducked to the far side of the dumpster and hunkered down to the ground, arms around her knees, panting.

Dark enveloped her. Moonlight lay like a scarf in front of the dumpster and against the next wall. Sounds of running came like shots and filled her ears. She squeezed her eyes tight, stilled her panting lungs.

"Where'd she go?" came a masculine yell.

"Shit, she's gone!" came another.

"Find her, take the next street, Barney."

"We'll find her," came a reply from a female. "She won't get away from us. We'll turn her into red meat."

Angie had no doubts that was exactly what they would do if they found her huddled beside the dumpster. It was a nightmare turned real and she was the victim.

The sound of pounding feet passed and was lost in the distance. The voices faded into the rich, black night. She could let out a breath now, relax and let her racing heart simmer down to a regular beat.

It was then a long shadow slid over her dark hiding place. She let out a small yelp that was bitten off. She looked up.

"That was a dumb stunt." Tyeson lounged in front of her squatting position. "Who thought it up anyway?"

Angie pushed up the wall and sidled sideways from the trap. She backed in a circle, her eyes never leaving him. "Get away from me."

"I hope you learned your lesson. If I were you I'd get back to Dana's car and lie low until this thing's over. They're out for blood, you know. There's going to be a real fight before the dance is over."

He knew she had come with Dana. He always knew everything. The image of him in his shorts standing before his brother's desk came back to her. A smile twitched at her mouth. Maybe he didn't know everything . . .

"I'll walk you back, how's that?" he asked, stepping forward as if to take her arm.

She jerked away, threw back her head, looked at

the deserted street. "Forget it. I can take care of myself."

"Can you now?"

That smirk, that smugness, it killed her, it made her want to blurt out what she knew. She had to bite her lip to keep from spilling the secrets out. She turned from him and started off down the sidewalk in the direction of the main street where Dana had parked. She heard the footsteps keeping pace behind her. If he reached out and touched her she was going to ball up her fist and knock out his teeth, that's what she was going to do. Even if he was much bigger and stronger and might do her real physical harm, she'd slug him first. And slug him hard.

"Dana's a jerk," he shouted at her back. "Look how he left you to fend for yourself."

She wanted to defend Dana, but not enough to dare to speak to Tye. She refused to be drawn into any sort of conversation with him, under any circumstances.

"He only wants to get from you what I got," Tye taunted.

She stopped in her tracks. Her shoulders began to shake and she could feel her teeth scraping and rattling in the ensuing fury. "Leave me alone," she said. "Leave me alone or I'm going to start screaming for the cops."

He jockeyed to the side of her and held out his hands palm up. "I gotcha. Let you walk this street alone, that's what you're saying. I can see that. Fine, go ahead, smartass. Go it alone, all by your lonesome, fight off the wolves—or is that *bears?*—if that's your thing." He skipped ahead of her, turning his back and sticking his hands in the pockets of his school jacket. His shoes clicked along the sidewalk. His silhouette grew smaller, turned a corner and disappeared.

Angie drew in a breath and let it out. The sounds of children giggling came from behind her and she turned to see a gang of little boys racing down the center of the street, their heavy bags of candy swinging at their sides. She loped off into the street and joined them. "Hi there, doing good?" she asked, pacing them.

"Yeah, great!"

"Hersheys! Big bars of 'em!"

"Double-Bubble gum," said another. "A handful! Want one?"

She shook her head and her wild sprayed hair bobbed like railroad spikes driven into her skull. "Nah, thanks. I'll just stay with you guys until Main, okay?"

They allowed as how they didn't care. They wanted to get to Woolworth's before it closed and she'd have to run if she wanted to keep up with them.

This she did while all the time watching for Clarksdale's blood-mad students to rush them from the lurking shadows between the buildings. She left the boys on Main and found Dana's Buick. She sat in the driver's seat, all four doors locked, and listened to "The Monster Mash" and other dumb Halloween junk songs on the radio while she waited for the dance to end and for Dana to come to the car in search of her.

Once Tye left Angie to her own devices, he walked to his car and brought out a black and white skeleton mask. He put it on over his face and grinned widely beneath it. It felt right to be Death. It felt good. It was his persona tonight, Death, and he knew exactly how to play the part—the biggest part ever to be his.

Now to catch up with the dancers.

He found them on Twenty-third Street, whipping along the tree-lined avenue that led into the heart of the business district farther on. He had watched Angie and Dana join the chain. He knew Dana's disguise and approximately where he was positioned in the snake. He began to jog along the sidewalk, catching up to them. When he reached the snake, he picked out Dana where he held on precariously to his third place from the tail end.

Tye rushed the street, his feet pounding, his mask in place. He broke in between Dana and the clown who held his hand in front of him. It was tricky, but Tye managed to grasp them both before the next snap of the chain. He was in place! He had Dana's fate in his hands. Literally. He laughed aloud at the very thought, the sound of his laughter blending in and lost with all the other squealing, happy sounds of the dance.

They rounded a corner, moved down Grudine Street. Tye held each hand in his own with a vise-like grip that had to be shutting off the blood to their fingers. So what. He wasn't letting go. Not yet.

The snake snapped and whipped. They were all thrown this way and that, feet leaving the ground sometimes, stumbling at others and having to be held up by the person in front. Tye judged there were still almost two dozen students making up the chain as it ripped along the hollow streets to fill them with loud screams and laughter.

Tye scanned the closest side of the street for his target. He needed a window. A big window. A huge plate-glass show window not too far set back from the curb. The thought of glass, splintered and sharp as knives, filled him with a feeling close to sexual arousal. He felt his head bloating with blood, his lungs expanding with cool air, his mind gorging with thoughts of revenge. Goddamn Dana. Goddamn him. Goddamn his interference, his slack-jawed, ignorant, naive blundering. He couldn't have Angie Thornton. If he couldn't stop Angie from going out with him, then he must stop Dana from going out with her. Goddamn his soul anyway, the son of a bitch. Had he kissed her? Had he touched her, the bastard? Had he stuck his slimy tongue into her clean, beautiful mouth?

Goddamn him to hell and back.

Pearson's Fine Furniture appeared a half block distant. The window. It was perfect. Huge, wide, faultless. Tye did his best to pull the entire end of the snake chain closer and closer to the curb's edge. He was able to get them a few feet from the sidewalk.

His mind zipped along as quickly as his feet carried him forward. He did not take his eyes from the show window. He saw the back-lighted living room furniture, the pale gray and blue swirls of cloth on the sofa and matching chair, the mellow sheen from the coffee table in front. Wind whistled in and out of his mouth like a cyclone. He allowed Dana and the other two behind Dana to whip back from the sidewalk they approached and then with exacting calculation, Tye hauled them in as if he were desperate to haul in a net of shark from the ocean. The muscles of his arm rippled from the exertion. They whipped forward, forward, and the momentum carried them flying across the curb, screaming, screaming NO NO NO and Tye let go. He let go. He broke contact with Dana's hand right at the point that would carry the boy careening across the sidewalk and into the plate glass window of Pearson's Fine Furniture.

The action broke Tye's stride and contact with the one in front of him. He fell to the pavement with a thud that coincided with the shattering crash of Dana striking the window face first. Tye rolled and came to his feet like an acrobat. He ran to the curb to look, to see how well he'd calculated Dana's running thrust into the unyielding glass wall.

He stood there with the other two boys who had run and then fallen as they hit the brick surface of the wall next to Pearson's glass showcase.

"Oh shit," one said.

"We gotta get him outta there," said the other, clambering over the spiked glass rim of the window into the store.

Tye cautiously stepped back in the shadows beside the window to watch as the boy who went in to help bent over Dana and tried to raise him. "Help me!" he called to his companion standing, staring in the broken hole.

That boy too climbed inside, cursing when he cut his hand open on the low sill. "He okay?"

"Not in here! I don't need help *in here*. Go get someone, for chrissakes, go get a doctor or the ambulance! This guy's bleeding to death!"

The boy stood looking down at Dana's bloody form for a minute before obeying. He jumped the sill and raced off down the street screaming hysterically for help.

Tye stood watch, out of view. He saw the boy inside lift Dana from where he lay headlong over the coffee table. He saw him drag Dana to the sofa, knock off glass with one hand, and lay his charge on the gray and blue cushions. He saw the cuts on Dana's arms . . . neck . . . face. Blood flowed by the pints, rolling in rivers down Dana's torso. The blood was as scarlet and shiny in the recessed store lights as red ribbon. It was brilliant against the muted colors of the expensive sofa where he lay. He saw Dana's surprised stare. His steady, unflinching stare into nowhere.

Dana was dead. No doubt about it. Yowzer, yowzer, as Brody would say. No doubt whatsoever.

Tye grinned, stuck his hands into his pockets and walked off.

He heard the boy in the furniture store window saying over and over, his voice weakening as the distance between them mounted, "For chrissakes, for chrissakes, shit, shit, shit . . ."

Let's see how much he interferes *now,* Tye thought savagely.

And then he began to laugh.

This would be Angie's last date. Her last dance. The final curtain on the hope for a normal teenage life of boys and dances and corsages and "fun." She would not forget again her real purpose or the danger that lay all about her like broken glass beneath bare feet. She knew something Dana might never have learned before the end. That life is full of precarious situations and the promise of snatched away happiness. In the midst of a solitary swim there can be rape. In the high excitement of high school rivalries there can lurk the threat of brutality and bloody, incomprehensible death. You couldn't trust the world. It fooled you into lazy assumptions. That Halloween was but All Hallow's Eve, a harmless, pagan, Americanized ritual. That life was forever and nothing could stop it. That games were just that, games, and not life-threatening.

Angie sat in the car with her father on the drive home to the lake and she cried. She could not talk. She couldn't answer her father's soft questions. She didn't know how it had happened; he knew as much as she. The snake broke. Three of them were propelled across the curb and into the storefront. Dana, unluckily, had gone through the window, couldn't stop to save himself. No one would admit to having been the one to let go of Dana on the tail end of the snake. All of them claimed there had been someone else there, but no, they couldn't remember what he was wearing or who he was. They were all wearing Halloween masks. They were certain they hadn't done it, that's all. Not one of them.

It was an accident. A terrible unjust accident.

As Jason Thornton drove his daughter home, he

listened to her sobbing and wondered what he could do to help her. Nothing was going to replace the boy. Nothing had replaced Susan either. But he must try something for she was his daughter and he loved her so much that he hurt when she hurt. He felt like weeping when she cried and ached for the loss of Dana Percy as she did. What could he do to help in some way?

Maybe he'd buy her a pet. He didn't know where this idea came from, but it pleased him. She had never had a pet, not even a goldfish. He'd get her an animal, a bunch of animals! He would, by God, find a way to lift her from the walking depression she had been mired in from the time they had moved here. Her health, he felt assured, required happiness and she would be happy or he would find out why. The idea of a gift, of pets, might be a stopgap measure to replace a dear friend, but it was all he could think to offer Angie. That and his great abiding love. It would have to suffice. There was no more.

Chapter
15

Dana's death left a hole in Angie's life that she could find no way to fill. She kept seeing his face in her mind when she least expected it. His shy smile loomed up from the depths of memory and it squeezed her heart dry as desert bone. The sensation of flying through the night wind when he had pushed her in the swing returned when she tried to sleep. She would catch herself floating up toward the moon and the stars and then back, back to where Dana put his warm palms against her shoulders and pushed. She kept remembering the day she had first met him when Tye dumped the cafeteria food over his head. The way he had calmly handled the situation, the way his eyes had sparkled even then as if he shared a secret with her and the secret was this: Tye might get in our way, but we will be friends no matter what he does to separate us.

The night she had left the snake chain she had lost him for good. Forever.

How many people, so young, so *needy*, lost the

ones they cared for the most? she wondered. And why was staying alive beginning to seem to her like a miraculous event? Could it have been her death, not Dana's, had she stayed connected in the snake dance?

Death was an unfathomable thing trying to make itself known to her. She supposed that was what it meant to be an adult: grappling with death until it was a tolerable idea, if never acceptable.

She realized she had never accepted her mother's passing and having not done so, she could accept less the loss of Dana. If growing up meant that she could more easily live with loss, then she was failing miserably.

Dana's face kept coming to haunt her. The warmth of his lips, the sweetness of his friendship, the kindness of his gaze. She thought she might go crazy if the dead did not go away to leave her alone. Carrying ghosts was so burdensome a load and, her strength, like a rope playing out between her hands, so limited.

She hid all these gloomy, unhappy thoughts from her father as best she could. He had his own ghosts tied to him, trailing his every step. On the day that she came home to discover he had thought of a way to dispel those ghosts, at least for a while, Dana's spirit loosened from her just a bit. She felt returned to the world of living, breathing, healthy beings. It was as if a shawl of depression had been flung from her shoulders and she was butterfly free, wings aflutter, heart palpitating a thousand beats a second. Scent and sight and sound and love flooded over her senses like a warm, sloppy wave birthing on a pristine beach.

Angie's surprise at her father's gift of the three pairs of rabbits was such that she began to twirl excitedly and clap her hands. In St. Louis she had never been permitted pets. Her mother thought them disease carriers and too much trouble in a busy household. Her father had never owned pets as a boy and cited the abundance of stray dogs and cats in their neighborhood as good reason why they should abide by Susan's wishes and not keep animals.

Angie had never spoken of this, but she had always yearned for a warm, cuddly animal to love and care for since the time she could walk. Some of her friends had pets and she envied them. Now she had her own!

She stood between the two large wire cages at the side of the house glorying in ownership. It was the ultimate gesture of love for her father to do this. Jason had gone to the trouble of building wooden legs to hold the cages off the ground and he had supplied her with army green tarpaulins to throw over the rabbit cages during bad weather.

In the cage to her right four grown New Zealand rabbits scampered for her attention. They were white and huge, large as fat furry cats. In the cage to her left sat a pair of snowy white long-haired Angora rabbits. These were a rarer breed than the New Zealands and they were her favorites. They looked even more like cats with their long silky fur that she loved to stroke and rub against her cheek.

She changed the water containers on each cage, filled the feeding trays with rabbit pellet food, and finally allowed herself to reach in and take each rabbit in turn into her arms for a session of cuddling.

Warm. Snuggling. Innocent. To Angie they symbolized everything good and clean in life. She had no idea pets could provide such comfort and contentment. She sat on the leaf-covered ground and spoke softly to the animals, naming them, delighting in their abrupt movements and sparkling, alert eyes. So what if she didn't possess a close friend or if she missed school activities? So what if she were alone and outcast when she could return home each day to the companionship and acceptance of these friendly creatures? They could not call her name or answer her questions; they did not solve her problems or assure her she would survive loneliness. But they knew her and they trusted her, and in a way that was enough compensation in a life that before appeared to be a burning desert of hopelessness.

"You're my pal," she whispered to the Angora doe in her arms. Its liquid eyes glistened, the inquisitive nose perked. "You're my real pal. I think I'll call you Little Egypt."

The doe buried its head beneath her arm. It sniffed and squirmed as if going down a rabbit hole into blessed darkness and then was still, its delicate breastbone rising and falling gently as it breathed against the side of her sweater. She would be covered with fur, she knew, when she was done petting Little Egypt, but it was worth it. She stroked its humped back, closed her eyes and surrendered to the sensation of satin flowing beneath her fingers.

Jason watched from a protective position behind the curtain at the living room's side window. He smiled radiantly, sure he had been right in his decision. That's all his girl needed—a hobby—something to interest her. *Now* things would fall into place. *Now* that she was on the basketball team and she had the rabbits to keep her company on the isolated lake, she would begin to blossom and become a part of the new world he had brought her to. *Now* he need not worry quite as much over his daughter.

He smiled until it felt his mouth would crack open his face. Love for the girl sitting on the ground outside with the rabbit in her lap filled him with an expanding emotion that physically seemed to burst beyond his chest out into the open. He could not remember being happier in years.

Tye sat in cold brown shadow behind a stand of fir trees several yards from the Thornton home. His mouth twitched intermittently in disgust. He saw the girl on the hard ground with her newest prize. He also saw the man at the window gloating over her. He wanted to puke. Kid's stuff, that bunch of rabbits. More evidence—as if he needed any—proving Angie and her father too, descended from peasant stock (as his father would say) and lacked the brains to pour piss out of a boot.

Angie couldn't be as smart as he once thought. Not if she were so easily entertained and made happy. He could *see* the effect the rabbits had on her. Looking at her face she reminded him of Mary in Michelangelo's *Pieta*.

He had flown with Brody to the New York World's Fair the year before and stood on the escalator with all the other visitors to get a glimpse of the master's handiwork bathed in blue light. It seemed to him there had never been a more beautiful woman than the carved Mary, nor a more beautiful man than the dead Jesus she held across her draped legs. He never expected to see a human being who reflected the sad but courageous visage of Mary, yet here she was cradling not a dead prophet in her arms, but a measly fat white rabbit. Stupid.

Brody told him Angie was planning something. Something he could not yet find a pattern to. Well, all was fair, and if she was up to no good, she was about to find out she was on treacherous ground. He knew what she cared about now. He knew what to take from her if she tried anything.

He would wait awhile yet to be sure she was scheming against him. And if he found it to be true, then Mr. Thornton would curse the day he thought to buy his daughter pets.

Don't cross me, Angie, he thought, moving back into deeper shadows for his return trek home. Don't you dare think about crossing me.

*   *   *

Each evening when caring for the rabbits Angie forgot about Tyeson Dompier and the emptiness he had caused to fall upon her soul. Each night when her father retired to his bedroom, she was reminded.

Stalking the Dompier house had become an addiction that provided roughly what her time spent with the rabbits furnished—a release from pain she could not even name. The nightly foray down the gravel road and onto Dompier land brought adrenaline surging until her brain felt semiparalyzed with anticipation. It did not occur to her to question why more people did not fall into the role of a Peeping Tom. It was enough that it worked for her. Keep on the move, never give up, stay busy, that's what she had to do.

She dressed, made the bed with the pillow body, and left the house. She blew kisses toward the rabbit cages as she passed them. It was silly, but no one would know.

The crisp wintering air awoke all her senses so that she heard clearly and distinguished the rustles from the trees near the lake and the whisper of wind through the dead cotton stalks. The night skies scored her eyes with whirling space splattered with a zillion worlds blinking indecipherable signals. She was never more alive than when sneaking through the dark like a wraith and discovering what transpired in the strange household set back and isolated from the rest of Moon Lake. Spying was so much fun.

This night she was dressed warmly in a down jacket, jeans, socks, and tennis shoes. Over her hair she wore the blue cap pulled down over her ears against the coming drop in the temperature as the clock ticked past eleven o'clock. She meant to explore the freestanding buildings behind the Dompier house proper.

Once across the field without incident, she headed for the rear of the house and away from the blazing lights in what she now knew were the parlor, the dining room, and Brody's workroom. The low quarters directly behind the plantation mansion must have been used for slaves, she guessed. She had read about them in history class. The building was made of the same slatwood construction as the main house though the paint was more weathered and peeling. Dead vines wound around the entry posts on the long porch, and the steps creaked as she ascended them counting as she went, one, two, three.

She grasped the brass doorknob, the shock of its cold causing her to let go momentarily. Again she took it into her hand and turned until the latch clicked free. The door whistled sharply as she cautiously opened it and stepped inside. She withdrew a flashlight from her coat pocket and shutting the door, flipped the switch. She swept the pool of light around the interior of the room. It was obvious no slaves or anyone else had lived here in decades. Cobwebs hung from the high ceiling and stretched across the corners of the room like filmy silver nets. A broken lightbulb dangled from a black, raveled electrical cord into the middle of the room. Backless and seatless chairs were stacked haphazardly across the far wall. The floor was plain, unadorned planks of the same kind that made up the porch.

Angie rubbed her nose to clear it of dust she'd stirred up on her entrance. She advanced through the door on her right and came into a large open kitchen with a crumbling fireplace and oven that took up one half of the end wall. Next to it was a massive black and silver woodburning stove covered with a thick coat of dust. Other odds and ends of furniture filled the remaining space. The room lacked an exit. She turned, swinging the light, and heard a gnawing, papery sound which stopped her. She listened, gathered it was rats in the attic, and moved across the living area through the opposite door.

In here she could hardly move. Old, dilapidated furniture barred the way. It was stacked and shoved, the legs of tables and the backs of easy chairs throwing misshapen shadows across her body.

So, she thought. Nothing much remarkable about the old slave quarters. Now for the rest of the outbuildings.

She left the house making sure to secure the door again. Behind and to the right of the quarters stood a barn that did not look as if it had been in use any more than the quarters. She quickly inspected it and found to her satisfaction that it held nothing but a rusted tractor with the tires missing off the rims, a few bales of wired and sour-smelling hay, and farm tools lying about the earthen floor like giant pick-up-sticks thrown down in a fit of pique.

Leaving the barn, she scouted a utility shed on the other side of the quarters, noting nothing out of order. There was a riding lawnmower, several push lawnmowers in differing states of ill repair, gasoline cans, paint cans, brushes, old baseboard moldings, rolls of chicken wire and barbed wire.

Wandering back to the house, she wiped her hands along her jeans to clean them. She stepped lightly and carefully for she could not use the flashlight here. She must feel her way, led by the beacons of electric light emanating from the house.

Windows besides the ones that she knew to belong to Brody's menagerie room were lighted on the other side of a concrete patio set up with wrought iron furniture. She moved toward those windows, curious to see something new in the house. She cringed to think she might happen upon a bedroom or a bathroom. That's not the area of their lives she cared about. She vowed to herself that were she to chance upon one of the Dompiers in either of those kinds of rooms, she would immediately leave off peeking inside.

Again the ledge was too high to see over. This time she took one of the petite black iron patio chairs and used it to stand on beneath the window. She lifted her head inch by inch until her eyes cleared the sill.

The kitchen of the house. That was a relief. A voice. Tye's! But where was he? She strained against the glass to see, stilled her breath so that it would not fog the window and hamper her vision.

"What do you think I should do?" she heard him ask plainly. She waited for a response, but none came. Was Brody with him or his mother, his father? She could see no one. One low-wattage light fixture shined down over a double stainless steel sink. A wood-grained Formica-topped table took up the center of the room, four brown Naugahyde chairs on rollers pushed beneath it. Darkness claimed the far area where she thought there might be the stove and refrigerator. He must be standing there in the dark. With whom, though?

"When I graduate," he said, "I think I'll head west and get out of this hillbilly burg. Daddy will pay for it if I ask him."

Angie had never heard Tye talk with such complete frankness before, not even to his brother. He was always hesitant even if what he actually said sounded perfectly plausible and honest. Whoever he was talking to now he must trust absolutely. She needed to know who that person was. It could be a major discovery, someone she could use against him.

She moved her head to the side panel of the window in order to see better. She thought she could make out Tye's silhouette, but she was not sure. She squinted. Listened, barely breathing.

"No, I don't want to go to college. Brody says I should, but what does Brody know? That stuff's a waste of my time. What do I need to make a living for? We've got money. I won't ever have to make a living, that's for jerks who have to do it. I don't want to be a doctor like Brody or a lawyer like Daddy. It bores me to think about it.''

He walked from the darkness into the kitchen. Angie ducked, afraid he had seen her. She cupped her hands over her mouth and nose and breathed the warmth of her palms into her lungs. Her fingers were numbing, the tips like chunks of wood. She must leave soon. A wind had come up and it brought with it a harsh, blistering cold. But she couldn't leave before she understood what was happening in the kitchen. Not before then. She'd freeze first.

She heard the squeaking of one of the roller chairs. She carefully peeked from the side frame of the window. Tye had his back to her. She was safe from detection and sighed easily. He sat at the table with his feet propped on the tabletop. He had moved a salt and pepper shaker to the side to accommodate his shoes. She still did not see his companion. Was someone else in the darkness at room's end? Why didn't he respond?

"You think I have looks, huh?" Tye asked, apropos of nothing. "I suppose you're right. The girls like me, that's for sure. All except Angie and Angie will get hers, don't you worry none."

Hearing her name caused her to duck again and shiver as she breathed from her cupped hands. What was he talking about? She would get her what? She wanted to shout at him. Was he ever in for a surprise! It was he who would be getting something and he wouldn't like it either. She was no longer his poor, unwilling victim. God, but she hated him. Smug, offensive little bastard, that's what he was.

"What will she get?" she heard him ask as if he could hear her thoughts winging their way to him from outside the window. "Why, I don't know yet. Oh, maybe I do. I have a plan too, you know. She's not the only one with the sense God gave a chicken.''

Angie peered over the sill, her eyes widening at the prospect of learning what kind of plan he had in mind for her. It was the first time she'd considered it. This was *her* game. How dare he be playing one too, one she knew nothing about! Hadn't he done enough to her? It was her turn now. Why else did she come out night after night on reconnaissance this way?

"But who cares about her?" Tye asked. Still there had been no answer to him. "That will all come in good time. I want to talk about afterwards. About the real future. I want to talk about what I want to do when I get out of this dumb country bumpkin high school, that's the thing on my mind. The guidance counselor's on my back about deciding what I want to do when I grow up." He laughed sarcastically. "When I grow up, the jerk says!"

A distorted shadow filled the doorway to the kitchen. A light switch was hit and light flooded the kitchen. Again Angie ducked and listened. She had seen in the split-second illumination that it was Brody who had entered.

"What're you doing in here again talking to the four walls?" Brody asked. "I get sick of this shit, Tye."

"Shut up, Brody. Leave me alone."

"Daddy wants you to go to bed. It's been hell getting you up in time for school."

"Tough titty."

"Tye, you're keeping everyone awake. Go to bed now."

"You're not my keeper. Go tell it to the Marines."

"Do you want me to call Daddy?"

A pause. A scrape and scuffling of feet. "No, I'll go to bed. *You* don't have to get me up anyway, I don't know what your problem is. This big brother craparoo gets on my nerves if you want to know the basic truth," Tye muttered.

"I don't want to know the truth. Now get outta here. I'm hitting the sack again, see if I can get back to sleep."

Angie saw the window go dark and slipped from the chair to the ground. Her fingers felt stick-like as she carried the chair back to where she'd found it. She hurried away from the house and into the dead field. The wind buffeted her until she had to tuck her chin into her coat front to keep warm.

All the way home she wondered at one thing Brody had said to his brother. "Talking to the four walls . . ." Could it be true? If so, why did Tye talk to himself? And why if his brother knew it, didn't he do something about it? People who talked to themselves weren't right in the head. Even she knew that and she wasn't a doctor. What could Brody be thinking, letting Tye rave to himself in an empty room that way? How bizarre could this family be and still function, that's what she wanted to know. Brody had to know Tye was unbalanced—*crazy*. Her father would call him unbalanced, a polite way of saying he was off his rocker. Brody also had to know his mother's naked dancing wasn't exactly your normal American family evening fare either. Or his father's way of ignoring everything around him. But Tye's talking to himself— that alone should have been enough to alert a doctor that something was wacky as owl shit in the hen-house.

Marveling, shaking with cold, wide awake with revelation, Angie let herself into the house and crept to her room.

Chapter

16

Angie knew she had gone too far and blown her cover the moment she opened her mouth to Tye in the cafeteria and asked him, "What are you going to do in the future, Tye? Keep talking to the four walls?"

Yet by that point she did not care anymore. Let him know she was privy to his home life. Let him suspect she had been outside the kitchen window that night. So what? He had stalked and watched her when she was unaware. She had merely turned the tables on him. Let him see how he liked it. She had enough ammunition now to ruin not only his reputation at Moon Lake High, but his father's law practice and his brother's hospital administration job too.

"What do you think you're talking about?" he asked.

Angie pulled open her purse and produced four photographs. They were not very good ones. All off center and the light was so dim you had to look closely, but they were proof, unmistakable proof. She handed them over.

Tye stood holding them, the first one showing his mother balancing on one leg, the other one in the air. It was obvious she did not know she was being photographed because she looked crazy. She actually looked out of her mind. That startled Tye the most, Angie thought while watching him. That he noticed for the first time just how insane his mother must be. Slowly he flicked aside the pictures one at a time and looked at them all. She waited impatiently.

His voice came out hoarse and low. "Why did you do this?"

"Why have you done the things you've done to me?"

"I knew you'd been at my house."

"But you didn't know I had a camera, did you?" She relished his vulnerable position. She wanted to press him to the wall. "You didn't know I'd be smart enough to get real evidence, did you? What do you think the city council and the police and the newspapers would say about these photographs?"

"You wouldn't . . ."

"I might. Why shouldn't I? Tell me a good reason not to."

"Angie, if you . . ."

"Go to hell," she said, snatching back the photos in one sweep and leaving him open-mouthed.

All she had to do was show the photos of Mrs. Dompier waltzing naked before her family every single night of their lives. If she did that it would be all over for the Dompiers on Moon Lake. Total and absolute destruction to their sleazy little lives.

So let Tye know she knew. It was time.

Once she'd asked him about talking to the walls it was as if kleig lights had come on behind Tye's eyes. They seemed to shimmer in their orbits, the blue intensifying to a deep, glassy blue. Then when she had shown him the pictures, he had turned as white and as ghostly as a cadaver. Let him suffer!

Finally she'd pierced his armor. By afternoon it would be all over the school that she and Tye were in some kind of mysterious feud and she was winning. That was the thing. She was on the move and winning. No one before this had left Tyeson Dompier speechless. That in itself was a victory of a sort. And now he knew his family secrets weren't inviolate. That was the best revenge of all, though it wasn't enough by a long shot.

She whistled as she walked, shifting her school books from one hip to the other. If he dared come down the aisle on the bus once school was out and say one word to her, she'd tell everything she knew, damn it. She'd shout it from the bus windows. She'd hand those pictures over to the papers. She would gladly watch the scramble Tye's father and brother would have to make to avert a town scandal.

She had him. It was dirty pool and her father would wring his hands and scold her if he knew, but anything, *anything* that served to unsettle Tye was worth any amount of risk. The only regret she had was that she was no longer invisible. Her trips to the Dompier house at night were now necessarily curtailed, if not completely out of the question.

She sat down in her seat in American Government and sighed. Too bad, she thought. It was just beginning to be fun. She wished she had been a tad more circumspect. She had not known what she would say to him until the second the words slipped from her mouth. She might have waited about the pictures.

No. This was the way. She hoped he was in the boys' bathroom vomiting. She hoped he would stay sick for a month.

*   *   *

That afternoon Varna began to gently question Angie. After school at least every other day and on most weekends, Angie had made it a habit to visit and pass time with the old woman. They talked about school work, forgotten days in the cotton fields, the Civil Rights Amendment, President Kennedy's and Martin Luther King's assassinations, parents, chess, Chubby Checker, the Nylons, and of course, Shakespeare. To find out what Angie thought, Varna asked her questions and in turn, the girl asked for advice from the older woman.

This particular afternoon, however, Varna sensed something new happening to Angie's personality and she wished to explore it. In her experience with her own children, when one of them began to act too spirited and talkative, it meant there had been a change in his life. Not always good changes. Children—and all people Angie's age were children to her—sometimes drifted into excitable phases that led them into bad habits, poor relationships, or disrespectful attitudes.

Then there were the always lurking addictions that ruined so many of today's children. Nowadays Varna heard that the young people had skipped right over experimenting with alcohol and were taking drugs. Things like LSD and marijuana. Out in sunny California where her own grown children had fled to seek their fortunes, she had received reports about rioting college students and something called "sit-ins" and something else called "flower power." Why, there had even been a riot and looting and killing in Watts where two of her sons lived, and for the life of her, Varna could not understand the erupting violence these days.

It sounded curiously unhealthy to Varna, this "revolution" she was hearing about, and she told her grandkids in long, elegantly scripted letters that if they even once fooled around with that kind of stuff she would personally fly a big bird out to the coast and switch their hind ends with a willow branch until they couldn't walk straight or sit down for a month.

She could not, of course, take a willow switch to a big, strapping white girl like Angie. Civil rights in Mississippi had not progressed to those lengths! But noting the change in the girl, she felt obliged to seek out the reason for it. It would be a shame if Angelina, alone and convinced she was a misfit, turned to those marijuana or LSD trips for relief from the pains of growing up. In fact, Varna would not have it, nosirree. If she found out something of that sort, she'd take a stripped willow branch down to Mr. Thornton and lay it right in his hand. Show him how to use it too if he was so backward as not to have any acquaintance with proper discipline. Yessirree.

"I see you been real happy last few days," Varna said, wading right into the thick of it.

Angie preened, straightening her back where she sat on the porch steps staring across the dusty road at the forest wall. "I've been feeling better."

"Going out with a new beau?"

Angie shook her head and her hair flew. "I don't care about boys. Dana . . . after Dana died, there didn't seem any point at all. He was the only one . . . I might have liked . . . Did you know that my Angora doe is gonna have babies?" she asked, changing the subject.

"That right?" Varna sucked the inside of her cheek. "Babies. That'll be an event for you, I'd guess."

"Absolutely. I read they have anywhere from two to eight in a litter. Imagine. Eight little Angoras. You'll have to help me think up names for all of them. They're supposed to be hairless, blind, and helpless when they're born," she added.

"They grow quick. Will you go to selling them then?"

"Nah." Angie laughed and tossed her head. "I couldn't do that."

"Then you'd best separate the boys from the girls. You'll have more rabbits than you can shake a stick at. You'll have a regular rabbit farm."

"I never thought of that. I'll have to get more wire and build some cages. I already made one new cage. For the babies coming, you know. I fixed up nests and everything. I busted my thumb with the hammer. See?" She held up a purplish thumbnail for Varna's inspection, laughing at her own clumsiness.

Varna let the conversation about rabbits sag, the silence draw out. It was not rabbits she was concerned about. Finally she said, "I been hearing some upsetting news from my kids out in the City of Angels."

"Yeah?" Angie squinted at her, then looked off across the road. "I guess you mean the riot this summer in Watts. That was terrible. My father had the TV on the news the whole time we were packing in St. Louis. They say it was the heat. And the . . . uh . . . poverty."

"Appears so. But that wasn't what I meant. The upsetting news had to do with all them kids taking pills and smoking funny cigarettes." She waited, watching the girl's face for a clue.

"Oh, that," Angie said immediately. "Yeah, I think that's crazy. People are getting hurt. 'Tune in, drop out.' Daddy says Timothy Leary's a nutcase. And we lost Janis."

"Janis?"

"Joplin. The singer. She OD'd."

Varna thought about what "OD'd" might mean and finally gave up. She should get a television set. Maybe she wouldn't be so behind the times. "What'd she do again, this singer girl?"

Angie looked over at her. "Overdosed. Drugs and liquor. Jimi Hendrix, too. Another singer. Played a wild guitar. He was black," she added, then blushed to the roots of her hair. Her father had told her not to say "Negro" anymore. It was considered an insult. Saying "black" made her feel funny. Doubly funny when said to a Negro woman. Why had she felt compelled to mention Jimi's color anyway? The whole race thing confused her no end.

Varna shook her head in wonderment. "Stupidity ain't got no color line, Angelina. It hits everybody equal."

Angie agreed with that. She tapped her feet on the steps to an Otis Redding tune in her head. It was a slow song, but she couldn't remember the words. Something about love. Something she didn't believe. She stared at the dust-coated trees. Though it was nearly Thanksgiving, everything was green as summer. "I wouldn't take drugs if you made me," she said, voicing her thoughts. "Some of the kids who smoke pot say it won't hurt you, but I think they've got brain rot."

Varna, relieved to hear this confession, nodded gravely. So it wasn't drugs. Then what brought about this abrupt change in the girl? It wasn't boys. She had not dated since Halloween. What could it be? The rabbits had cheered her, and Varna thought Mr. Thornton must be a smart fellow to have lucked on the idea, but something else had come into Angie's existence to make her so bubbly. Especially after the sudden, awful loss of that nice boy who died in that tragic accident on Halloween. What could it be?

"Ole Tyeson hasn't bothered you no more, I take it?" she asked carefully, feeling her way.

And then Angie said something that set the old woman back on her mental heels.

"He knows he better not. I'll tell everyone about how his mother dances every night without a stitch on." She had turned to Varna, smiling grandly as if bestowing a surprise gift.

Varna sucked in her breath. She blinked slowly. "You know about that?" she asked. "How do you know about that, girl?" Her voice rose. "He knows you *know* about that? Sweet baby Jesus!"

The queenly smile faded. "What's the matter? You're the one who said she was a dancer, that's what you said, Varna, and then you quoted something Shakespeare said. I remember it. I figured you knew about what she does at night from working there once."

Varna clasped her hands together in her lap. It was her turn to stare across the road into the gathering evening shadows engulfing the treeline. "I never told you about the naked part," she said. "Nobody who knows them folks go around talking about 'em. I thought you understood that. You can't ever breathe a word of it. And if Tyeson knows you know and you ain't friends . . ."

"Friends! He's a lowlife, rotten . . . bad . . . I'd never be his friend, not after what he . . ."

Varna turned back to her. "Not after what? Tell Varna, it's for your own sake, Angelina. I got to know."

Angie lowered her gaze to her feet. She picked at one dirty shoelace. "I can't tell you. I . . . can't . . . tell anyone."

"He done something bad to you, is that it?" She was rising from the steps, her anger growing in strength, her voice gaining in volume until it was like thunder rumbling from low-lying clouds. "What did that no-account do to you? I heard tell of what he's done to girls and women, him and that brother of his. I know what that boy's capable of doing, and if he did it to you, I'll . . . I'll . . ."

Angie skipped off the steps down into the yard. "He didn't do anything! Nothing! Let's forget it, okay? I'm handling Tye. It's my business, it's no one else's problem. No one's!"

"Angie, wait. Come back here, girl. I got to know more. I got to know how you seen his mama dancing that way. Come back . . ."

But she was gone. Rushing down the road toward home lickety-split, feet puffing up little dry clouds of white gravel dust in her wake. And if Varna was any judge of children, the girl was weeping like one beaten half to death.

Now it was all out in the open. It was worse than she'd imagined, far worse. She could have done something about a drug habit, but what could she do about this? Angie must have gone down the road in the night and peeked into windows. That was the only way she would discover the naked Mrs. Dompier. What else did she discover, Varna wondered worriedly. And how did Tyeson find out she knew one of the Dompier secrets?

Surely she had not . . . told him. She wouldn't . . . do that, would she?

"Oh Lord, Lord," Varna whispered into the twilight. "How much more misery can you let Satan smite this poor girl with? How much more can a child take and still survive? Where is your mercy?"

Tye could not rid his mind of the pictures of his mother dancing so unaware she was being watched, being photographed, being caught in moments of insane abandon.

He parked in the Thorntons' drive. No one was home. He was certain of that. If they came home and caught him, no matter. Nothing mattered right now except clearing his mind of the naked images of his mother.

He stepped out of the car and went to the trunk. There he rummaged until he found the tire iron. He hefted it in his hand, enjoying the balanced weight of it. He slammed the trunk lid and strode to the side of the house where Angie kept the rabbits. He did not pause for a moment's reflection. No time for that sort of thing any longer. Payback was a bitch and she was riding him strong, urging him with a whip.

He went to the first cage and struck the center of it with the tire iron. It crumpled and shook. The two rabbits inside set up a racket to alert their fellows. Tye struck again and this time the shoddy thin strips of fir wood broke and the wire gave and one of the rabbits was splattered in a corner. The other one was caught by wire and screaming, its pink mouth open, white teeth showing, eyes rolling. Tye hit again and silenced it.

He moved to the next cage and struck it a blow that rattled his arm socket. The cage sank to the ground. He stood over it battering and battering. The rabbits screamed as if they were being boiled alive. Their cries pierced his eardrums and made him want to smash them flat, flat, flat. Blood flew and spotted his face. When the rabbits there lay still, he moved on. His face felt made of stone. He had nothing in mind, but the picture of a naked woman, his mother, caught out in a lewd pose.

At the cage housing the long-haired rabbits, he halted and stood there with the tire iron raised above his head, the wind rustling in his ears. They were huddled together as far from him as they could physically manage. They were shivering and screaming intermittently as if he were touching them with electric prods. He reached in and withdrew one by the ears. He held it high and watched the back legs kicking. He swung with the iron and caught the rabbit on the side of the head. Tremors ran down the length of its long, silky pelt and then it was dead. Tye put this one at his feet, straightened and immediately attacked the remaining long-haired rabbit. He smashed it into unrecognizable pulp before he stopped. Once through, he went back to the first cage and began methodically breaking the cages into pieces, knocking them down to the ground, stomping them with his feet.

Out of breath and drained, he looked over his work and was glad. He retrieved the one rabbit he had knocked in the head and went to the car, threw it inside on the front seat. He dropped the bloody tire iron on the floorboard. He started the car and drove home.

He felt better than he had in many long days. He felt avenged.

Varna pulled on white gloves and adjusted a black pillbox hat in the milky horse-collar mirror hanging on the newsprint-plastered bedroom wall. She was not comfortable in the girdle; it pinched at the tops of her thighs like a pail of scared crawfish. But this would not take as long as a Sunday service at the Grace Baptist Church so she expected she could stand the aggravation for the duration of her mission.

She walked steadily toward Jason and Angelina Thornton's house. She checked her Timex wristwatch now and then. She knew their routines, their comings and goings. Mr. Thornton arrived home from his teaching job in Clarksdale between four and four-fifteen of an evening. And Angelina had a late basketball practice to attend today. It was now—she checked to be sure—four-thirty. She had watched for his car to turn into the drive before starting out.

She neared the house almost in a pant, furious with her bulk and how it slowed her. The weight caused her to breathe heavy when she had to walk a far piece. Not only was she breathless, but the girdle was putting a powerful squeeze on her vast stomach. The crazed crawdads had moved up around her waist, pincers working away.

She knocked at the front door and when no one answered, she circled the house to the right where Angie kept the rabbit cages. There she came upon Jason Thornton standing in shock, gibbering to himself, a bloody Angora doe in his hands. He did not glance up at her approach.

"Mr. Thornton? What's happened here, Mr. Thornton?" She looked wildly around at the destruction. Cages bashed, wire hanging crooked, splintered wood, rabbits, rabbits lying scattered, scattered and bludgeoned about the ground. "Oh, God."

"This one was pregnant," Jason mumbled. "It was Angie's favorite. I don't know . . . I don't know how . . . why . . . I don't know who . . ."

Varna put a hand to her heart to still its erratic fluttering. It felt as if a band of small feet were thudding against her rib cage. Her temples throbbed and her vision went in and out. She closed her eyes to block out the blood and fur, the staring flat pink eyes that looked at her from the trampled earth. The chill of the day wrapped her in its frosty fingers, bringing her to herself.

She opened her eyes and took the man's arm. "We have to clean this up before Angelina gets home from basketball practice, Mr. Thornton. She's not to see this. We have to do it right now. Let me help."

His eyes locked with hers, his daze giving way to anger, and he staggered back as if only now noticing he was not alone. "Yes," he said in a fierce voice. "I'll take them to the woods. I'll bury them. I'll get the shovel from the garage."

Varna nodded and stripped off the white Sunday-go-to-meeting gloves, slipping them into her black patent leather pocketbook. She bent and lifted one of the dead animals by the bloody ears. She walked off a ways and retrieved another one. By the time Jason had returned with the shovel, she had piled the little cold bodies onto one broken square of chicken wire for disposal. He crushed the wire ends together and walked off into the nearby woods, the shovel dragging the ground behind him.

Tyeson, she thought, as she worked getting all the cage pieces. You're a demon, she thought. " 'My mind is troubled, like a mountain stirr'd; And I myself see not the bottom of it,' " she said. *"Troilus and Cressida*, act three. Sweet Suffering Jesus."

Brody's workroom was dim and green as a room under water. The lamp had not yet been turned on. Tye entered quietly and stood before the desk where his brother worked before he noticed he was not alone.

"You startled me! Don't creep in here that way, Tye," Brody admonished.

"I have something for you," Tye stated almost shyly.

"You do? What is it?" Brody sat back. He picked up the unlit cigar from the ashtray and slipped it between his teeth to chew on.

Tye brought the white, long-haired Angora from behind his back. "Here," he said, holding it out.

Brody sat forward, frowning. "A rabbit?"

"It's a rare breed, I think. It has longer hair than other rabbits. It looks like a cat. You don't have one like it in your collection."

"Where did you get it? We don't have Angoras in Mississippi."

When Tye did not answer, Brody took the dead animal from his hands. "It's nice, Tye. Still warm. I need to get to cleaning it right away."

Still Tye did not answer. Brody glanced at him. "You do try, don't you?"

Tye blinked.

"You know, sometimes I think you really try. It's a shame I don't know how to love you more for it."

Tye stood silently, blinking. His offer made and accepted, he turned slowly to leave the room.

He heard his brother thank him for the gift as he shut the door. He wished Brody had understood what the gift meant and how much it had cost. He wished his brother had not told him the truth about how small and shallow his love was.

Chapter
17

Angie played a Bob Dylan song over and over, mouthing the words. Concentrating on the lyrics kept the other thoughts at bay—those troubling, acidic thoughts that groaned and seethed just below the surface like mercury in a heated thermometer.

Dead.

No, not to think of it. Not to imagine what the scene must have looked like when her father came home. No.

She could make it. She knew the face of violence, had the opportunity to scrutinize it up close, millimeters away, in full and glorious technicolor, Panavision, wide screen, stereophonic sound. And she had survived the contact. Would always, some way, survive.

Bludgeoned.

Belong to no one, she singsonged as Dylan wailed in his plaintive nasal voice. Belong to no one and no one belongs to me. That's the trick. Cut all ties so no one can hurt me. Keep moving. Keep moving, that's the only way.

Bloody carcasses, buried in cold ground.

Did Tye want her down in the hole that he was in? Yes, he did. Yes, it was the truth, unvarnished and cold as rock in winter. And she was going to join him, too, in that hole. He had gone too far, taken from her all she would allow him to take. If fighting back meant following him to the mouth of Hell, she would not hesitate one step. Throw back the gates! Let loose the flames and get on with the gnashing of teeth!

Dead. All dead. Buried deep underground, like her mother, like her hope. The unborn litter, the helpless, hairless and blind. Dead.

"Angie? Baby?" Her father stood in the doorway to her room, the hall light framing his stooped shoulders. He reminded her of Eliot Ness on "The Untouchables" slouching in the shadows, a hangdog look on his square-jawed face. "Honey, don't let it hurt you this way. You've been playing that song over and over. I don't think it's . . . good . . . for you."

She smiled sadly and reached out for the needle arm on the stereo to lift it from the record for the last time. "Okay, Daddy. I'll turn it off now."

"The police said they would try to find out who did it."

She nodded. Of course they would try, but never succeed. And of course she could not accuse Tyeson. Then she would have to go into the whole story, explain why anyone would do this. She'd have to tell about the rape. Then about how she'd spent nights creeping around the Dompier house. No, that wasn't possible. It wouldn't make any sense to the police.

She took the Dylan record and slipped it into its smoothly worn album jacket.

"I'll buy more rabbits for you," Jason said.

She shook her head. She stared at her father until

he glanced down at the floor. "All right," he said. "I won't buy more."

"Thanks, Daddy. Don't worry. I'll be all right."

I'll never be the same again, she thought.

"Sure you will. Sure you will, baby."

He hardly ever called her "baby" anymore. It made her feel small and vulnerable. She waited until he cleared the hall before she placed her hands over her face and wept for the first time over the loss of her pets.

Varna Jenkins again dressed in her Sunday best and began walking down the gravel road away from her home. As she passed the Thornton residence, she gave it but brief attention. She could not help anyone there. The only help would have to come from the culprit who had murdered the rabbits. And that was Tyeson Dompier. She knew the source of the evil without ever talking with Angie. And she knew how the girl must be devastated by the massacre without seeing her face. Something had to be done. If Tye had raped the girl and now was creating his own brand of chaos in the wake of Angie's interference into his family life, then someone had to speak to the boy.

She knew him. When he was but two years old she had been employed as the household cook. He was not a bad child—not in the beginning. He was willful, but some of her own children had been willful. That was no sin. But as she watched him grow up in his curious family with a much older brother and a mother and father who were not quite living in the real world, Tye began to exhibit strange, violent preoccupations in his childish games.

Countless times she had tracked his every move in the backyard while she baked and slaved over the hot stove in the kitchen. While she peeled apples, she saw him take a hammer to his toy metal cars and crush them flat. While she rolled biscuits, she saw him build castles and moats and towers in the dirt—intricate, fantastic designs that fired the imagination—and then stomp them into unrecognizable oblivion. While she washed stacks of dishes and pans, her arms in soapsuds up to her elbows, she watched him progress from the destruction of toys and creations to the mutilation of insects and the arson of property belonging to other family members.

He made no attempt to keep any of this behavior secret. It was as if he did not care about her opinion or he deliberately wanted to show her, show *some-one*, the growing power he wielded over his world.

Often she had spoken to him about his destructive nature when he was a child. It was certain no one else would. "Now, Tye, you know your mama spent a lot of money for that toy. Why would you want to ruin it?"

And he would skewer his mouth into a disdainful little pout and say, "Aw, Mama don't care about this old toy. I can do whatever I wanna do with it." Then he would smile a smile to charm the birds from the trees.

Or she would say, "Tye, pulling the wings off grass-hoppers and the legs off crickets is a downright mean and ugly thing to do. How would you like it if some giant came along and ripped off your arms or legs?"

And he would reply, "You're just a nigger. Niggers don't know nothing about nothing. Get outta my way before I tell my mama you ain't doing your job and she fires you and gets someone to cook for us who knows how to make something besides collard greens for supper." Once he was old enough to talk to her this way he no longer tried to charm her. Instead, he would spit near her feet and walk away leaving her to stare after him, her heart full of concern for him, full of anger at his unjust attitude.

So she knew this boy. And she meant to talk to him one more time. It would be the last. If need be, her next stop was the Clarksdale sheriff's office. Tyeson Dompier had passed beyond the pale; he was no longer defiling and robbing life from the insect world. He was steamrolling over an innocent little girl, his preoccupations now large enough to encompass rape and killing. She suspected he had come to this impasse long before he met Angelina Thornton, but she hadn't proof before. Something now had to be done in the name of decency.

Brody Dompier answered the front door. He stood gaping at her massive, black taffeta-dressed presence. "Well? What is it, Varna? If you're looking for work, there isn't any here."

"I'm not looking for work, Mr. Brody. I've got business with your brother, if you please." She shifted her pocketbook to the other hand.

"What kind of business could you possibly have with Tyeson?" He inched the door closer to him, ready to shut her out.

"I can't tell you that, Mr. Brody. It's private business." She stood firm, gripping the handle of the pocketbook as if it were the handle of a sword.

Brody cocked an eyebrow. "Private, is it? Oh well, if that's the case . . ." He gave a patronizing smile that made her want to slap him. ". . . Tye's out back somewhere . . ." He waved his fat hand in the air above his head. A diamond ring glittered. ". . . I don't know. You'll have to go find him."

Varna nodded and turned on her heel. She almost said "thank you," but withheld the automatic response. Brody had never been among her favorite people and in her book, he did not deserve the benefit of her courtesy.

Circling the house (Brody could have asked her inside and let her out through the kitchen, thereby saving her time and effort, but she had not expected it), she came to the corner and paused. Walking on soft ground in her patent leather pumps was a difficult maneuver. The little heels sank deep with each step. And of course, the girdle pinched like live coals all around her waist and thighs. One day she would throw the damn thing in the trash pile and burn it. Be done with vanity, she told herself. You are an old woman, Varna Louise Jenkins. You haven't the energy to be vain.

"Tyeson?" she called out. "You back here, boy?"

Her words carried on a breeze and disturbed the quietness. She plodded across the seared grassy expanse toward the barn. Tye had his hiding places. But she knew them all. She would have her say if it took her the rest of the afternoon hunting him down to do it. "Tyeson!"

His name echoed into the cavernous structure of the abandoned barn. She glanced quickly at the open stalls, the small loft. It smelled of decay in here. She wrinkled her nose. Hay rotting, packed earth beaten down with hooves slick with manure and urine. She turned and left, glad to be outdoors again breathing in fresh wind.

She pulled open the door to one of the utility sheds. She did not call his name. He was not in sight.

At the old slave quarters she had to hold onto the rickety porch rail to get up the three steps. She stepped carefully across the dry, splintery boards. "Tyeson, you in there?"

The door, swelled out of shape from damp, squealed and stuck when she pushed it open. She was forced to turn sideways, sucking in her belly and holding her breath, to get inside. Here the must and mildew of age assaulted her nostrils. She sniffed, coughed to clear her throat. "Tyeson? Boy, you better answer me. What I got to say to you is important and if you don't hear it, somebody with a gun and a badge is gonna hear it. And that's the Lord's truth."

She waited, listening for his voice. The setting sun cast the front room of the quarters in bronze tones. The chairs stacked against the far wall looked to be painted in a layer of gold. There was majesty even here in a place where her people had lived lives of sheer misery, beauty where the spirits of pain and mental suffering rose up against the walls year after year looking for an escape from bondage.

"Tye, you come out now. Varna's not messing with you no more. I'm getting too old to climb up to that attic, if that be where you at, or down into that root cellar, if you down there."

"So what do you want?" came the eerie, disembodied question.

"Come out here where I can see you," Varna demanded. "I ain't talking to the air."

Tye laughed. "Why not? I do. That's what they say, 'Tye talks to the fucking air, he's so nuts.' "

"You watch your mouth, boy. I don't like that kind of language. And who is it says that to you, anyway?" Varna knew about this peculiar idiosyncrasy of the boy's—talking to himself when he thought he was alone. She had seen him do it in years past. The first time she caught him, she thought it merely odd, a child speaking to a fantasy friend. After that, she realized he had something seriously wrong with him. But there was something wrong with the entire family, always had been. If they all took to grave-robbing or drinking blood while wearing purple velvet capes, it would not have surprised her in the least.

She heard a scraping of furniture along the floor of the other room. He stood in the doorway to the kitchen, his hands and clothes covered with dust streaks. What was it about the old quarters that drew the boy? It seemed to her even the woods or the fields were cleaner places, more wholesome places for being alone and thinking things out.

"Who're you gonna tell? And what're you gonna tell them?" he asked.

Varna knew there was nothing for it but to wade right into the matter. "I'm not thinking of telling anyone if you'll stop. Right now. Just stop and leave that girl alone."

"Angie? She's your friend, isn't she? What's she told you?"

"She didn't have to tell me nothing, Tye. I guessed most of it. And I was at her house yesterday when her father found the dead rabbits."

"So?"

Varna sighed. She opened her purse and withdrew a white lace-edged handkerchief. She mopped her face. The room was cold, but she was suddenly hot all over as if she were within proximity of a blazing bonfire. She wanted to pull at the legs of her girdle, free it from where it squeezed her crotch in an elastic vise, but Tye would laugh at her. She could not let him have an upper hand. She must work from a position of strength with the boy. Anything else and she was lost.

"I know everything," she said, bluffing him, for she realized she did not know for certain all he might have done.

"Do you?"

"I know you probably took that girl against her will . . ."

"She tell you that?"

"No. She didn't have to. I knew something was wrong for a long time now. I just didn't know what."

"Bullshit. I never laid a hand on her. She says different, she's lying."

"I'm not going to argue with you. I'm going to tell you what I know and I'm asking you to stop it."

"You don't know nothing."

"I know that Angie came around here and found out something you didn't want her to know. I know she told you about it." She paused and shook her head, still marveling at the girl's audacity. "And the day you discovered it, you came to her house when no one was home and, to punish her, you killed every single one of her rabbits. You beat them to death like the horrible little monster you are. I know that. And it *will* stop."

Now she was cold, so cold her ill-fitting dentures chattered like something coming to life in her mouth. She wrapped her arms around her body and swayed slightly onto her heels.

Tyeson looked at her. He kept looking at her. Not with hate or anger, emotions she had expected, but with an unswerving, uncaring, do-your-worst kind of look. It made her shiver; it made her afraid. She would have preferred he fight with her, deny the charges, even threaten to call in his mother and father on the situation to protect him. She was unprepared for his bland, so-what attitude. She feared she was not going to get the promise she had asked for. Would he really force her to take it to the authorities? And how could she do that if Angie forbade it?

"Is that it?" he asked finally.

"Tye, will you leave her alone or do I have to go to Clarksdale and tell the sheriff what I know?"

He blinked several times. "You can't do that. No one would believe you."

"They'd believe Angie."

"Stay outta this." His first passionate statement since the conversation began. It buoyed her.

"Will you stop?" she asked again. "I want a promise. And I don't want you to break it."

"Get out." He turned his back on her and disappeared into the interior of the cluttered kitchen.

"Tyeson!"

"Get out or I'll throw you out."

Varna dropped her arms at her side. Her face fell, the wrinkles and jowls taking up their normal positions across the bones of her skull and beneath her wide chin. "I suppose I have to go to Clarksdale," she said in a voice hardly above a whisper. "The boy won't listen to Varna, Lord."

She turned to the door and squeezed her bulk past the impediment it posed. She held tight to the rail and went down the steps to the yard. She shook her head. She thought she could make him give the game up and she'd been wrong. She had not seen him in over two years and it was apparent to her now Tyeson Dompier was more man than boy, more crazed than sane, more lost than even the archangel Lucifer whose pride came before the Fall from the right hand of God.

Tomorrow she would fulfill her promise to Tye. She would go tell her story—the whole story that began years before in the Dompier household—to the sheriff.

It was the only choice he had left her.

Chapter

18

It was midnight, dark with no moon. Cold outside, a wind whistling off the lake and whipping beneath the house with enough force to make the pilings groan in their buried cement casings. The windowpanes rattled, the squares of glass vibrating with each new gust.

Angie lay on her back in bed listening to the wind and wrestling with the urge to leave the house, enter into the screeching darkness.

She turned onto her side and stared at the windows. She listened to their cracklings as if she might decipher a code. She imagined the tortured writhing of the trees lining the lakeshore, the whitecap surf coughing spume into the air. There were demons loose.

She fell onto her back again, her eyes wide open though she could not see the ceiling above her head. Every time she thought of Little Egypt lying beneath the sod of the forest, she experienced a muscle spasm in her legs that moved the blankets into different humped shapes. When she thought of Little Egypt

177

and the graves of the other rabbits, she thought of her mother also in a grave where they had left her in a St. Louis cemetery.

Was the wind blowing there? Did the stone angels and heavenly cherubs dance across the manicured mounds, giving solace to the dead?

Did her mother know of her daughter's life and the dreadful turns it had taken?

Angie imagined her mother as a spirit since her death, a waif-like presence that hovered nearby anxious for attention, lonely and hoping to intervene. She had not thought of her that way since moving to Mississippi with her father. It was as if she had allowed her to remain behind in their old home where she would grow tired searching for them and return to her rightful place, the grave.

Angie had not brought her mother along to the South. And now she needed her more than ever.

The lure of the midnight walk came on Angie again and she could not remain still. She flopped onto her stomach and buried her face in the pillow to blot out the night sounds. It was crazy to want to go to Tye's house tonight. She would have to brave the nasty weather, half freeze to death in the November wind to gain . . .

More information, a small voice answered.

And do what with it?

The same thing you did before, the voice said.

But look what Tye did when I told him what I knew. He knows. He knows.

Look what frenzy you drove him to, the voice said. Notice what fury you set upon him.

I can never repay him now. He's too clever and he's extremely dangerous, he might . . .

Suffer, said the voice. He might suffer the way he makes you suffer. Learn from him. Find the chinks in his armor and drill until cracks appear. He knew you loved the rabbits so he killed them. What does he love? What means something to him? Break past his defenses. Hurt him.

It's cold out there, there's a cold wind . . .

No colder than where you lie helpless, said the voice. Are you willing to let him win? If this were one of Varna's chess games, it would be stalled in a deadlock, no further moves possible without serious loss. Haven't you already lost so much it's worth one more move? You want to let him win by default just because of a cold wind?

"No," she muttered aloud, throwing off the covers and slamming her bare feet to the chilly floor.

"I'm no loser."

She hardly felt the wind at all until she reached the Dompier house from across the stubbled cotton field. Then it was as if after having crossed the distance between the two houses during a daydream, her senses suddenly came alive. A blast of wind drove down the neck collar of her down jacket and made her stop dead where she walked in order to survive a bout of shivering. A metal filling in a back tooth thrilled with an electrical shock of cold when she drew in a deep breath. She winced and bit down, tonguing the filling to warm it again. She stuck her hands into her pockets, startled that she had forgotten her gloves. The skin on the backs of her hands felt raw from exposure. Her nose dripped and her breath fogged before her face. Insane! What possessed her to do this? What might she accomplish?

And yet the lighted rectangle of window drew her, moth to flame, and she hurried to get a patio chair for standing. The light came from the kitchen where she had last watched and listened to Tye talking to himself. She wanted to see him, *must* see him in this secret way again. It seemed that the scenes she spied through windows were reality and everything else a fantasy. Inside the house life moved and breathed and progressed into each moment with a preciseness like clockwork while outside the house she stood on tip-toe trying to catch a fleeting glimpse of what made the earth move. In the beginning the people within the house were stage actors playing to an audience of one, playing for her sole benefit. But now the stage was reversed; she was the actor, they the audience, their milieu the real world, strange and bedazzled as it appeared to her, an outsider.

Wait! Wait! What was she thinking? Something was happening to the way she thought and it had begun with her father telling her of the death of the rabbits. Nothing that had occurred since then could jog her from this treadmill of morbid explanations of how the world worked. Her mother might be spirit, but she did not hover about like a ghost. She was with God. That's what Angie had been taught and she believed it. Tyeson had not run her into a chess game dead-lock, forcing her to make the next move. And the people in the house were not more real than she, more in tune with reality.

Still, since she was here she might as well glance inside, satisfy her curiosity before calling it a night. She had been idiot enough to come this far, she might as well peek inside. She stood holding on to the sill, pressing against the house, her nose to the glass. The room was empty. She etched every item in the room into her brain. The chairs, standing just so against the table's rim. The sink dully gleaming in the overhead light. The drip of water falling in slow motion from the faucet lip even as she watched it gather into a droplet and break free, pulled by gravity.

After a while she felt the cold again and stepped down from the chair. She walked the length of the house, the chair in her stiffening fingers. She stood it below the window looking into Brody's workroom. She climbed aboard and looked inside, searching for Tye. What she saw caused her breath to freeze in her throat. She gripped the ledge until her knuckles turned white under the strain.

Brody, his back to the window, sat at his desk manhandling the remains of a white rabbit, a buck, a large, dead, floppy-eared Angora buck she recognized instantly as Little Egypt. Brody had one of her rabbits she thought buried in the woods next to her house. No, no, he couldn't stuff Little Egypt, not one of her own. She could not allow it.

The obscenity of it, the beastliness . . .

"Hello, Angie."

Angie fell from her precarious perch to the ground, the wrought iron chair kicking from underneath her feet and landing on its side. Tye stood over her, his school jacket snapped tight, hands in his pockets, the wind blowing his black hair at a slant from his forehead.

She stood shakily and backed away from the house.

"Don't go. You've only just got here."

"Stay away from me."

"Believe me, I intend to. You don't have to be afraid."

Something wrong with his tone of voice. Mechanical.

"I'll leave now," she said but did not move to go. She kept seeing Brody stretching apart the slit belly of her rabbit, scraping at the inside of the skin with a scalpel-like instrument that winked in the light.

"What did you want to see tonight? Maybe I could go inside and satisfy your every desire."

Something wrong with his eyes. He didn't blink. He stared through her.

"You didn't have to murder the rabbits," she said. "You had already done enough to me. *They were just innocent little animals! You didn't have to kill them!*"

"Why have you been spying on my family?" He took a step closer. His voice hardened.

"You didn't have to bring one of them to your brother to stuff like a damn trophy." She backed away a step.

"You made sure I found out about your spying," he said, ignoring her protest. "You wanted me to know."

"Yes! Yes!" She shook with fury, her hands flying from her pockets, doubling into fists. She rushed toward him to pound his chest, but he stepped aside and pushed her out of the way. She turned, fists raised. "That's right, I wanted you to know. I've watched you every night for weeks. I know about your crazy naked mother and your father with his books and pictures and your brother with his terrible hobby of stuffing poor, dead animals. I know everything. I watched you talking in the dark, talking to yourself about going out west, about never worrying about making a living because you were rich and no one cared what you did with your miserable, stinking life!

"And I'm here to tell you that you won't get away with this. You've gotten away with everything, haven't you?" she screamed. "Haven't you?"

A tapping at the window interrupted her. She turned her head to see Brody watching them, Little Egypt's corpse dangling from one raised fist pushed up against the bright window.

"You all need to be put into an institution," Angie lashed out. "Your brother, your parents, but most of all you."

"And I suppose *you're* going to be the one to do that?" he asked with a smug smile of skepticism.

If he had not smiled she could have borne any sarcasm, any filthy thing he wanted to say to her. But she could not countenance his knowing grin. Again she rushed him and this time he was not prepared for her move. She hit him full on with the heels of her hands and sent him pinwheeling backwards across the barren, windswept yard. She kept going, running now, her feet carrying her beyond his grasp into the cotton field. Stubs of cotton plants, stiffly frosted with ice, sliced through the thin rubber soles of her tennis shoes and broke the skin on her feet. She screamed, more in the agony of confusion and despair than in pain, but kept running without a backward glance until she cleared the field and reached the relative safety of the gravel lake road.

She halted, out of breath, her feet on fire. She leaned over, hands on her knees. She looked behind her at the black fields to be sure she had not been followed.

She saw the scalpel, the flayed skin of Little Egypt, the studious way Brody scraped and scraped meticulously at the hide. She saw Tye accusing her of trespassing as if her sin came anywhere near his own, as if he had every right to protest her harmless spying.

The pain of her stabbed feet brought her to herself and she hobbled the rest of the way home. The wind drove at her back, each gust pushing her stumblingly forward, flinging her hair from her neck and ears, licking the bare skin with an Arctic tongue.

Keep on the move, she admonished herself. You can bandage the stab wounds, you can stanch the flow of blood, you can heal yourself. At least you aren't dead. At least Brody doesn't have your body scraped inside out, ready for the sawdust and a wooden trophy stand.

She opened the front door carefully and slipped inside the warm house that smelled of tonight's dinner of vegetable soup. In the bathroom, the door closed, she began to minister to her bloody feet, refusing to cry when the alcohol burned and the bandage was wound around the reddened punctures.

Chapter

19

Varna moved the white castle into position on the chessboard. She withdrew the captured black knight and set it gingerly on the side of the coffee table. She sucked in her cheeks, content to have made a fine move. In theory, she was supposed to want all chess pieces, black or white, to win. When it came to the black knight, however, she never mourned its loss. In the shaped plastic she saw the black horse on its hind legs, rearing. On his back she envisioned the person of evil. More than ever this person was the boy, Tyeson Dompier. When he was finally captured, she was always more at ease.

The raging wind outside kept her awake. That and the hot tea she drank and the mission she needed to do on the morrow.

She glanced at the orange wall clock shaped like a rooster one of her sons had sent for her birthday. It was two in the morning. Outrageous. She would never be able to get up in the morning and dress herself for an audience with the sheriff if she stayed up much longer.

Newspapers glued to the walls of the living room were alive, rippling and flattening as the wind slipped through the cracks of the house. Varna hugged the patchwork quilt around her shoulders and stood. She circled the table and sat down in the easy chair where she could make the next move for the black side of the chess game.

She had tried to read all evening. Neither her beloved Shakespeare nor the beautiful imagery and language of the King James version of the Bible could keep her attention. Thumbing through Shakespeare's *The Tempest* she discovered one quotation she committed to memory. Most days she memorized a half dozen passages. In act four, scene one she found: "We are such stuff as dreams are made on, and our little life is rounded with a sleep."

Around ten she gave up trying to read and made herself a pot of tea, brought the quilt from the bed, and sat down to play chess. She should have known her brain would not simmer down when engaged in game. Playing chess brought her most alert, her mind plotting five and six moves—sometimes more—ahead, her wits tested by the rigors of trying to outmaneuver the last move she made on the other side of the board.

Wind caught under the overhanging eaves moaned like a man trapped in the jaw of death. Varna nervously glanced at the solid black blocks of the windows. She lifted the flowered saucer that held her cup of tea and brought it close to her face so that she might inhale the aroma and at the same time warm her chin from the steam. Soon she needed to poke another split oak log into the pot-bellied heater standing in the corner. When she finally went to bed the fire would burn out and she would wake to a freezing house that creaked and popped from the contraction of timbers. Daily it was more difficult for her to force herself from beneath the nest of highly piled quilts and build a fire for the start of a new day.

She was old. She felt age whittling at her spirit each day. "Old Varna," she said aloud, raising the saucer and cup again to bathe her face in its aromatic heat. "You getting good for nothing but the scrap heap, old woman. 'Crabbed age and youth cannot live together. Youth is full of pleasure, age is full of care.' Old William knew whereof he spoke."

No one needed her except maybe the child down the road. Once that was taken care of . . .

A sound of splintering wood caused her to snap her head to the right to stare at the back door. Tea sloshed from the cup into the saucer.

Varna placed the tea on the table and rose, adjusting the quilt as a cape. "Who's there?" she called, advancing through the kitchen to stand in front of the door leading to the backyard.

A simple slide bolt held the door locked. She could see no evidence of damage, but she had not mistaken the sounds of forced entry. "Speak up," she yelled. "What you want with Varna? You boys know I ain't got no money. I been poor as a church mouse all my life. Now you git outta here."

She expected it was some of those Hylander boys belonged to James, the deacon of her church. His boys were known to be bad about breaking in and robbing folks. James Hylander beat them nearly every single week of their lives and they still sneaked out late at night to terrorize the older widows living along Moon Lake Road.

"You hear me? By God, I'll go get my baseball bat I have to. Your daddy will break your backs with a stick he finds out you come messing 'round my house this way! Varna's one old woman you ain't gonna get no satisfaction from, you hear me? I ain't got one silver dollar you can steal." Actually she had several silver dollars hidden in the bottom of her chiffonier between stacks of sewing material, but the Hylander boys couldn't know that and she sure as Baby Jesus wasn't about to tell them.

She stood waiting, impatient now that they be gone. A weariness was settling in that was heavier than the quilt on her shoulders. She felt as if finally she could go to bed and be able to sleep through the rest of the night. Just as soon as the tomfoolery outside was sent on its way.

As she glared at the door a movement down by the doorknob caught her attention. She moved closer, staring as the broad, silver blade of a knife inched between the door frame and door, the point aimed in the vicinity of her midsection. Varna stepped back, her mouth opening with surprise. A knife! How dare those bad boys! They had never been known to bring along a weapon before. The cowards always roughed up the old women they robbed and scared them witless without needing anything other than their fists and the palms of their hands.

Wind screamed past the eaves. The blade slid back and forth, sawing the air. Someone was simply showing her he had a knife. He was not yet trying to get the door open with it.

Varna stepped to the stove, removed a clean, black skillet from the cold burner. She moved back to the door and, heaving with all her might, struck at the blade invading her kitchen. The entire door shook under her attack. The blade disappeared.

"Now git outta here!" she yelled. "I'll have your daddy skin you alive for this and you know it."

She thought she heard laughter and it made her anger spiral out of hand. "Laugh at me, will you?" she mumbled, turning, the quilt flying. She slammed the skillet onto the stove hard enough to jar her elbow and left the kitchen. In the bedroom she turned on the light and drew back the feed-sack curtain hanging over the door to her tiny closet. Inside she felt around hat boxes and suitcases and stacks of bath towels until she felt the shape of the baseball bat handle. She grasped it and dragged it into the light. She sighed while looking at it, then turned to leave the room when the window behind the headboard of her bed shattered inward with a resounding crash. Glass scattered all over the bedspread and tinkled to the bare floor on either side. Wind shrieked through the opening. Like ribbon banners fluttering at a parade, the rose-colored curtains whipped the sides of the wall.

"You little bastards!" Varna covered her mouth with a hand, sorry she had cursed, furious they had made her lose her temper to such an extent. Next they would have her taking the Lord's name in vain and for that she would never forgive them.

A trill of laughter came through the broken window, fading slowly into the distance as it was overpowered by the freight-train voice of the wind.

It was now that she wished she had a telephone. No one but the white people along the road could afford one, but Bless God, if only she had a telephone she would have the scoundrels locked up faster than they could say Jack Sprat. Robbing defenseless old women of their pitiful life savings, destroying property, trying to frighten the elderly into submission so they could get liquor and gambling money. She would bash their fat heads in before she let them scare her tonight, that's what she would do.

"You c'mon through that window, boys. I'll swat open your skulls like smacking a ripe watermelon!"

Again she waited, colder now, the wind zipping past the bed and folding her in its frigid fingers. She would be up all night finding enough cardboard to cover the window. She would need the hammer and carpet tacks. She'd probably catch her death of pneumonia . . .

The front door rattled. Varna turned woodenly, her calm a mantle more useful than the quilt. Her obsession with chess was paying off. She knew nothing if not how to concentrate on the moment. If she went in there to check, one of them might climb over the window onto her bed. If she stayed put, one might get the latch broken on the front door and sidle in like a mongrel dog, teeth showing, hair on end.

She looked quickly at the window. It was a black tunnel leading out into the darkness. Before they could climb inside, they would have to get over the impediment of the high, cedar headboard. She had time to check the front.

She moved swiftly for all her great bulk, the quilt loose and falling behind to the bedroom floor where it lay in a heap. She reached the door in time to see the knife blade again, its movement having a life of its own as it snaked up and down the frame searching for the latch. Rather than a bolt, this door had only a metal hook latch high up. The blade would disengage it. The intruder could get in easily.

Varna planted her feet and swung the bat. It glanced off the door frame inches below the knife blade with a loud crack. The blade vanished in a flash of light.

Varna moved back to the bedroom without hesitation. She stopped to watch the window. No face appeared. No hand crept over the headboard. Where were they? She stepped back to straddle the threshold between the two rooms, looking back and forth from the broken window to the front door.

"Marshall Hylander, can you hear me, boy?" Marshall was the eldest, the leader of two younger brothers—idiots if she had ever seen one—Macy and Matthew. "You don't go home, stop bothering me, somebody's gonna get hurt and I guarantee you it won't be me." It occurred to her that she might not be dealing with the Hylander boys. They had never

acted like this before. If not them, then it had to be
. . . must be . . . Tyeson. She should have known.
Now the slow stalking kind of threat made sense to
her. It was Tye's style. The other boys were ruffians
and thieves, but this endless terrorizing was not something they indulged in.

She paused for a response. "I can wait long as you
can. I got nothing pressing to stop me." This was
untrue, of course. Whoever it was he was taking a toll
on her endurance. A tiredness that threatened to cause
collapse had taken hold of her. She wished to sleep
for a year.

A crash from the back of the house brought her
upright and made her grip the bat. She rushed to the
kitchen in time to see the slide bolt cracking loose
from the screws in the wooden frame. She hauled
back with the Louisville Slugger and slapped it flat
against the door. The resulting sound was like a powder keg blowing, breaking all through the house.

Seconds later she heard noise at the front door
again. "Lord Jesus," she whispered. "This be wearing me down."

She placed a cane-bottom kitchen chair beneath the
back door knob to secure it. She hurried through the
narrow living room to the front where the broad blade
of the knife slid up and down, up and down, an
eyeless searching for the hook.

"Blast you to hell!"

Varna knocked at the knife with the bat, missing it.
She wondered how long this was going to go on. She
wondered if she could outlast the invader of darkest
night.

Chapter

20

"There's some ill planet reigns: I must be patient till the heavens look with an aspect more favorable."

Varna read this line in Shakespeare's *The Winter's Tale* and decided it applied directly to her situation. She would memorize and add it to her lexicon of quotations.

The house had been quiet for half an hour. Having hauled the easy chair over close to the doorway between bedroom and living room, she took up vigilance with the quilt again draped over her square shoulders and *The Complete Works of Shakespeare* in her lap.

"There's some ill planet reigns," she repeated in her mind. Oh yes, yes, Mine Bard, even at Stratford-on-Avon there must have been times when an evil planet ascended to rule. Like the grand playwright she admired, she could do nothing beyond waiting for the heavens to show more favor, to shine down benign.

Until then she watched the windows and doors from her vantage point after reading each few sentences from the current play she studied. While nailing pieces of a cardboard box over the broken window she thought she saw the shadow of someone lurking outside. If she had not seen one of Satan's disciples, she might have taken the silence to mean she could go to bed and forget about intruders. But a thin veneer of unease prickled her mind: He might still be there plotting entrance and theft.

At her back the fire in the stove crackled and warmed the quilt. She caught herself nodding off between dialogue in the play and shook her head to clear it. The rooster clock ticked off the long minutes into eternity, lulling her. It was ten after three o'clock and she could not remember being so weary that even the Bard put her into a dozing trance.

Minutes later when the second hand on the wall clock had moved to twenty-two after the hour, Varna's chin dropped, her mouth opened slightly to emit a soft snore, and the blade of a knife slipped through the envelope space between front door and frame. It moved stealthily up and up from doorknob to latch hook, encountered the obstruction with a light click, paused, and with a grating of metal against metal, raised the latch from its hook.

Varna woke suddenly and let out an explosion of surprise. Her gaze riveted on the door, the knob turning. She dropped the book from her lap as she stood, wide awake now, her earlier anger as nothing compared to her present wrath.

"Get out of my house!" She reached for the bat. It slipped from beside the easy chair where it was propped, clunking solidly to the floor. She bent to retrieve it, feeling blindly, her face turned toward the door.

She heard his voice before she saw him.

"Hello, Varna. How could you mistake me for a Hylander fool?"

Varna froze in place, the bat now firmly in hand. She decided not to let him suspect she had known; it did not seem to her that it would help her situation. Better he think her stupid and confused.

"I couldn't let you go to the sheriff tomorrow." He entered the house dressed all in black from neck to foot. The formidable black knight. In his right hand he carried the broad-bladed knife. In his face was the hollow-eyed look of madness.

Taking possession of her scattered senses, Varna straightened from her crouch and brought the bat around in front of her wide belly to hold it firmly in both hands. "You won't stop me, Tyeson. I have to do what's right. No one has ever done what's right by you. That's why we are where we are tonight with you unlawfully breaking into my home and threatening me." It occurred to her he might not be able to understand anything in the state of mind she saw reflected in his handsome, young face. "Are you listening to me, boy? Can you understand the wrong you've done and hope to do?"

He stood just inside the open door, the winter wind swirling in, eddying along the bare floorboards. He reached out with his left hand and shut it. He did not move toward her and for that Varna was thankful. She did not wish to hurt the boy. If she could, she would help him.

"I killed the rabbits," he said in an oddly pleasant manner.

"Yes, I know you did. That was a terrible thing to do to Angie." He spoke sweetly of murder and it chilled her blood.

"I raped her. She wouldn't love me."

"That was a sin," Varna said with fierce conviction.

"But I've done it before. It doesn't matter, really. Everyone knows it doesn't matter. It happens all the time." He gestured with the knife in an offhand way, dismissing terrible and sinful things.

193

"You did what before, Tyeson?"

"Killed and raped. Raped and killed."

Varna shivered at the thought of a boy accepting his sins so fully. Her back ached. Her legs were numb from lack of circulation. She thought of a quote from *The Merchant of Venice*. She recited it to the boy, thinking he might still possess a minimal vestige of sanity. " 'Truth will come to light; murder cannot be hid long.' "

"I killed Dana Percy on Halloween night."

Could this be true? Was Tyeson now confessing to actual cold-blooded murder?

"He took out my girl. He shouldn't have done that," Tyeson said dreamily. "I couldn't stand the thought of him touching Angie. Of her . . . liking him . . ."

I do not wish to hear this, Varna thought, inwardly wincing. "Tye . . . I think you should go home and I'll come down tomorrow so we can talk things over." What she meant was she would have the sheriff talk with the boy. Lock him up, that's what she meant to have done to him. "It's too late for you to be out."

He cocked his head to look at her quizzically. "You don't get it, do you?"

"Oh, I understand that . . . you have killed someone, Tye."

Tye nodded, satisfied his confession's moral was clear to her. "The thing is, Varna, I'm going to have to kill you, too. You know that."

"You're crazy, boy."

"That's very possibly the truth. I don't mind admitting that's a possibility." He stepped forward, then stopped again. "But don't you ever say it again."

"Why would you want to harm Varna?" she asked. "I'm not your enemy."

"You've always been my enemy. Even from the time I was a little kid. I saw how you looked at me, how you judged me. And now you know about Angie and you know about Dana. You know so *goddamn much.*"

Varna raised the bat higher to ward him off. "You didn't have to tell me about the boy. Everyone thought it was an accident."

"Why not tell you?" He took another step nearer. "You won't live to repeat it. I didn't come here and camp out on your porch steps in the freezing night just to tell you the story of my life. I came to . . ."

" 'There is no sure foundation set on blood,' " she screamed at him, the pulse jumping in her thick neck. Panic, she thought, I'm letting him see how scared I am. " 'No certain life achieved by others' death.' *King John,* act four."

The quoting of Shakespeare halted his advance. It threw him into confusion. He rolled the knife handle around and around in the palm of his hand and his brow furrowed in thought. "There is no foundation set on blood?" he asked. A sad smile formed. "There's no foundation anywhere. I've known that since I was born. There's no God and no heaven or hell. There's no law and no punishment and no reward. If you were so smart, you'd know that, you stupid old woman."

Varna could not wait another second to strike. If she waited, she would be in mortal jeopardy. She moved like a powerful earth machine geared high. The Louisville Slugger bit into the air over her shoulder as she raised it to clout him across the head. She brought it down with all her might, but even as the bat swung, he had moved out of its way, leaping past a table laden with dime-store knickknacks. Dollar statues of angels and the Messiah fragmented into a blizzard of flying glass and porcelain that peppered Varna's wild silver-streaked hair.

She whirled, raising the bat again to the attack. He

had taken up stance in the doorway to the darkened kitchen. He still smiled. The knife glittered in lamplight. Outside a dog howled in the far distance.

" 'Tis strange that death should sing. I am the cygnet to this pale faint swan who chants a doleful hymn to his own death.' "

"Stop speaking riddles, old woman. It's not going to help you."

"Nonsense." She came for him, plodding forward, each heavy step in determined cadence. "It has always helped me against the blight of Satan's minions. I will show you God's might and God's will."

His insulting laughter drove her the remaining few feet and then she swung . . . missing . . . missing . . . his bright, shiny teeth by a fraction, the momentum behind her swing carrying her into the very boundary of his traitorous arms.

Varna did not feel the knife sink into her soft gut. She had no indication of having been stabbed until after she had fallen to the floor, felled like a giant sequoia standing tall and strong as a skyscraper one moment and lying flat, beaten into the dust the next.

She tried to rise, but a weakness consumed her limbs so that she floundered, legs and arms splaying. It was then, after the effort to stand, that she felt pain, the most awful pain running from near her navel through her innards to the edge of her spinal cord. She gasped, fearing what she already knew. That she would die. That she was dying. That a boy mad with his own demons had shoved the knife—broad, wide blade, a butcher knife, a killing knife—into her stomach and somehow managed to extract it and her life with it as she dropped.

"Lord, lord . . ." she muttered, again pushing with her will to get legs beneath her, arms to lift her torso from the cold, cold floor.

Tyeson squatted next to her motionless form. "It's better this way," he said calmly.

"You . . . you . . ."

"You got in my way. You never should have done that, Varna. You can't threaten a Dompier. We have too much to lose."

She raised her cheek from where it kissed the floor. She moved her shoulder up and back. She stared down at the growing puddle of incredibly red blood inching beneath her chest. If she could get her arms to moving, her legs to obey. Her fingers twitched. She heard a door creak open, felt the gust of wind sweep her prone body. It fingered her ears and neck, the bare skin on her legs. She heard the door slam shut, felt the wind vanish and a stillness overtake the house. Alone. And dying.

Move, she thought. *Move.* If you can move, you can survive this most bestial of deaths. We are such stuff as dreams are made on, she thought, such stuff as dreams . . .

Above her head the coffee table holding the chess set had gone undisturbed in the battle. If she could reach up, knock off the chess pieces . . .

Such stuff as dreams . . .

If she could do it, make her arm reach up, break out of the paralysis the massive dying body imposed on her . . .

She shut her eyes and called on God to help her if He could not save her from joining Him tonight. She concentrated on her right outstretched arm. She pulled. It moved. She meant for it to rise. *It would rise!* She sought help and she would have it or she would die cursing all future races of man forever, forever.

A loud clattering made her open her eyes. The worn chessboard hung over the side of the maple coffee table. Pieces lay all about her. Her vision blurred in and out. Where was . . .

Such stuff as dreams . . .
Where was the piece she needed?
Such stuff . . .

There. She spied it. Right beside her fisted hand,
Bless Jesus. The black knight, the thief in the night,
the raper of girls, the killer. Calling forth more effort
than she had ever asked for in her life, more than
when birthing children, picking cotton in hundred
degree sunshine, and more than when her husband
died in her arms, Varna tried to open her hand and
take the chess piece. It was so close. It meant so
much. It might mean the life of others, of the girl
Angie, of ones after her. It meant justice could be
served and there had been so little justice in her years
on earth.

Eyes closed, so tired now, so tired she might sleep.
Yet she had something she must do. Didn't she? It
was important she remember. Squeezing her hands,
she recognized the strange, humpback feel of the
knight pressing into her palm. She'd done it, oh God
and Good Sweet Jesus, she had done it even though
she did not know how.

What matter? She had it. They would know. They
would stop him.

Such stuff, she thought, such stuff . . .
As dreams are made on . . .
Our little life . . .
Is rounded . . .
Yes, Lord . . .
With a sleep.

198

Chapter
21

Saturday morning dawned luminous as burnished pewter. The bitter cold northerly wind of the night before had moved on across the state. In its wake Moon Lake shone still and bright as a resplendent spread of blue-gray satin.

Jason Thornton asked Angie to accompany him to Clarksdale for grocery shopping. He thought the trip would do her good. "Thursday is Thanksgiving," he said. "You can help me pick the turkey and all the trimmings. We could try to make that great carrot and raisin salad your mother always had for holidays."

"I'm sorry, Daddy. I don't feel like going." She toyed with a bowl of Shredded Wheat, her appetite sinking lower with each passing minute.

The radio in the living room was tuned to Clarksdale's most popular station. The announcer urged his audience to buy a new car from McFee's Chevrolet. "You can't go wrong with a McFee!" he chirped.

"Are you sure, Angie? We could do some window

shopping, too. Christmas will be here before we know it and I haven't a clue to what presents you'd like."

Christmas, Angie thought, dunking her spoon to the bottom of the bowl and bringing up what appeared to be wet dog food. Who needs Christmas? Our second Christmas alone together without Mom. If it's like last year, we shouldn't bother. After opening presents we both cried, remember, Daddy?

But she would never talk about this. Her father tried so hard to make her happy.

"I'll put on a load of clothes to wash," she said. "I have some homework . . ."

Jason sighed and sat at the table across from her, a pen and writing pad in his hands. "Well, if you won't go, then help me make the grocery list. Except for turkey and cranberry sauce, I don't know what we need."

She felt sorry for him, almost sorry enough to go to Clarksdale to help him shop. But not quite. "Sweet potatoes," she said, trying to remember what they ate on Thanksgiving every year of her life. "Brown sugar and marshmallows for the potatoes. Carrots and raisins for the salad." He wrote these ingredients on the pad. "Chicken bouillon cubes. Celery." She paused to think what else they needed to make dressing for the turkey. "Sage if you want the southern dressing Mom always made for you." He wrote down sage in big, capital letters. "Eggs. Cornmeal. I don't think we have any," she said, picturing the contents of the pantry shelves.

He looked up from writing. "I wish you'd go. You know what we need."

She dropped her spoon in the cereal with a plop and turned her head to look out the window at the shining lake. If this show of obstinacy did not work, she would go to her room and stay there. The thought of spending hours choosing food and Christmas gifts held about as much appeal as working on a Mississippi chain gang.

"All right." He sighed and bowed his head to the task. "Go on. What else?"

"I think that's it. Don't forget the cranberries, the whole ones in the can, not the jellied sauce or fresh cranberries like Mom got. I don't know how to cook them."

He folded the pad of paper in half and put both it and the pen into the pocket of his flannel shirt. "Great. Then I'll be off. Is there anything you need for yourself?"

She thought about tampons for her period due the next week, but she couldn't tell her father to buy them for her. Since her mother's death she had gone into the drugstore to buy personal articles for herself. There were all sorts of private areas in her life shut away from her father. Not the least of which was her ongoing war with Tyeson Dompier.

"No, nothing," she said. "I don't need anything. But thanks."

He bent to kiss her cheek. When he straightened he said in a mock authoritarian tone, "Now eat your breakfast so you'll grow up strong and straight."

She smiled as he left the kitchen. She was as strong and straight and *tall* as any woman ten years her senior. Maybe she should stop eating altogether. It was a cinch she was going to stop having Shredded Wheat for breakfast. Maybe she could try grits, the southern favorite morning fare. Her father liked grits. Her father, she concluded, liked nearly everything in the world. She wondered sometimes if he had come into life full-grown, bypassing adolescence and puberty, his taste for variety instilled in him from the moment of conception. She had never seen him push aside any food—as she was now pushing away the cereal so that it set on the other side of the table. He even seemed to prefer godawful things like liver and spinach and, yuck, raw oysters on the half shell.

She stood from the table to watch her father leave the driveway. On Saturdays other girls were already preparing themselves for seven o'clock dates at the drive-in two miles outside of town or the Bijou Theatre on Clarksdale's main drag. They had boyfriends. They cared about clothes and lipstick and perfume. Girl things. Stupid things.

What did she care about? Rabbits, dead ones stolen from her, the game of basketball only because she was agile and quick, music, if it was loud enough. If it had a good beat and you could dance to it, like those kids on Dick Clark's "American Bandstand" always said. She smiled again at her own sardonic wit.

She saw her father back the car onto Moon Lake Road, wave at her, and leave a floating band of white, motionless dust behind as he headed for town. She turned from the front window to tackle the breakfast dishes and then round up a load of laundry for the wash, but before she reached the kitchen she stalled, biting her lower lip in perplexity. *Rabbits. Dead ones stolen from her*.

How could she look forward to Thanksgiving and turkey when her life was in such turmoil? How was she to attend to everyday affairs like the housekeeping chores she shared with her father after having seen Brody cleaning the carcass of one of her animals? The important question: How could she let them get away with it?

In all the books she read women were victims. They rarely took their destinies into their own hands. This peeved her no end. Even in *Wuthering Heights* and *Pride and Prejudice,* women let themselves be used and abused. All in the name of love, of course. Austen and Brontë were wonderful women writers, but they gave the world some wimpy heroines.

Veering away from the kitchen, she reached the hall closet and snatched down her blue down-filled jacket from a hanger. She shrugged into it, zipping it to below the collar.

To hell with washing dishes and clothes like some Victorian paper doll character. Angelina Thornton would find a way to make the Dompier family pay for her suffering.

She needed Varna. Varna knew just about everything. Angie had run away from her after admitting part of the truth. Why must she run anymore? Now that someone knew Tye's crime, someone who might help her seek proper revenge, all she had to do was ask for that help. Be honest about everything that had happened since she moved to Moon Lake. Let one other person help her bear the weight of the secrets which threatened to send her into a depression from which she might never recover.

Yes, there was hope. In Varna there was the last best hope. There must be a path out of the labyrinth Tye had placed her in. With Varna's wise guidance, that path might be unearthed for her to follow.

Angie no longer carried the transistor radio with her everywhere she went. The new one her father bought was better than the one she broke (she would not think of that, *would not* think of it), but for some reason she rarely listened to it.

Now as she walked down the gravel road to Varna's house she missed the solid square weight of it in her pocket, the little plastic earplug spearing the right side of her head with high-decibel music. The music, she realized, often served as an alternative to thinking. When her brain was flooded with rock and roll there was no call to think. The music substituted for that function.

But she must think. Tyeson evidently had done

plenty of thinking and scheming. When he killed the rabbits he spared one of them to take to his brother for only one reason. He knew she'd return to his house and peek through the windows. He wanted her to catch Brody in the process of taxidermy.

That he considered every avenue that might bring her pain was the reason he had been so successful. She would now think as he did, scheme as nastily as he, take precautions to work out plans in advance in minute detail so that she would never again be surprised.

Leaves were scattered across the road from the trees lining the lakeside. A few branches lay in the roadway ditch from the wind the night before. The sky, overcast with a pall of gray, reminded Angie of winter days in St. Louis when it threatened to snow. Mississippi, a state where it never snowed, seemed to suffer all the same drawbacks winter brought with it without the benefits. She could never make snowballs to throw or snowmen to laugh at. She would never see the lake's thick green firs laden down with blankets of shimmering white. She would miss the snow. Just one more segment of her life that had disappeared with nothing worthwhile to take its place.

In the bleached, dim light of the day she trudged up Varna's porch steps. Time for truth. All of it.

Raising her fist to knock on the door, she noticed that it was not fully closed. Frowning, she placed her fingertips against the wood and pushed gently. The door creaked open on unoiled hinges.

"Varna?" Angie called. "Your door's open . . ."

She stepped into the ruined mess of the usually tidy room, her frown deepening. Shadow here hid the scene of destruction from her until her eyes adjusted and began to pick out furniture. Her gaze moved over the downed table, the broken bibelots, the chess set missing from the coffee table . . . the . . . the body lying on the floor beneath.

"Varna!"

She hurried to her friend and knelt beside her. Varna lay on her stomach, her head turned to the side. *Dead.* There was no doubt in Angie's mind that she was kneeling before a dead woman. In the faint light from the window Angie saw the seepage of blood that had spread into a semicircle from beneath the body and coagulated there. Taking her hands from her mouth where she had been biting down on the knuckles, she reached out with palsied fingers to touch Varna's cheek. Cold, the skin of the face like a rubber mask stretched over the bones.

"What happened to you?" Angie whispered. "Oh Varna, what happened!"

Turn her over, she thought. No, don't, don't touch her, call an ambulance, hurry home and call . . .

She knew the old woman was dead and no one would be able to bring her back to life. It was senseless to hope for anything. She knew that. The lesson had been imprinted on her many times already.

Angie cringed remembering all the death surrounding her life. Her mother. Dana. The rabbits. Varna. Everyone and everything she cared about always died and left her.

She opened her eyes and looked upon Varna's quiet corpse. It felt as if her heart was being squeezed, flattened dry, set loose inside her chest to sink like a petal blowing to the ground in a wild, crazy wind.

Where was the blood coming from? How did this much blood come from one human being? She must turn her over, find the wound.

She reached for Varna's shoulder and pulled at her tenderly. She was too heavy. She would need both hands and much of her strength in order to move her. She tried again and Varna's outstretched right arm came up from the floor stiffly. Angie saw that Varna's hand was made into a fist.

Oh God, she couldn't turn her, she couldn't stand it.

The room began to whirl and tilt. Angie scrabbled backwards on her knees away from the body. She felt glass sticking into her hands before she stood, turned, and flew through the open door, down the steps, and onto the road sobbing, droplets of blood leaking from her hands as she raced toward home.

Jason Thornton stood silently across the living room at the front window looking out. Angie sat in a chair, head bowed, hands in her lap, answering the sheriff's questions in a droning, tired monotone. The sheriff sat next to her in her father's favorite TV chair, his tan uniform crisp with starch, his badge shining on his left breast pocket. He was a young man in his mid-twenties who might have been handsome except that his face was in the process of being ravished by a virulent case of acne that threatened to move down and engulf his long scrawny neck. Had Angie the emotion left to waste, she would have felt sorry for him. He seemed like a nice man caught up in something he had not been prepared to handle.

He spoke with a soft southern drawl. He had been extremely circumspect in his questions, taking into consideration her youth and fondness for the deceased.

"Well," he said and it sounded like *walll*, ". . . it looks to be a case of homicide, but there was nothing taken." He turned a gold wedding band on his finger while contemplating. "Whoever did it didn't come to rob her."

There was nothing for Angie to say. She wanted to leave the room and go to bed the way she had done when raped. This time she might not get up again if she didn't have to.

From the corner of her eye she saw the young sheriff stretch out one of his long legs and push a hand into his pants pocket. He withdrew something and held it out for her inspection. She lifted her head and stared at a black chess piece lying in the center of his palm. "Have you seen this before?" he asked.

"It looks like one of Varna's chess pieces. She liked to play by herself. She always had a game going." Something about the particular piece nagged at Angie's brain. Something Varna had said once . . .

"I found this clutched in her hand. That bothers me. It appeared that she reached up and knocked the game off the coffee table or maybe it fell during the struggle. But what I want to know is why she took this specific piece and held onto it. Don't you think that's pretty strange? Could it have meant something?"

Angie stared at the piece, thinking, feeling some odd bit of information lurking just beyond the reach of memory. "I . . . that's the black knight . . . I . . ."

"Yes? What is it, Angie? What does it mean? You know, don't you?" He asked these questions in a slow, deliberate way.

Jason turned from the window and looked at his daughter. The room was so quiet Angie could hear her own breathing. She cast back into her mind to find the day she had sat with Varna at the chessboard. Varna had picked up the black knight and said . . . She was talking about . . . the Dompiers. She said the black knight . . .

Angie came abruptly to her feet. "It's Tye."

"Tie?" the two men chorused.

"Tyeson Dompier. He lives a mile down that way." She pointed toward his house. "Varna told me once that she thought of Tye as the black knight and she didn't like the black knight. It symbolized everything bad—death, destruction, evil." She turned to Sheriff Newton. "Tye killed her. I know it now. That's why she got the chess piece and held onto it so hard even when she was dying. She was trying to tell us it was him, that he stabbed her to death. I know it was him!"

The sheriff looked astounded. "Walll now, that's a pretty harsh accusation, Miss Thornton. The Dompiers are well known in this vicinity. Besides, what would be the boy's motive? We're talking about murder here."

"I don't know his motive, I don't know how he thinks, but he's nuts, I know that. How can you explain she was holding the only piece on the board she gave a name to if he didn't do it?"

The sheriff glanced at the black knight, palmed it, put it into his pocket. "We'll talk to the boy. We'll find out what this is all about. I want to thank you for helping us out, Miss Thornton. I know it was difficult for you. Mr. Thornton." He stood and nodded at Jason. He walked to the door as they watched.

Angie's sudden understanding of the secret Varna held in her dead hand had swept over her like fire ignited with gasoline. Yet it was obvious to her the sheriff did not have much confidence in a Dompier being a murderer. What had she expected anyway? She knew Tye's family hold on the town of Clarksdale. No one could name a more prominent family in the entire county. Tye's father was an attorney! How could she get the authorities to believe her?

"Wait, let me go with you," she called, hurrying to the door to join him.

"Angie!" Jason called. "Let it go."

She glanced at her father. "No, I won't let it go. He doesn't believe me. I want to be sure he questions Tye. I have to be there."

The sheriff stood just outside the door looking from her to Jason and back again. "It's all right, Mr. Thornton. I want her along to check Tye's reaction to the chess piece and the accusation. Come along.'' He gestured for her to follow him to the police car. ''We'll go right now.''

Angie grabbed her jacket and rushed outside. All she could think about was the black knight. Varna left them the clue to her death. It was up to her to make the sheriff believe it. Maybe her appearance at Tye's door with a policeman would shake Tye so badly he would make a mistake or confess to the crime.

Varna had no enemies. Her house had not been robbed. She had been stabbed in cold blood and only one person at the lake could have committed murder.

Now Angie did not have to plan a way to make him pay for all his sins. His monstrosity had led him to his own downfall.

Varna, in her death, had been able to point the finger at the callous soul who wielded the knife. There could be no justice left in the world if her last effort went unrewarded.

Chapter
22

Brody and his mother, Jessica Dompier, sat stiffly in the drawing room with Sheriff Newton and Angie. There was the scent of roses in the air from a bouquet arranged on the end table nearest the company. A fire crackled from the depths of a fireplace flanked by brass andirons.

"I'm sorry Father can't be here to greet you, Sheriff. As you know, he's away on business until Thanksgiving. Are his services needed at the courthouse?" Brody innocently asked. "We can call him in Jackson if need be."

"I would really like to speak to your brother, Tyeson, if that's possible," the sheriff said. "This matter concerns him."

"What do you want with Tyeson?" Jessica asked, rising from her chair until her son motioned that she sit. Angie noticed she didn't seem to know what to do with her hands. She alternately rubbed the palms together and interlaced the fingers.

"Yes, what has your visit to do with Tyeson?" Brody repeated.

The sheriff sighed and rolled the wedding band on his finger. "I would rather talk to him, if you don't mind, Mr. Dompier. Is he about?" He glanced through the doorway as if to catch sight of the boy hiding there in the shadows.

Brody looked at his mother and cleared his throat. "Uh . . . Tye went with Daddy. He's always liked to shop in Jackson when our father's on a business trip. With school out for the holidays it was a perfect opportunity."

"That's too bad," the sheriff said, turning to look at Angie, blinking hard. "When will he be back home, do you think?"

"They'll return Saturday. Now what is this all about? I think my mother has a right to know, Newton."

Angie noticed the change in the tone of voice and the dropping of the young sheriff's title. Her heart sank. She couldn't keep her mouth shut any longer. "I don't think Tye went anywhere," she said before the sheriff could continue. "Where was he last night?"

Brody turned slitted eyes in her direction. "Are you asking the questions now?" He looked pointedly at the sheriff. "Tell me what exactly it is you want."

"Walll, there's been a death . . ."

"A murder!" Angie interrupted.

"Yes, Miss Thornton's right. There's been a murder on Moon Lake Road. Varna Jenkins, the Negro woman who lives about a mile and a quarter down the way. I remember she once worked here, didn't she, Mrs. Dompier?"

Jessica nodded, her hands clutched around the chair arms like claws digging into the fabric for firm purchase. It was the first time Angie had seen her clothed. It still seemed odd. She kept seeing her naked, pirouetting around the room, the stereo blasting Mozart.

"What has this woman's death got to do with us, Newton?" Brody asked, losing all patience with the sheriff's insistence on speaking to his mother when it was perfectly clear who was in charge with his father absent.

"I am only conducting my investigation, Mr. Dompier . . ."

"And you aren't making it any easier," Angie again interrupted.

Newton nodded his head, but did not look at her. "She's right. You're not being very forthcoming and that makes my job harder to perform."

"Perform?" Brody laughed and glanced at his mother who giggled with him. "Since when did you perform, Newton? I'll have you remember that my father contributed heavily to your last campaign for office. It would be wise for you to recall who you are speaking to. It sounds to me like you're treading on shaky ground coming here to question my brother about a 'murder.' Why aren't you down at the Hylander farm questioning those rowdy nigger boys who are always robbing and beating up Moon Lake's old women? What's got you coming here wanting to interrogate Tyeson?"

Newton stretched out his leg and fumbled in his pants pocket for the second time that day. He drew out the chess piece and held it out to Brody. "This is why I'm here, Mr. Dompier. Miss Thornton says Varna called Tyeson the black knight. She had this clutched in her fist when we found her body. I find that interesting, don't you?"

Brody stared at the chess piece for some moments before glaring at the sheriff. He stood, his mother stood, and finally Newton and Angie were forced to stand with them. The silence in the room was a palpable thing pressing in on the foursome standing in the shifting, firelit shadows of afternoon. Angie trembled at the confrontation of power taking place between the young sheriff and the heavyset, infuriated Brody. One thing was evident. She should not have worried about Sheriff Newton's ethics. He did not let the Dompiers in any way intimidate him.

"You know your way to the door," Brody snapped between clenched teeth.

"I'll have my husband call you," Jessica frostily stated, turning with a ballet-like snap and leaving the room with a swirl of striped velvet skirts stirring the air in her wake.

"Thank you most kindly for your time, Mr. Dompier." Newton took Angie's elbow and guided her to the hallway where he let them both out. Once down the steps he said, "I'm sorry you had to witness the Dompiers' breach of good manners, Miss Thornton. I have never been on the best of terms with Brody. I think he opposed my appointment even though his father, it's true, was a big supporter."

"Do you think Tye's really with his father in Jackson?"

He shrugged. "Walll, that's something I have to find out, isn't it? Now let me drive you home."

Angie sat in the white police cruiser, her mind a jumble of thoughts on the way home. She did not believe for a minute that Tye was out of town. He might have been in the kitchen talking to himself or in his room, listening through a cracked door. But he couldn't have been in Jackson when the murder occurred. A dying woman did not lie.

"Can you arrest Tye when you find him?" she asked. She stood just outside the open car door in front of her home.

"Right now what we have is called 'circumstantial evidence,' I'm afraid. Now if the dead woman had left a note or something or we had fingerprints at the crime scene . . ."

"Did you check for fingerprints?"

"We have a man coming up from Baton Rouge to do that. There's no one in my office who's qualified. He'll be here tomorrow."

"And if you don't find fingerprints? What if he wore gloves or something?"

Newton looked through the windshield. "Then we have circumstantial evidence and that's not enough to convict. Tye's underage, he's a minor, too, that's a problem. The law presumes one is innocent unless proven guilty, Miss Thornton. So far all I have done is conjecture and question. The thing that bothers me is Brody's antagonistic attitude."

It was all shaping up, Angie thought, just the way Tye would like it. No one ever got him for any of his deeds. She had not reported his rape when she should have. She had told no one she knew he killed her rabbits. And now even though Varna left a death message for the living, it might turn out to be useless. How could this be? How could he go on getting away with every evil thing he wanted to do?

"Good-bye, Miss Thornton. Thank you for your help. If I need something else I'll drop by again."

She watched him drive away. The wind picked up and it brushed the fine hair from her face, drove leaves across the road toward the cotton field. She looked toward Varna's house and felt her throat constrict. Empty and bereft it stood as a lonely, dark outline against the lowering sky. She wondered if Varna's children in California had been notified.

She had not missed someone so much since her mother died. There was no one left for her to talk to, to ask advice from, no one to fold her in a warm, motherly embrace.

Wiping the welling tears from the corners of her eyes with fists, Angie went inside to see her father. She wanted circumstantial evidence explained to her.

She needed to know how easy this time it would be for Tyeson Dompier to get out of reaping what he had sown. Were the scales of justice really so heavily tipped against the victims of this world? If so, what could she do about it?

"What possessed you?" Brody screamed. He pushed Tye backwards and kept moving in on him. Tye retreated until he hit the back of an empty horse stall. "Have you lost complete control of your senses?"

"Brody, I didn't do it . . ."

"Don't give me any of that 'I didn't do it' stuff. Do you think I was born yesterday? Do you think I don't know you? That old woman left them a clue!"

"That's ridiculous." Tye wiped his nose and kept his eyes off his brother's furious face so as not to provoke him.

"Ridiculous? It may be, it very well may be, but that girl down the road you've been messing with has Newton all heated up about questioning you. What's gonna happen when they learn you didn't go with Daddy to Jackson? What are they gonna think when they discover I *lied* for you? You've put us all in jeopardy, don't you understand that? Daddy's the damn district attorney! Jesus. What about me and the board of directors at the hospital? What about your family, Tye?"

"There's lots of stuff the hospital doesn't know about you." Tye flinched after saying it, but he would not be yelled at and accused without recourse even though it meant he bring up his brother's morbid interests in sedated patients.

Brody kept silent so long that Tye chanced a look at his face. He wished he hadn't. Brody looked as if he might explode. His cheeks puffed and reddened, his nostrils flared, his lips pulled back slightly from his teeth.

"What I've done might be shameful, but what you've done is psychotic."

"Psychotic?" Tye let out a little squeak of disbelief. "I think you're looking through the wrong end of the telescope, Brody. You won't take any flak about your own little perversions, will you? I had to kill old Varna. You just don't know how she threatened me. She said she'd go to Newton and tell him everything she knew."

"And what did she know?"

"She knew I raped Angie. Angie must have told her. Varna said she would tell the sheriff. She was going to do that today if I hadn't stopped her. I told her to stay out of it, but she wouldn't listen. I *had* to do something."

Brody slapped him across the face with a stinging blow. "You didn't have to *kill her,* you stupid son of a bitch! I could have bought her off. I could have sent you out of state. I could have gotten to the girl. Anything but this."

Tye held one hand over his aching cheek. He felt with his tongue on the inside of his mouth where a tooth had cut the flesh. He turned his head and spit blood onto the ground.

"Don't hit me, Brody. Don't ever hit me." He no longer cringed against the wall of the horse stall. He stepped out, forcing Brody to do the same. His eyes turned the color of storm clouds and there was murder there.

Brody turned in an agitated circle. He began to pace the length of the darkened floor of the barn. "We're going to have to send you away, Tyeson. It's too much for me to handle any longer."

"You got Daddy to threaten me with that before, Brody. I'm tired of everyone telling me they're going to find ways to hurt me or take me to jail or put me into clinics. Don't tell me that again."

"You'll have to go willingly, of course, we don't want any more problems," Brody continued, having paid no attention to his brother's statement. "We'll find a nice, comfortable place where they'll give you the best of everything. You stay in a year or so and we'll come get you, let you finish high school somewhere else. Find someone to live with you."

"I'm not going into an insane asylum."

Brody paced, his hands at his back. "That's not what it'll be. It'll be just a sanitarium, a resting place where Moon Lake's authorities can't reach you. You'll be protected until this whole mess is dropped and forgotten."

"Brody?" Tye moved across the open lane of the barn from the old horse stalls to the mildewed pile of hay where a pitchfork lay.

"Mama and Daddy found a pretty good place a long time ago. It was in Memphis, I think. Or was it Chattanooga? They use all the new therapies and they even have a golf course and a swimming pool. It's one of the best places. We need to call them right away, see if there's any vacancies."

"Brody, don't talk about that," Tye warned.

"Of course there's always the New Orleans clinic where Mama stayed those months after you were born. It was successful. At least, mildly successful," he corrected. "We might look into that."

"Brody, stop it."

"Shut up, now. We have to make plans. Newton's going to keep coming back until he can talk to you. In your present state of mind I wouldn't be surprised if he had you confessing within fifteen minutes. The Thorntons are going to be on his back until he gets you. If you've been put away, he might let it go. We have to make sure he lets it go. I know Daddy will agree with me. I'm going to call him at the Jackson Hotel, see if he's in yet . . ."

Before Brody reached the big closed door of the barn he let out a bloodcurdling scream. His back arched and his hands scrabbled behind him to dislodge the pitchfork piercing the fabric of his gray suit, white shirt, muscles, ribs, and heart.

He fell face forward to the earth with a body-shaking thud and was still.

In the midst of the ever-creeping darkness of the November sunset, Tyeson Dompier stood prayerfully waiting for the courage to squat down beside his only brother. He had to see about him. You couldn't let someone you loved simply lie in the dirt leaking blood.

Finally he drew in a long breath and stooped over Brody. He felt along the folds of his neck for a pulse. He brushed the thinning hair from his brow. He stood and, putting both hands on the handle of the pitchfork, one foot on Brody's back, jerked the buried tines from the flesh. More blood oozed from the row of holes.

Tye needed to do something about that leakage.

He could sew the wounds shut. That's what Brody did to specimens that had been wounded.

Inside the house Tye spent several minutes gathering together all of Brody's taxidermy instruments. He carried the tray to the kitchen, paused to find a plastic tub in the cleaning pantry, and arms loaded, returned to the barn.

Undressing his brother was a tedious job. His belt wouldn't unclasp and his slacks wouldn't come off his legs until Tye removed his shoes and socks. His tie snagged with the knot tightening. Finally exasperated, Tye used a scalpel to cut the tie and shirt from Brody's inert body.

Once unclothed, Brody lay on his bloody back upon the hay-strewn floor staring at the roof timbers. His legs were spread, feet pointing in opposite directions.

His penis was gray and shriveled, hiding in a thick mat of hair like a paralyzed mole in a bush.

Tye sighed at the work to come, but knew it must be done. How could he, he asked himself, bury this man, this flesh of his flesh, this one he had so loved? How could he allow the body to decay and putrefy, the skin splitting open and releasing gases and fluids? If he stuffed Brody, then he would never lose him . . . never be without his company. He understood now Brody's obsession with the hobby of taxidermy. It was the preservation, throughout a lifetime, of things beautiful and irreplaceable.

He stared a full minute at Brody's steady opaque gaze. Where would he find the glass to replace those pale blue myopic eyes? Perhaps he could use large marbles. He could not leave the sockets empty; it was too frightening to contemplate.

So to the task.

To the task.

Tye felt for the scalpel. His eyes filled. Tears overflowed down his cheeks and dropped, plip, plip, onto his brother's hairy chest. It looked as if morning dew had settled upon the corpse.

Tye straddled the body. He put the sharp edge of the scalpel against the skin at the top of Brody's sternum. He pressed down and drew the blade in a straight line down between the ribs, across the swollen belly, through the navel, down across the abdomen into the hairy crotch where the blade hit bone. Blood welled from between the layers and droplets formed until gravity pulled them down sloping irregular paths of Brody's barrel chest.

Tye put the scalpel again in the same position at the top and, following the sliced flesh, he pressed harder until the blade passed through muscle and, in places, sank into viscera so deep Tye's knuckles pushed against the skin. Next he made a lateral cut across

Brody's ponderous stomach so that the incisions now made a cross. Everything inside bulged up against the opening as if seeking escape.

Dropping the scalpel into the hay, blinded now by tears, Tye forced his hands into the split in the chest cavity and pulled with all his strength until he heard the ribs crack and give. The sound reminded him of early fall when his father sat cracking pecans in the palms of his hands. He opened the chest, slid his hands down the cut and pulled open the abdominal walls. He reached into the warm body first to snare the heart. It would not give in to his probing fingers or grunting jerks. He had to use the scalpel to cut it loose.

Swinging his leg off, Tye bent over the task full of serious concentration. He brought out loops of mottled intestines, pieces of lung tissue, what looked like a liver but might have been a pancreas or a gallbladder. He flung these slippery hot *stubborn* organs into the plastic tub for later disposal. None of it would come free of the body without a fight. Tye looped the coil of intestines over his arms and tugged, breaking it in spots, then catching hold of the broken end. His blood-covered hands slipping for a firm grasp, he tugged out the rest.

He was covered with blood and with offal. His clothes were soaked. Had he been able to smell himself, he would have gagged. All around his knees and Brody's body the hay was coated with pools coagulating in the cool air. Flies, discovering bounty, clouded over the pair upon the floor.

Tye realized after a time that the sound he had been listening to was the sound of his own sobbing.

He realized further that he would never be able to completely and expertly clean and scrape out the shell of the man he called brother.

The sun set; the barn darkened to pitch. He worked

by touch, too impatient to go in search of a lamp. He felt things within the rapidly cooling body cavity he thought might still be alive and imagined they pulsed against the abrasiveness of his fingers.

Before he knew it he was crawling around on the barn floor scraping and hugging hay to his wet shirt-front and scrabbling back, feeling for Brody in the dark, feeling for his slick opening where he stuffed and tamped down the hay as best he could.

And still he wept openly, loudly, unabashedly for he was not doing this well, in fact, he was doing a terribly sloppy job, and Brody, Brody was laughing at these pitiful efforts, chortling at how clumsy, how inept, how asinine, how *crazy* everything had become while night swept down from heaven and covered over the sadness of the whole corruptible, contemptible, condemned earth.

Love.

Tye knew once and for all it had created an abomination.

Chapter

23

In a trance, Tye left the barn and returned to the
house. Not until he stood in the kitchen—and he had
no idea how long he had been standing at the sink
staring out the window—did he awaken to his state of
disrepair. Where he stood, blood marked the floor. A
path led from the back door to where he'd become
immobile.

Shaking himself, admonishing himself for slovenness,
he went to the downstairs bath and stepped clothed
into the shower. He undressed there and washed down
a dozen times with soap. He walked naked to the
laundry room, finding clean clothes and a pair of
sneakers.

He had only finished cleaning up the kitchen floor
when he heard his mother's voice.

"Tyeson, have you seen Brody? I needed to speak
to him and I can't find him anywhere in the house."

He saw she wore a velvet dress, the bodice a muted
shade of aquamarine, the skirt rainbow stripes of
color that flowed to mid-calf like a prism falling from

her waist. She was a beautiful woman, he thought, elegant and graceful. Her body was a finely tuned instrument with muscles that moved her through rooms like a jaguar moving through lush foliage in a jungle setting. He wondered suddenly if his father still made love to her. His father seemed too dispassionate about everything in his life, except his "collection," to consider sex important. In reality, even his job suffered because of his preoccupation with concentration camps. Brody said this made him a mediocre attorney. It would surprise Tye if his parents ever had sex anymore.

He suspected the keepers of this zoo cared little for the baser animal instincts. Brody thought sex disgusting and periodically went into months of withdrawal from women. "The sex drive is a built-in time bomb. The thing that gets all of us in trouble in this upside-down world. I'd like to do without it permanently one day."

"I'm the only normal person in this family," Tye had answered him.

Jessica stared at her son patiently. When she received no response she repeated, "Tye, have you seen Brody? I need to talk with him."

Tye squinted at her. "Brody?" A vision of his brother's body lying facedown on the earth of the barn blossomed in his mind. It must be a waking nightmare. Images of blood, buckets and gallons of blood came to him. He trembled all over. He was sick. He did not know what was wrong.

He shook his head. "I don't know where Brody is. I haven't seen him."

His mother frowned. "He said he was going to find you just a while ago. Didn't he tell you about Newton and the Thornton girl coming by?"

Tye shook his head again. "I haven't seen Brody."

"All right. If you see him, tell him I've gone to lie down in my room. If I'm napping, he can wake me."

"Mother?"

She turned back. "Yes?"

"Would you dance for me? Just one dance, please? I . . . I would like to see you dance."

"I don't feel like it right now, Tyeson. I'm tired. The interview with Newton sapped all my energy. I feel as if a vampire had sucked my blood. I wish your father were here. I feel . . . vulnerable . . . when he's out of town.

"While I'm lying down, do not under any circumstances answer the door or the telephone, do you hear me? You're supposed to be in Jackson with your father. I'll let Brody explain it to you."

He watched her disappear into the hallway and imagined her graciously mounting the stairs to her room, the colored velvet sweeping behind her. On the surfaces of the Louis XIV furniture in her room sat photographs of a younger woman wearing her face, dressed in tights and a tiara, dancing upon a smoky stage. White satin ballet shoes hung from a wall hook. She had been a budding dancer in New Orleans before she married, but something had happened, Brody told him once when he was younger, something snapped in their mother's mind long before they were born.

She had been a pampered and spoiled southern belle from a fine old family in the French Quarter, but her ancestors carried the seeds of madness in their line. Her uncle was institutionalized; he thought he was Ponce de León. He affected knee britches and sleeves with ruffled cuffs. Several of her first cousins suffered varying degrees of paranoia; one of them killed the mailman, convinced the civil servant was delivering a device that would link him with a surveillance satellite over the North Pole. Her own mother, Tye's handsome, aristocratic grandmother, in later life was treated for manic-depression. As an old woman she alternated between wild euphoria and glum, silent periods where she would not speak to anyone no matter how they pleaded with her.

"It was unfortunate that our mother chose to marry our father. I believe I would not be remiss in stating he is an obsessive-compulsive personality. Therefore, brother, we," Brody concluded, "are direct descendants of a gene pool rife with delusion artists. I have been fortunate in not displaying outward symptoms. This cannot be said for you."

"That's a rotten thing to say," Tye said, deeply hurt. "There's nothing wrong with me."

"You, Tyeson, have just made a remark that is proof of your own instability. The mad do not know they are mad. But don't worry about it overmuch. As long as Daddy is functional, he'll protect the family's secrets. All the bones will remain in the closet. His father, after all, owned nearly the entire county around here. Privilege and wealth is most helpful in providing a shining coat of respectability. As long as we stick together and don't let outsiders get too close, no one need ever know."

An overpowering feeling of suffocation gripped Tye on remembering the conversations he'd had in the past with Brody. All that psychological jargon, just meaningless nattering. All those clichéd labels for behavior none of the Dompiers actually believed. He staggered from the room. He held onto the staircase looking up it for help from the dreadful memories that kept flooding his mind.

"Mother . . ."

She was in her room, napping. She had told him that some time ago, he could not remember when. It might have been yesterday or this morning or merely minutes ago. Time was increasingly less germane to the process of living. He could not tell, for instance, how long it took to make a trip to the barn and back.

Was it hours or was it minutes that he worked at the foot of the stairs to make everything perfect?

What had his mother and Brody discussed while he wasn't present? Had it been her idea to send him away?

He trod the stairs softly, his shoes muffled by the carpet runner.

Why did she dance naked every night? Was she an inherently cruel woman? As a child she made him lust for her. Was that not intolerable?

He moved down the hallway to her room. He stood before the closed door with his palms pressed against the wood.

Was she responsible for all of this? For how he felt about Angie? What could be the catalyst for untold anguish? For unfulfilled longing?

He turned the doorknob and quietly opened the door. He stepped inside the shadowed room and halted, watching how the moonlight played with her naked limbs upon the bed. It caressed the curves and softened the angles. He heard her breathing. He smelled her perfume.

"Mother?" he called.

She stirred. "Would you like to lie down with Mama? Are you tired?"

"I'm tired, Mother," he confessed. "So tired."

"Then come lie with me. We'll rest together until Brody comes back."

"Yes," he said. "Rest. It's late."

He saw her neck swivel so that she could see the bedside clock. "It's only seven-thirty, Tye. But we'll have a late dinner. Won't that be nice?"

"Can you come with me for a minute?" he asked.

"I thought you were going to lie down for a while."

"I will. I will. But I want you to see something downstairs. You only need come to the landing. It's something very special."

He heard her sigh as she swung lithe legs over the bedside. She stood and moved with balletic grace through the moonlight to his side. "What is it, darling?"

He led her from the room and down the hall. At the landing, she leaned against the banister and looked down. A sharp intake of breath caused her to stiffen. She brought both fists up to rub her eyes before looking again.

"I found Brody," he said, peering over the railing to where his brother, hastily sewn together, sat propped against the far ivory wall, his spindly legs spread out before him. Tye had washed and groomed him so that he appeared to be a stark white ghost of his former self. Stray straws poked through some of the large red raw stitches running down his gut.

"Brody never showed me how to really do it right," Tye complained sadly. "I should have taken more interest."

Taking his mother's shaking shoulders, he steered her to the head of the stairs.

"Oh Tye, oh Tye . . ."

"Dance, Mother. Dance for me."

He let go her shoulders and pushed with both hands on her cool, white naked back. She tumbled head over heels, her scream a long, drawn-out spine-shattering cry. She lay at the bottom of the stairs. Still. Silent. All is done, Tye thought, relieved.

"That's fine," he whispered. "That was a beautiful last waltz." He applauded, his handclaps echoing in the empty mansion back to him.

He moved through the house as a zombie would. He reached the back door and flung it open. He wore his jacket, but the evening was lengthening and a freeze was predicted overnight. He shivered, hugging himself. He eyed his choices—the barn or the slave quarters. For some reason he knew he could not go into the barn. It was as if an invisible giant stood guard at the doors warding him away.

He lurched toward the old quarters, hands buried beneath his armpits to keep them warm. Once inside the dusty, unheated building, he made for the cob-webbed attic where he could wrap himself in a shred-ded quilt and wait for Brody to find him. He feared whatever news his brother had to tell him.

Brody might want to send him away from the fam-ily, away from Moon Lake.

Brody was a doctor and he'd always said he would know when it was time any of them needed to apply for treatment.

Brody was a classic, self-styled son of a bitch. Tye realized if he hated him with one more ounce of his strength, he would gladly murder him and be rid of his high-and-mighty superiority forever.

After arranging himself in a corner of the attic, the quilt wrapped tightly around his knees, he slipped into misty reverie. Ancient scenes from the past formed in his head and clung there demanding his attention.

In the first ghostly display he saw the young Tyeson, the boy child dressed in shorts and a summer shirt. Dirt was smeared on his chubby cheeks and ground into his knuckles and knees. He had been playing outside with sticks and branches and mounds of newly turned earth in the cotton field until he noticed it was evening and supper time. Strangely enough no one had called him inside and asked him to wash. He walked through the echoing house. A mysterious strain of music wafted from somewhere and he followed it as he would follow a string lying on the carpet to find where it was tied. He stood just outside the parlor where his mother shockingly disrobed like an actress playing a role.

"Mama," he whispered. "Oh, Mama."

She had taken off silk stockings and a garter belt.

She had taken off a pearl-white slip, bra, and panties. She went up onto her naked toes, arms lifted heavenward, eyes following them. Then she stepped out into the room on a strand of the music and hung there, a perfect teardrop of female flesh suspended upon an invisible wire. She then broke the stance and turned slowly, slowly toward him as if she felt his eyes upon her. She smiled angelically. "My baby," she cooed. "Come and watch Mother dance, sweetie. Come join me in a dance."

He hung back, baffled at what he saw, at the tone of her voice, at the strangeness of finding her this way. It was not right. He knew it. There was a kernel of disbelief screaming way inside, trapped way inside, and it tore him apart with the wrongness of his mother unclothed, calling to him.

"Don't be afraid," she said, her voice still dovelike, seductive, a ruffled wing spreading upon the surface of the air. "It doesn't matter about clothes," she said. She held out her long white arms to him and bent to receive his chunky little boy's body. "Nothing matters when the music plays." She enfolded his stunned, sweat-stained face into the marble-smooth round nakedness of her breasts.

"Nothing matters," he said now into the gloom of the cluttered attic. He had always known the truth.

She had not really cared about him even when he was small. She never said it. His father had never said it. No one had to voice the truth when it was there bright and fatally pocked as the moon for him to see.

The mist cleared and Tye was left without memory. He was left alone with the thing that walked in his mind.

And this is what the thing said: What do you do when the world doesn't care? When no one cares?

The lake will never go dry, the stars will remain at

their stations, the winds blow constant, but no one cares if you live or die. If you die your thoughts die with you. That's one of the blessings death bestows. Those thoughts that plague and lay ruin to a mind vanish into the wind and visit the stars, but they don't bother any living thing ever again. Silence might be worth giving up breath and pain and loneliness. Confusion and empty dreams and loneliness.

He stared at the near rafters of the ceiling until he could see beyond into the drifting starry night.

The litany returned and his mind revolved with the universe.

What do you do when the world doesn't care? When no one cares? What is it that you can possibly do about the bitter truth found at the center of a life?

Chapter

24

Angie sat in the oak tree swing dragging her feet along the ground, watching brown leaves swirl and eddy into the field as the wind picked up in strength. Across the street, lights shone from the windows of her home. Jason Thornton prepared dinner for two. Angie could almost read his mind. Susan, dead and gone. The return home to Moon Lake, Mississippi, nothing but heartache and despair for his daughter. Animals slaughtered. A neighbor knifed. Danger and death dogging him every step he took. Nowhere could he find the peace and safety he needed to provide for his family.

Beyond the sloping land behind her house, Angie could see a strip of the lake beaming beneath the freezing glare of a new moon. On Thanksgiving Day her father would take her to lunch in Clarksdale, too depressed to ask that she prepare an elaborate meal. They would pick at the food and try to make conversation without mentioning Varna or the boy down the road.

Tomorrow Varna's relatives might arrive from California to see about funeral arrangements. Tomorrow the fingerprint expert being summoned from Louisiana would dust the house of an old, poor black woman.

Without the lights from Varna's house shining out in the night, the lake was shrouded in an unrelenting, uninviting blackness. The Thornton home appeared to be a lone dwelling in a lost, forgotten land made of dead fields and a single, icy lake.

God, she hated it here. She hated the South, the provincialism of the area, the small-mindedness of the people. She hated the bigotry and the ease with which they made her an outcast. She hated the decadence of the wealthy and the bitter poverty of the poor. She hated losing so much for so little reason.

She hated with such huge feeling that it would not surprise her to see the stubbles in the field catch fire and turn into an inferno from the heat of her projected wrath.

"Stand up," a voice coldly ordered. "Come with me."

Angie jumped in the swing. She came to her feet, whirling around. Tye. "Get away from me!"

"Can you see this?" he asked quietly. He held out the blade of a knife to her.

Her gaze became riveted on the blinking stainless steel. "Yes," she said, catching her breath.

"This killed Varna. Do you want it to kill you?"

"No."

"Then come with me."

"Where are we going?"

"For a walk, that's all." He gestured and she turned, stepped out toward the road.

"Can I go tell my father I'm going for a walk? He'll be calling me inside in a minute."

"No, just head down the road past your house."

She could barely stand to have him at her back.

She kept imagining the point of the blinking knife sliding in between her shoulder blades. She discovered she was hunching her shoulders against just such a phenomenon.

She was walking funny. She swallowed funny. She licked her lips and wondered why she could not think.

Of course. It was her heart. It had frozen dead with fear upon his appearance and without its warm, circulating blood her brain was slowly dying.

"I don't want to go," she whispered. The wind caught her protest and blew it away.

"You never cared," Tyeson said. "I gave you a chance. Now it's too late and it doesn't matter anymore."

"What are you talking about?" She was yards past her home and the darkness crowded in. She could smell the sweet, clean scent of the ruffly water mingling with the heavy green smell of wind-washed conifers.

"What are you talking about?" she repeated, raising her voice and hearing it near the shaky edge of hysteria.

"You betrayed me," he said simply. "Brody betrayed me. They all did in the end, that's what I remember now."

Talk to him, she thought, he's crazy so just keep talking to him so he can't use the knife the way he used it on Varna.

"How did I betray you?" She felt him prod her from behind with the tip of the blade and she walked faster, face forward into the wind that swept down the moonlit road.

"You turned me away. You chose Dana as your boyfriend. You never liked me."

This she could not deny. "How did Brody betray you?" Another prod that caused her shoulders to jerk

233

forward in automatic response. Oh God, she thought, why hasn't my father called for me yet? Where *is* he?

"Brody meant to send me to a hospital. This time he was serious. This time, together, they would have done it."

"Where's Brody now? Let's go talk to him about it," she said, looking back over one shoulder at the stalking shadow.

"You can't talk to Brody when he's dead! Weren't you listening to me? They'll be burying him in a deep grave soon. Just like they buried Dana after I killed him. I know they will even though I tried to do a good job of sewing Brody up again. Mama too. I wish Daddy were home and this could be done with finally, because you see, it doesn't matter when no one cares if you live or die."

Brody dead! Mrs. Dompier dead! Dana killed by Tye? No! It couldn't be true. She awkwardly laughed out of nervousness. He slapped her back and made her stumble forward.

"Don't laugh at me," he warned.

"Brody's not dead," she said, holding tight to a dwindling reserve of reason that asked of her she talk to him as if he were sane.

"Brody died with a pitchfork in his back," he said calmly. "It was something I forgot for a while this afternoon, but then I remembered.

"Mama died at the bottom of the stairs. She fell. I pushed her and she fell down and down just like a tumbling ballerina. She danced, you know. She loved to dance. But you know all about my mother. You saw her dance before."

"Tyeson, you can't be telling the truth. These are all lies. You mean to scare me."

He came alongside and took her arm, dragging her against her weight into the shelter of the trees. "You're coming with me," he said between gritted teeth. "I will leave no one alive to talk about me after I'm gone. *No one.*"

"Where are we going? What do you want with me? I'm not going to talk, I swear it!" Sweat flooded her pores and soaked the back of her shirt beneath the down jacket. Her teeth chattered from the pervasive dread trapping her head in a rattling vise. The dread was growing until she expected it would be a wall that isolated the two of them from the real world of her melancholy father cooking dinner while believing she sat in a child's swing beneath a bare oak tree. What hated wonderland had captured her? It could not be . . . could not be! Not Varna. Not Dana. Not Brody and Tye's mother. Not *Angie Thornton!*

She ducked to escape being stung by limbs snapping back on Tye's passage through the undergrowth. She tried to jerk free from his hold on her arm, but his fingers bit deeper into the muscle of her forearm so that she involuntarily cried out.

Suddenly they entered a clearing and when her vision cleared, she recognized it. It was where he had watched her swimming in the lake. Where he had raped her. She had not come here since, but the place was seared in memory. She turned her face away from the spot where he had taken her.

"Angie, don't turn your face from me. I want to see your face. I want to see all the faces that betrayed me, that laughed at me, that wanted to chain me down and see me die alone."

The wind whooped through the tops of the trees. The sound filled her ears with a roar. She straightened her back and faced him, but could not bring her eyes up to look into the face of madness. She stilled her racing heart, drew in a lungful of the frigid air. "Tye, you're sick. You don't even know what you're saying you're so sick. I don't know if you have murdered Dana or your family, but I do know you killed

Varna Jenkins. The police will soon know it for sure, too. You'll have to pay for that. You don't want to keep killing. Life means something. God gave us life. You're not God. You can't take it away."

"Don't try to tell me anything. Remember Dana? I threw him through that window. I was hoping it would kill him and it did. But it didn't stop there. You never gave me a chance." He ceased talking and looked at her with a pained expression. "Will you kiss me? Will you hold me?" he asked in a plaintive little boy's voice.

I could, she thought quickly, but if I do, he will stab me. While I hold him he will bring the knife up and bury it in my chest. This I know if I know nothing else. How many had he killed? And had they all died because of her?

"Come back with me to the house," she urged. "It's cold here. It's dark. We need to go home."

"You won't kiss me. You won't hold me," he pouted.

For a brief moment Angie's hatred and fear changed to pity. She nearly reached out to touch him, to try to take the knife from his dangling hand.

The moment passed, flashed by in a flicker, and she found herself stepping back, circling, as he came toward her, his arm rising into the air above his shaggy head, his dark eyes hooded in shadow. "You are nothing! No one!" he screamed. "I don't know how I ever thought different. You told Newton I killed Varna, didn't you? You want them to put me in chains too, don't you? Just like Brody. Just like my mother." He cackled and it made the hair on the back of Angie's neck stand up.

"Tye, please, listen to me . . ."

"It's the funniest thing in the world," he said, closing in on his prey now, stalking her as if she were but a rabbit locked in a cage. "The funniest thing in all the world when you find out no one cares. It gives you so much freedom.''

What could she say? That she cared? He would not believe her. He was beyond reaching and she realized that nothing she could say would alter the blazing savagery of his passion to kill. She must run.

Run.

Bolting from the place where she had stood like a wild thing sniffing escape from the hunter, she was on the move.

''Wait!'' he called after her in outrage.

She heard the pounding of his footfalls behind her. He had left her no direction to flee except toward the lake. She saw it loom up from between the trees like an ebony saucer. Farther out in its center where there was no protection, miniature waves, whipped by the wind, rolled over one another to reach shore.

Run. But where to? screamed her mind.

To the lake, take the lake, dive into the freezing lake because you have to. There isn't anywhere to go but to the waters.

Snakes. Moccasins. Lying in wait for her, a nest of venom and fangs, a watery bed of death.

And at her back a knife plunging, plunging . . .

Unless she dove, unless she plunged, plunged into the deep, into the oily darkness.

''Stop!'' she heard him scream just as she spread forth her arms, thumbs side by side, head bowed, canvas-clad feet lifting from the ground, the water coming at her, the frothy murk enfolding her, encasing her in liquid ice.

Jesus. Oh God.

Down and down.

Down the staircase, he had said. Like a ballerina in a last dance. Killed his mother. It was true.

A booming assaulted her eardrums and still she pulled through the water, breath held, eyes open to a world of eternal blackness. How far down was she? How far out had she swum? Were there snakes here to tangle her and keep her forever in their writhing, slimy, loathsome nest?

A burning began around the tips of her ribs and she imagined fangs buried around the delicate bones. The burning inched upwards rib by rib until it set fire to her entire chest and still it labored up into her throat and threatened to pop her eyes from their sockets.

Too far down. She must have air!

She felt a hand grasp hold of her ankle and slip free. She kicked, turned her body in a slow somersault, hoped with all her heart she was able to choose which direction led to the surface, to life. Bubbles slipped from her nostrils. Her pulse thumped with deafening noise. She reached up to her face, put fingers over her nose like bars and again let a bit of precious air blip from her shrinking lungs. The bubbles rose. She was heading for the lake's surface.

Thank God. Oh, thank God.

She kicked frantically and waved her encumbered, jacket-sodden arms to pull for the top. Tye and the threat he presented had entirely skipped her mind. Nothing stirred in her head but the need for air, the fear of drowning, the yearning for sky and unwavering stars overhead.

She burst from the water like a cork from a bottle of champagne. Her momentum carried her on a journey into the atmosphere where everything shiny swirled in outlandish configurations. She drank in air in gargantuan gulps, hiccoughing, spitting, crying all at once as she bobbed up and down, arms flailing against the gravity which pulled her neck and chin down again into ice.

"Angie . . ."

He said it so softly that she thought she imagined her name whispered by the throaty wind.

"Angie . . ."

She flapped at the waves, trying to turn, trying to see where he called from. She could see the shore off in the moonlight, the trees there presenting a solid wall planted against the sky.

"Tye, we'll drown, we'll both drown . . . !"

A muscular arm came around her neck and dragged her backwards so hard her feet came flipping to the surface. She screamed and latched onto him, her fingernails digging into the wet, woolly fabric of his high school jacket. "Don't," she begged. "We'll drown, we'll . . ."

He slipped under and for a scant second she faced the heavens, saw the moon new and full and mercilessly watching earthly struggle. And then she took a deep breath, closing her eyes and surrendering to the impelling tug that carried her down into the depths of Moon Lake.

Down and down, his embrace that of a lover's.

Down . . . Down . . . Swirling waters closing off her ears, stinging her eyes, whispering to her of death in the deep.

Give up, she thought she heard Tye say into her ear.

Let us die here together, he said.

Don't struggle anymore. It's cold and deep and soft in this place with me.

Her back hit bottom first, feet following as they thumped into a thick layer of mud. She moved her arms in slow motion and her fingers encountered lake weed and things alive and squirming in the depths. Was she feeling snakes?

She twisted, the burning starting in her lungs, tickling each rib in turn as oxygen depletion took its toll on her system. She caught his arm and brought it over her head the way she had been taught in lifeguard class. Her thoughts were foggy. She kept thinking she heard him speak aloud to her. *Don't go,* he said. *You can't leave me here.*

She found her feet and pushed mightily, arms held up for the surface once more. She felt his fingers tenderly encircle one of her ankles. She kicked back and forth with frenetic energy, but his grip tightened, a circle of iron binding her to the slushy lake bottom. She lost air in the struggle and her lungs burned brighter, so bright she thought if she were to look down she would see them lighting up the water like neon signs on an otherwise dead city street.

Christ, he would drown her now! He could hold his breath longer, he could outlast her!

Think. Think how to free herself. Think before her brain fogged to the point of no return and she surrendered to him.

If only she had something, a weapon, something to hurt him with. She pulled her hands against the drag of the water and stuffed them into her coat pockets, feeling for a pencil, a pen, anything to use against him. Nothing!

She withdrew her hands, her mind drifting aimlessly now in waves of panic. She felt over the front of her coat, remembering, remembering the safety pin she kept pinned inside the lining for emergencies. For times when she might lose a button or rip a seam and need it. Her mother . . . yes, her mother had taught her that . . . to carry a safety pin . . . for emergencies . . . girls always faced emergencies . . .

She thought she might black out before she ever got the pin unclasped from the material. His hand crept up her leg, pulling her down to him to sit upon the mud. Water weeds swayed before her face, caressing her skin and the lashes of her eyes.

Free! She quickly bent the metal of the safety pin, turning in one last burst of determination to fight him for her life. She reached out for him in the water, stabbing and stabbing. The pin bent. It went into the material of his jacket and she felt him jerk away. She lay over him on the lake bottom now, striking where she thought his face might be with the tiny bit of sharp metal. She felt him loosen his grip from her waist and she immediately floated up. His air bubbles followed, surrounding her as she rose with them.

She surged upwards and was loose, free, plowing forward sleek as a bullet, water rushing past her face, plastering her lashes to her cheeks.

Let me live, she prayed. Let me reach the top and make it home. Take me from this beastly watery hell and deliver me from evil. As I walk deliver me . . . as I walk through the valley of the lake deliver me . . . deliver me . . .

The wind struck her a hammer blow and scorched her lungs down to every cell. She spluttered, treading water, catching precious gasps of air.

The shore looked as far distant as the underbelly of the disinterested moon. A long way down the shoreline she saw the lights of her home beckoning. She caught more air, then went back under, slipping off both shoes. Came up for air. Went back under and unzipped her coat. Caught air, went back under again fighting with the wet material until she had the right arm free. Treaded water, caught breath, looked for Tye, expecting his advance at any moment. A tiredness seeped into her legs, her arms, her heaving chest. She struggled to free her left arm and immediately struck out across the wavelets toward land.

Tears merged with lake water.

She lacked the stamina to watch for, much less fend off, an attack. If Tyeson Dompier caught her now she would give him what he asked. She would go with him to the hellish, weedy, murky depths and make her bed of rest.

Finally she lay on her back and kicked, too tired

even to move her arms or hands. Her entire body was a block of ice and nonresponsive to demands. Only her feet and her eyes and the churning bellows of her lungs could be moved to action.

She lay on the pebbled, wave-lapped shore minutes before realizing she was alive.

She heard her father calling frantically.

"Angie! Angie!"

She began to wail, her head cushioned on tiny stones, her eyes closed, until he found her.

Sheriff Newton found Tyeson Dompier's swollen body three days later where it washed up on the other end of Moon Lake. He had already discovered Tyeson's mother, Jessica, at the foot of the stairway in the Dompier mansion. Her neck and a dozen bones were broken. Brody sat propped against the wall of the entrance hall, his carcass a grotesque naked form stuffed with straw. Upon investigation, Newton stumbled across Brody's innards filling and slopping over the sides of a plastic dish tub in the barn. Vultures and other winged scavengers had strewn the stinking intestines across the hay.

Some said these were just ends for a family so depraved. Some said they might have deserved worse. Not one soul on Moon Lake or in its environs, upon reading in the newspaper the full story from the girl, Angelina Thornton, felt sympathy for the Dompiers.

Joseph Dompier, Tye's father, returned on Thanksgiving Day to receive the news of his dead family. He broke down weeping and had to be hospitalized for three weeks in a clinic of his choice in New Orleans near his in-laws. He subsequently closed the Dompier house, resigned his post with the city of Clarksdale, and took up residence in a Bourbon Street flat.

On Christmas Day Jason Thornton suggested he and his daughter move back to St. Louis. Swapping one unhappiness for another had not been the enlightened decision of an intelligent man. Running and hiding from heartache had been the worst idea of his life. He had to learn to live. He had to accept loss. How could he set an example for his daughter if he couldn't do that? Would Angie like to go home, he had asked, taking her hand in his own.

Yes, she had immediately answered, hugging him to her. She would like that. She would like that better than anything else in the world.

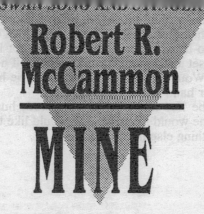

Robert R. McCammon

MINE

Robert R. McCammon the most innovative storyteller of our time has thrilled millions with his chilling vision.

Now, in his first Pocket Books hardcover, MINE, Robert R. McCammon brings you to the edge with his riveting tale of psychological terror and unrelenting suspense.

MINE is the shocking story of Mary Terrell, aka Mary Terror, was once a member of the fanatical Storm Front Brigade of the radical 60's. Now Mary lives in a hallucinatory world of memories, guns, and murderous rage. And when Mary's delusions lead her to steal a newborn baby from a hospital room, the horrifying odyssey begins.

**NOW AVAILABLE
IN HARDCOVER
FROM POCKET BOOKS**

POCKET
B O O K S

60-01

Innocent People Caught in the Grip Of
TERROR!

These thrilling novels—where deranged minds create sinister schemes, placing victims in mortal danger and striking horror in their hearts—will keep you in white-knuckled suspense!

☐ **TAPPING AT THE WINDOW** by Linda Lane McCall 65846/$3.95

☐ **SPIRIT WARRIORS** by Devin O'Branagan 66774/$4.50

☐ **LIVE GIRLS** by Ray Garton 62628/$3.95

☐ **GHOST STORY** by Peter Straub 68563/$5.95

☐ **HOT BLOOD: AN ANTHOLOGY OF PROVOCATIVE HORROR** Edited by Jeff Gelb & Lonn Friend 66424/$3.95

☐ **DEATHBELL** by Guy Smith 67434/$3.50

☐ **GOAT DANCE** by Douglas Clegg 66425/$4.50

☐ **VIDEO KILL** by Joanne Fluke 66663/$3.95

☐ **BLOOD LEGACY** by Prudence Foster 67412/$3.95

☐ **UNHOLY COMMUNION** by Adrian Savage 64743/$3.50

☐ **THE COMPANION** by Ken Greenhall 66410/$3.50

☐ **CRUCIFAX** by Ray Garton 62629/$3.95

☐ **THE TROUPE** by Gordon Linzner 66354/$3.50

☐ **HEX** by Stephen L. Stern 66325/$3.95

☐ **THE PRIORY** by Margaret Wasser 66355/$3.95

☐ **SCARECROW** by Richie Tankersley Cusick 69020/$4.50

☐ **SATAN'S SERENADE** by Brent Mondham 67628/$3.95

☐ **BLACK HOUSE** by Adrian Savage 67250/$3.95

☐ **THE DEVIL'S ADVOCATE** by Andrew Neiderman 68912/$3.95

☐ **DARK FATHER** by Tom Piccirilli 67401/$3.95

☐ **BREEDER** by Douglas Clegg 67277/$4.95

POCKET BOOKS

Simon & Schuster, Mail Order Dept. TER
200 Old Tappan Rd., Old Tappan, N.J. 07675

Please send me the books I have checked above. I am enclosing $_____ (please add 75¢ to cover postage and handling for each order. Please add appropriate local sales tax). Send check or money order—no cash or C.O.D.'s please. Allow up to six weeks for delivery. For purchases over $10.00 you may use VISA: card number, expiration date and customer signature must be included.

Name _____

Address _____

City _____ State/Zip _____

VISA Card No. _____ Exp. Date _____

Signature _____ 351-15

...LING AUTHOR OF
_ AND STINGER_

McCAMMON

McCammon,
ers of horror,
:ales of terror and

.... 66484/$4.50

N .... 66482/$4.50

.... 69518/$4.95

.... 66483/$4.50

.... 70717/$5.50

.... 69265/$5.95

.....62412/$4.95

OUR

r Dept. RMA
appan, N.J. 07675

POCKET
B O O K S

I am enclosing $_____ (please add 75¢ to cover
appropriate local sales tax). Send check or money
six weeks for delivery. For purchases over $10.00 you
customer signature must be included.

_____

_____ State/Zip _____

_____ Exp. Date _____

_____50-07

When I first saw Matt's photographs, I was excited because they captured some of the raw energy of the city. Sometimes in a big city it feels like everyone is rushing by with no time to talk. But if you look around, there are so many ways in which people are trying to communicate, trying to say, "I am here."

Like an Inukshuk on a frozen tundra or paintings on the walls of caves, someone is leaving a message behind. In the city messages are left on brick walls, garbage bins, billboards, park trees and many other things. As you walk down the street words appear, unexpected, unbidden, like random pages from a concrete diary. Who are they addressed to? They are addressed to you — the person who lays eyes on them — and you are compelled to read them.

Once you've read them, you've become part of the conversation. They've engaged you, maybe only momentarily, a passing thought, or maybe they conjure up a whole series of thoughts.

You've become part of the silent and yet noisy urban dialogue that is teeming all around you. The city is talking and you're talking back.

Joanne Schwartz
2009

When I first saw Matt's photographs, I was excited because they captured some of the raw energy of the city. Sometimes in a big city it feels like everyone is rushing by with no time to talk. But if you look around, there are so many ways in which people are trying to communicate, trying to say, "I am here."

Like an Inukshuk on a frozen tundra or paintings on the walls of caves, someone is leaving a message behind. In the city messages are left on brick walls, garbage bins, billboards, park trees and many other things. As you walk down the street words appear, unexpected, unbidden, like random pages from a concrete diary. Who are they addressed to? They are addressed to you — the person who lays eyes on them — and you are compelled to read them.

Once you've read them, you've become part of the conversation. They've engaged you, maybe only momentarily, a passing thought, or maybe they conjure up a whole series of thoughts.

You've become part of the silent and yet noisy urban dialogue that is teeming all around you. The city is talking and you're talking back.

Joanne Schwartz
2009